REST IN PEACE
BOOK THREE:
STARTING OVER

Evelyn Sciarratta

I have so much to be thankful for. First, I am thankful for my family who from day one placed their imprint on my heart and continues with new additions. I could never imagine not having them in my life. They have been my rock into the future after their dad's passing. I am thankful for my granddaughter Payton Sciarratta, daughters-in-law Krista Sciarratta and Shawna Sciarratta for their generous contribution and gift of time with their knowledge of the computer. And what would I have done without my editor Sarah Andrews? Without her talent, my novel would never have seen print. Sarah, I can't thank you enough.

CHAPTER ONE

Clay Chadsworth was living in a bubble of happiness after his marriage to his beloved Sloan. But that bubble burst when, less than a year after the wedding, his father Phillip revealed the truth of Clay's and Sloan's origins. Now Clay's life was a nightmare. Sloan was aware that something was dreadfully wrong when her husband suddenly stopped providing her much-needed dose of uninhibited sex. Her flesh was in constant torment from the need of fulfillment. Ignoring Clay was becoming unbearable, but this would be her only out until he told her what was troubling him.

The social event of the year was a huge success. Sloan proved to be the belle of the ball. Clay could not have been more proud had he not been her husband/uncle, his hand in motion more times than the hands on a clock. Congratulations finally wound down when the last of the party guests said their goodnights and good-byes.

Clay's arm was wrapped tightly around Sloan's waist when the door shut for the night.

Sloan's radiant smile vanished as quickly as his arm. "I'm exhausted. Do you mind sleeping in another room?" She had her back to him when she said good night.

He had been receiving a cool response from her for several days. He feared questioning her; afraid of the answers he might receive. He watched as she gathered within her hands the sides of her ball gown and carefully mounted the stairs.

Sloan had several evening dresses from which to chose. Her personal consultant suggested a no-frills, strapless moss green silk gown by Christian Dior to complement Sloan's impressive green eyes. The hairdresser and makeup artist decided her hair should be swept up and folded in an array of curls and swirls secured in place by an emerald headband. Diamond and emerald earrings with a matching necklace completed the ensemble.

She was well received by everyone, until the women noticed their husbands clambering for her attention. Jealousy raged in the eyes of the women.

Clay was dealing with his own jealousy, not giving a thought to others.

He was relieved when the night ended; he too was worn out, his dancing shoes not in use as he tirelessly removed Sloan from the arms of reluctant partners. Had she a dance card it would have been filled at the start of the evening. She had a smile for everyone, excluding Clay. He had not made love to her in days. That had to be the reason for the cold shoulder. She was a wanton creature. He introduced her to the wonders of lovemaking and then shut off the supply. Something like giving a child a taste of chocolate and then telling her she can never again partake of the fine delicacy. Clay had to use the talent he was given. He would no longer listen to his conscience; he had a duty, not only to Sloan, but himself as well.

Sloan had just stepped out of the shower; her skin glistening from the moisture. She was reaching for a towel when Clay caught her from behind. He did not say a word: actions speak louder. She willed her body not to surrender, but it refused to listen to the voice inside her head. The touch of his lips played over her backside, and she turned, welcoming everything he had to give. It had been much too long; her body screamed for attention. Clay's arms caught her up into his; he no longer had a conscience. The belle of the ball will remember this night; he will keep giving until she winds down and pleads for rest.

Sunday morning was fast approaching twelve o'clock noon. Clay watched his wife sleep while he had none. When she awakens will words be exchanged or will silence continue? He slowly rolled away, giving her full use of the bed. He stepped into the shower, fully aware that when

Sloan did awaken her cold shoulder could still be in use. Lies that start out small become your standard of living, controlling your very existence. Clay knew if they didn't talk soon, there would be no going back to what they had in the beginning. The towel absorbed the water that clung to his body; he then addressed the issue of readying himself for the start of a new day. He had a confession; he would tell all.

Sloan was awake when Clay approached her bedside.

"Babe, we need to talk. Something is troubling you and apparently it has to do with me. All last evening I was on the outside looking in, and let me tell you that is a feeling I can do without. Talk to me, please."

"You just took notice there is a problem? Where have you been the last few days?"

"Would 'busy at work' suffice?" He kept skirting around the confession.

"Clay, this is not the time to play games. You may as well come clean; I know you lied to me."

"If you could give me a hint as to what you are referring to, then maybe I could oblige. Seriously, babe, I have no idea what you are talking about." Did he lose his confessional voice?

"I was listening on the extension when your father called, only you said it was a disgruntled client. Does that ring a bell? Do you want to take it from there?"

A great liar learns quickly to think fast.

"Okay, I tried deception, it didn't work. Courage is also something I find lacking when it comes to delivering bad news." Clay had earlier taken a seat upon the bed facing Sloan but not touching her. Now he gently took her hands into his.

"Dr. Marshall, our family doctor, suspects my father has a cancerous growth. I'm sorry, babe; I know how much you love him." With that atrocious story, he managed to break into tears. The tangled web continued to weave.

"Oh my God, Clay, please tell me it's not true. I can't bear another loss." She went into his open arms, and they wept together. Tears emptied, she had something to say.

"Clay, how could you keep something like that from me? I love your father. When were you going to tell me, when he was on his death bed?"

He wiped his eyes dry.

"Babe, I have no excuse—call it selfish. I'm not prepared to go through another tragedy; besides, the tests could go in his favor. I chose to wait and see. Can you forgive me?"

She had a quick comeback. "Of course I forgive you, only because I can understand your reasoning, but from this day forward don't ever keep anything from me again. The next time there may not be forgiveness."

Clay had made his choice. He will be classified as a deceiver; there is no turning back.

Sloan scrambled out of bed; a shower was the only known device to relieve stress within. She had to see her father-in-law. She would provide the comfort and understanding he would need in the days ahead. She would insist he live with them, so she could be his caretaker.

Clay had not moved from his position on the mattress. He felt the burden of guilt weighing down on him. In the days and weeks ahead he would take that guilt and turn it into anger: anger against the one person he could never live without.

While blow-drying her hair, Sloan yelled out for Clay to call Gus. Gus's position as chauffeur required that he be on call twenty-four/seven, though you could count on one hand all the times his services had been required at night.

"Clay, you need to call your father and tell him you told me about his condition. And tell him we are on our way to visit, and I won't take no for an answer,"

Clay calmly stood, and the mattress reclaimed its natural contour. His walk to the phone was slow. He had to deliver Sloan's message to the one person whose integrity could not be questioned, the man who taught him to always walk the straight and narrow. So much for honesty.

Phillip picked up on the third ring.

Clay began, "Well, I see you made it home okay. I just wish you would have spent the night here.... Yes, I know, no one's bed is like their own. Father, I called for two reasons. The first is to thank you for all the work you put into making Sloan's party a spectacular event. It will continue to be an affair to remember. The second reason for the call is, I had to tell Sloan about the conversation you had with Dr. Marshall. She knew something was up; I couldn't put off telling her. I'm sorry. But now that the party is over, there is no excuse for putting off the biopsy. Like I told you before, tumors are not always cancerous. We have to keep a positive attitude."

Sloan began tugging on the telephone cord. She would finish the conversation.

"Hold on a minute... Sloan has something to say."

Taking the phone, Sloan said, "Phillip, I don't want to hear one word out of your mouth, we're coming over. What you need is someone to take care of you. We'll see you in a bit. I love you." She did not give Phillip a chance to say anything other than a mumbled "Okay."

Clay would have to dig a deeper hole for the crap to fall into; he prayed his father would realize something alarming had happened and follow his lead.

Sloan could not keep her thoughts to herself. Clay's head was killing him, so that he could barely focus on Sloan's moving mouth. (Guilt can do that and much more.)

"Clay, how can the doctor suspect cancer when there is no absolute proof? I think it outrageous to put a person through something so horrifying without fact."

"Father noticed a lump on his breast over a month ago but thought nothing of it, but now it has grown in size, causing him alarm. He saw the doctor over a week ago and was told breast cancer in men is extremely rare, but not to take it lightly. Father refused to put a damper on your welcome party by focusing attention on himself. So let's continue to follow through with his wishes and keep the visit strictly social. If and when he decides to talk, we'll be there to listen, okay?"

"Clay, I can't just sit by and do nothing. All I want is to comfort him — is that so wrong?"

"Babe, he knows you'll be there to help if the need arises. You're jumping the gun by assuming the worst. I prefer to keep my mind-set positive until the test results prove otherwise. Come on, put on a happy face; the grim reaper is not what my father should be greeted with."

Gus could tell the atmosphere lingering around his employers was heavy with anxiety. Something was brewing and he could not shake off the feeling; he knew it had something to do with the confidential conversation more than a week ago between him and Mr. Clay, quickly followed the next day by the inquisitive Mrs. Sloan.

Phillip had been standing at the stove finishing up with the makings of his homemade chili when the call from his boy came in; he turned the temperature control knob to simmer, contemplating the baffling call. Whatever was going on involved Sloan, but what was more mysterious was the topic of cancer, his cancer. They were on their way; he would remain calm and not give way to speculation. If possible, he would corner his boy for an explanation.

Gus was lucky: a parking spot was available. He would have a long wait for his passengers' return.

The buzzer sounded and the recipient responded. When the door to Phillip's apartment opened, Sloan fell into his arms, hugging him as if he would not last through the night.

"Wow, now that's what I call a hug."

Sloan did not blink; her show of tears would remain floating on her eyelids. Clay was not clueless; he knew she was ready to bawl. She definitely had a severe problem with tears. He had to provide a cover.

"Hey, are you two going to block the door all day?" he asked.

Sloan backed off while Phillip held the door wide open. His boy also greeted him with a hug while whispering in his ear, "I'll explain later." He pulled away, giving his father a look only they would understand.

"What did I do to receive such an honor, seeing my best girl two days in a row? It has to be the smell of my chili reaching far into the Hamptons."

Everyone's laugh was sincere. The conversation was light as they consumed the chili. Sloan was puzzled; Phillip was acting as if his life was not in jeopardy.

After the meal, everyone pitched in and put the kitchen back in order. All three, arm in arm, strolled into the great room. The warmth and scent of logs burning in the fireplace gave an inviting atmosphere. Phillip led them to a round table surrounded by chairs that was used for playing games or eating; it allowed them eye-to-eye contact while engaging in conversation and enjoying a sociable drink.

Conversation centered on Sloan's party. Phillip was proud of her and told her so, noting how she turned every man's head. She blushed while Clay held his tongue.

Clay wondered how long it would take before he blackened men's eyes. He was agitated at his best friend Garth's drooling attention towards his wife. Taking his friend aside, Clay had told him, "You better cool your tool before you have nothing to work with." He could still see Garth laughing, for he thought Clay was joking until

Clay told him it was a warning: the next time he would have to get on his knees and pray he could still perform. He got the message when Clay shoved him away.

Phillip kept going on and on bragging about his girl, while his boy for the first time in his life felt like hitting him. This woman could cause Clay to do great bodily harm.

Sloan had heard enough; she was at her father-in-law's home for a reason. She butted in on Phillip's ravings.

"Phillip, I wasn't supposed to say anything, but I can't sit still acting as if nothing is wrong. I'm sorry, Clay, but this needs to be out in the open. We are family and family stick together through the good times and work through the bad. Phillip, we need to talk about this cancer scare of yours."

Clay could not believe Sloan went against him, but then thought better, for if he could not control his tigress in bed, he surely could not control her actions out of it.

Phillip realized he had acquired cancer overnight, and he understood he had to go along with this farce. He would let his boy do the talking; he was the one with the facts.

As Clay took over the conversation, he kept his eye on his wife. She was getting used to that look. It spoke of the teachings you give to a child: speak when spoken to. This should not and did not apply to her; she had put away all things pertaining to a child.

"Father, again I apologize. Sloan could tell by my actions I wasn't myself. I did some research on breast cancer, and it's unlikely that is what you have. Dr. Marshall is only being cautious, that is the reason for the biopsy. I pray you agree and follow through with the test."

Phillip would have to bide his time until tomorrow. He could not wait to hear his boy's explanation.

Sloan was greatly relieved when Phillip stated he would not put off having the biopsy, but he also denied her request to be present when the test was performed.

"Honey, I'll tell you what, let me get though the test and when the results come back negative, which I know they will, we can then celebrate, okay?"

She smiled in agreement, what else could she do?

December was in its ninth day. The blustery cold forced Sloan to stay indoors. She hated the long months that winter brought. She was sitting by the telephone, hand placed on the receiver, fear getting the best of her; today Phillip would be told the results of his test. She prayed there would be a celebration.

Was Clay acting the devoted husband, comforting her anxiety while he hid his own concern? Of course not. His work could not or would not be put on hold. Earlier that morning she had pleaded with him to stay home.

"What if it is bad news? I know I won't be able to keep it together. I'll just upset him further. Please, Clay, stay with me?"

"I should stay home and walk the floors, possibly all day. I can't do that; I need to keep my mind focused on other things."

She remembered how she'd tried to shame him: "Your father chose to stay home, but you can't. What if the results are positive and your father asks to speak with you, seeking your comfort, and I tell him work was your priority? Can you imagine how that would make him feel?"

Clay ignored her, readying himself for work. Sloan continued to follow him from room to room, never giving her mouth a rest. He finally made it to the front door. His kiss was sincere though hurried.

"Babe, as soon as you get the news, call me. I love you." And with that he was gone.

She had begun to sob. Her loving husband had changed; the compassionate side of him had vanished. The morning too had disappeared; afternoon was taking its toll on her nerves. She could not take it any longer; she reached for the phone. The ring blasted her ear.

"Phillip, is that you?"

"Bring on the champagne. Tonight we celebrate." Further words were not heard. All Sloan could do was weep with joy.

As he replaced the receiver Phillip turned to his boy. "She fell for it, but from this day forward we will have to cover our tracks more carefully. I don't think I can go through another cancer scare."

Their laughter was contained within Phillip's office. They made their decision; they will live their life never feeling the pains of shame.

As the three of them gathered that evening to celebrate, the only sounds heard were the clicking of the champagne glasses, plus an additional toast of secrecy to never again speak of Phillip's cancer scare.

Clay for twenty-eight years had headed the start of a new generation, and like the last, this one too will be covered in a veil of deceit.

CHAPTER TWO

Harriet stayed home from the hospital to care for Ben. She thought he would never stop complaining. She tried cotton stuffed in the ear, but it did not work. Earplugs would have been much better, and she was seriously thinking of driving to the pharmacy to acquire some.

"I wish I had a dollar for every time someone told me there's hardly any pain. I'm sorry for crabbing, sweetheart, but trust me, it's all bullshit. I would have taken my chances keeping my goods in working order before I would ever do this again."

"Ben, I think you should call Dr. Roland. It's been more than twenty-four hours since the surgery; something else could be going on. I personally think if you had followed his orders and taken the prescribed pain medication today would have been a good day, but what do I know, I'm just the wife."

"God, you are making such a big deal about taking something that makes me sick at my stomach. I can do without that added discomfort."

"Great, then I can be besieged with your whining. I'm tired, Ben, I've been up all night listening to your complaints. Please take the medication or I'm going to visit the babies."

"Does it look like I'm holding you back? Just go. I can take care of myself."

Who would have thought they would argue? Just say the words "I do" and married life swings into full gear.

Harriet opened the closet to retrieve her winter coat, handbag and keys and mumbled good-bye. This day started out badly and it was only 9:00 a.m. Ben was in his so-called pain mode and did not acknowledge her.

Pain can turn a kind and gentle person into someone unrecognizable. By early afternoon Ben will have returned to his normal self, although he had ruined Harriet's day.

She drove to the hospital in anger, but had Harriet searched her heart, she would have realized a hunger was raging inside her, causing her to take it out on an innocent. She was desperate for the feel of Phillip beside her; her need for him was consuming her very existence.

She washed her hands and pushed through the door to the NICU. As she passed the nurses' station she could hear her recorded tape playing in the background. Hannah, Taylor and Nicholas were awake and eyeing their surroundings. In a mere two weeks they would be ten weeks old and ready to go home. Her anger dissolved as she went to the now open incubators and kissed each of her babies' tiny hands and feet. The nurses were surprised when she strolled in; she had called earlier telling them she would not be in that day.

Harriet was grateful the babies were more accepting of the bottle than the breast. Breast milk had been stored and frozen when she was producing more than enough, but that supply was quickly diminishing. Soon they would have to go on formula. She made the decision to accept the inevitable: she would stop breast-feeding. There would be no way she could breast-feed three babies with no help when they came home. She alerted the babies' NICU nurses she would stop pumping that day.

She spent a total of three hours cuddling, feeding, changing and talking to the babies before it was time to head home. She decided to stop and pick up something to eat for later in the day. The stove would not feel her hands that evening, but maybe the microwave would.

Ben was in a very receptive mood, a smile to welcome her home, his pain at a tolerable level. She accepted his kiss, giving him as much of her as she could.

"Sweetheart, I was a real jerk taking out my frustration on you. I should have taken the medication. If I had, all would have been well between us. Please forgive me."

"Oh Ben, it's not you that should be asking for forgiveness. I should not have behaved as I did. It's just that the life I knew has disappeared, and in its place is marriage and babies. It finally caught up with me and it's beginning to overwhelm me. I need time to myself, to figure out what to do about it. I would like to go away for a weekend before the babies come home. Would you object?"

He was not only surprised but shocked. Was Harriet trying to tell him she was sorry she had married him? He had to be careful with his reply.

"Sweetheart, whatever you want is okay by me; take all the time you need. It would take a dummy not to realize the excessive amount of pressure you've had to deal with. I don't know if I could have held up as well. You do what you need to do to make things right." Ben's gut began to tighten its grip. His sweetheart had him backed into a corner; fear of the unknown had stepped into his life, and he did not like it.

"I was also thinking of hiring in a couple nannies to help in the care of the babies. I could call a few agencies that specialize in that field; of course, this is with your approval."

Ben began to calculate the cost of possible airfare if her weekend excursion included a flight somewhere, and God only knows the cost of two nannies. There was no way they could afford one nanny, let alone two. Burying his head in the sand would not help in the discovery of money.

"Sweetheart, I have no trouble with a weekend away, but unless I get a huge raise, which is unlikely, there is no way we can afford nannies. I'm really sorry."

It was time for Harriet to expose her wealth. They had by this time taken chairs facing each other. The discussion was heavy, and the food they only picked at lay on the sofa table. She reached over and touched his arm.

"I have something to show you. I think you will be pleasantly surprised." She rose and headed towards their bedroom. Within seconds she was back, presenting Ben with a list of her holdings. He looked up, puzzled.

Harriet was in good spirits, no doubt because she had the means to escape into her monthly plan, the sin of adultery.

Ben's hands were shaking. The figures before him staggered his imagination; his wife had millions secured with investments. He was at a loss for words. Where had she acquired that amount of money? Surely not from holding someone's hand and seeing their future. He had to ask, and he was stunned at her answer: the money was payoff for the kidnapping of her son Clay.

Harriet apologized for not telling him sooner. It was not as if she were trying to hide something, she just truly never gave it a thought. Money for more years than she could count was always at her disposal.

She had an additional document; it was a copy of her notarized will.

Ben unfolded and read the legal paper. Everything Harriet owned would be divided equally among him, Marc and their babies Hannah, Taylor and Nicholas. During her stay at the hospital, she had a lawyer from Macon County draw up the will. When the lawyer was finished with her request, he came to the hospital for Harriet's signature.

Ben could find no justification to deny either request; Harriet could literally come and go and do as she pleased. He would look at his wife in a different light. If he wanted to continue to be a part of her life, he would have to give in to her demands. He would grow to despise her money. He was now sorry they had married; had they not, he was sure they would still be passionately in love.

Of the many things on Harriet's mind, the one thing that annoyed her the most was Ben's collection of personal items.

"Ben, we have yet to tackle the boxes from your home that seem to have taken permanent placement against our living room wall. We need to clear these away before the babies come home. You can rest while I sort through them. It will be your decision what's to stay and what gets thrown away."

When Harriet was through carrying out dozens of boxes still filled with non-essential items for trash pickup, all that remained were two small boxes of Ben's non-negotiable useless items and a green metal lock box.

"Ben, why in the world would you pack and bring a mountain of boxes to my house when you knew they would be thrown out? Is your time not worth something?"

"It's a man thing; everything you threw out was the essence of me. I guess I'm worth nothing."

"Ben, you are the one that kept throwing your hand about and telling me to discard everything, so place the guilt where it rightfully belongs." Harriet had taken care of his responsibility and now suddenly it was her fault his things were junk. She gathered the remains of the food; she was again becoming testy. She would feel much better when order was restored; chaos was not a part of her demeanor. She decided it would be best to store Ben's non-negotiable trash in a storage locker behind the house.

Those things will never again see the light of day.

The lone item now facing her was a very small green metal lock box. She held it and politely asked, "Ben, I have no idea what you have stored in this container, but whatever it is, I think it will be much safer in my secured box. Do you mind?"

He took the container from her hands and turned it upside down on the now cleared sofa table so the contents spilled upon its surface. Harriet started laughing and could not stop, and yes, she was pissing him off. Finally she spoke, holding her hand over her mouth to prevent another outburst.

"Ben, you have got to be kidding. Is any of this worth anything other than the obvious one-dollar silver certificate?"

"Like I told you before, my life was kept simple: what you see is what you get. Are you dissatisfied?"

Harriet could not have understood any better had Ben hit her over the head with the container.

"Honey, please forgive me. I have shown no respect for things that apparently are of great importance to you."

He was looking down on the possessions that meant more to him than life itself. His father's cherished pocket watch that he considered a lifeline, and the dollar bill that was its companion. A flattened quarter also occupied the space, this from his father's working days on the railroad. The most recent items were two letters: Cindy's to her parents and the other from Cindy's mother Sarah.

Ben held his father's watch in his hands, tears gaining speed as they fell from his chin. His father was like no other man he had ever known. His days of remembering were many. The long walks through spring, summer, fall and winter. His father holding tightly to his hand, pointing out things he thought were important in a young boy's eyes. A bird chirping, a kite sailing in the wind, a leaf fluttering to the ground, a squirrel sitting on a park bench munching on a tossed peanut, catching a grasshopper and then letting him go after he spat tobacco, catching a fish with only a bamboo stick, and never ignoring puddles of water. The joined efforts of making mud pies that streaked Ben's giggling face and that of his father. And the memory of rolling his first snowman, the only one in town whose body parts were never positioned where they were supposed to be.

Ben was grateful for those thirteen years, for there are those who will live a lifetime never knowing the kind of sacrifice that comes from that degree of love and devotion. He wiped away the tears, but never the memories.

Harriet's laughter was replaced with tears; she was beginning to believe she was suffering from postpartum depression. She loved Ben and yet showed no compassion. She desperately needed time away to get her head on straight. She knelt at his feet stroking his tear-streaked face. He held her against his chest, gently caressing her back; he understood there could be no actual penetration for several weeks, although foreplay was permissible. He had the will to endure, she did not.

Harriet's body demanded to be fulfilled from the intense satisfaction of foreplay and the explosions that follow. Phillip had more than proven he was the one to take care of these wanton desires. She would place a call to him the second Ben returned to work.

Destiny was working hard in her favor.

The phone rang.

Harriet removed herself from Ben's warm embrace. The phone would ring another three times before she picked up the receiver.

"Hello." There was a brief hesitation before she cried out. "Oh my God, I can't believe it! Is it really you? It's been years. How have you been?" Harriet's ear was plastered to the receiver; a more joyous smile could not have been witnessed. She was bouncing about the room, asking question after question, answers tossed about.

"Marnie, you must have been sent by God. I'm desperate to get out of this house. How would you like to have some company for a few days?"

Ben's head jerked in her direction. She was desperate to get away from him. That was the message he received. *She asked for a weekend, now it's a few days?*

Harriet lingered on the telephone for well over an hour. The conversation was nearing its end when Ben heard her make plans to leave the day after tomorrow. She would meet up with Marnie in Chicago, end of discussion, end of call. Ben had no say; Harriet was the decision maker, and he was her obedient husband.

Harriet rushed to his side. He wished that show of exuberance was for him and not for her friend.

"Ben, that was Marnie on the phone. You must remember, I've spoken of her many times. Gosh, it has been years since we've spoken. I feel as if a cloud has been lifted, showing a sunny side to my life. This is exactly what I need to get my life back on track. I'm sure you heard when I plan to leave. Do you think you can take care of yourself?"

She continued to rattle on and on. Ben remembered well the last time she had shown this much excitement: it was when Hannah, Taylor and Nicholas were born. Each day since had spiraled downward.

"I was taking care of myself long before you came into the picture; I'm sure I haven't lost my ability." He did not raise his voice, and Harriet appeared not to have heard his comeback. He was shocked that she made no mention of the babies. She would be gone for days; how could she turn her back on them and run away?

"I'm not running away from my babies, Ben. How dare you think such a thing." She was at it again, reading his thoughts; he wished he could turn off his thinking cap.

"I need to get away. I truly thought you would understand. If you do not, that is your misfortune, and if you persist in this discussion we will just end up arguing, and that is something neither of us wants. Ben, look at me. I love you, you must believe that if nothing else, but I'm hurting. Please do not make me feel as if I'm deserting you and the babies."

Ben quickly changed his attitude, willing his mind from thinking, *She could leave and never come back.*

"You are right. I'm behaving like an ass and being selfish to boot. You take all the time you need. While you are away I will call and make arrangements with the agency to send as many applicants as they have for the nanny positions. You will have to trust me in my selection. Hopefully, when you return you will have all the help you need."

There was little doubt Ben pleased her with his reply. Harriet began to kiss him nonstop until the doorbell sounded. She quickly righted herself and moved towards a mirror that was positioned above a small table that sat beside the Chippendale chair. She ran her hands through her hair and with a tissue wiped away the remains of her lipstick. She opened the door to a handful of neighbors.

Among the residents only one was chosen to speak.

"We pray we are not intruding. We are not here for you and Sheriff Ben to be bombarded with endless questions. There is plenty of time to know all there is to know about the babies. We are only here to deliver a truckload of gifts. The townspeople that were involved wanted them delivered before the babies' release. This way if something were overlooked, you would have plenty of time to shop. So, if you will kindly step back, we will bring them in."

Harriet was joined by Ben. They stood side by side holding hands as the presents began to take up space. Ben's offer of help was declined. The babies' room had been painted a pale yellow bordered by kittens, puppies and butterflies. Puffed replicas were grouped and placed on two of the walls. Cribs had already found their place within the room. Two rocking chairs lay in wait for the warmth of their mommy's and daddy's bodies.

Harriet had given Ben a list of items he was to pick up when he was up and at it. Now that list, and so much more, had been taken care of through the kindness of their neighbors. True to their word, after the last of the gifts was brought in the neighbors departed, but with a promise:

"We will be back when you all decide it's the best time to visit with the babies. Until then, behave yourselves." They left giggling.

Harriet and Ben stared at the humungous tower of baby items, everything duplicated in threes. They would not be visiting a store anytime soon.

"We should have told them to put all the items in the spare bedroom. So much for insight. Well, we may as well get started; I don't want to be looking at this clutter when I return," Harriet said.

Harriet began clearing Ben's prized possessions off of the coffee table. They would be placed with hers, but no sooner had she picked up Cindy's letter, than she felt as if her hand had been burned. The letter fluttered onto the floor. She tried to rub away the pain when the presence of Cindy and her slayer came into focus. Ben did not notice; he was already collecting, as instructed by his wife, the lightest of the gifts. They would be placed, as again instructed by his wife, in the spare room. He had no recourse; his wife was the person in command and would remain so.

She calmly stated, "Ben, Sarah was right. Cindy was murdered."

He dropped the gifts as he turned to face her. He was shocked at her statement. She reclaimed the fallen letter. It was now warm to the touch; the message was already received.

Ben had always been amazed at Harriet's revelations, never knowing when her ability would surface. She reached for a chair; she was waiting for the strength to continue.

Ben went to her side, his knees making contact with the part of the floor that was carpeted. He took her hands into his.

"Sweetheart, please tell me you can see the person responsible for her murder."

"Ben, it's a woman and it's someone Cindy knew."

Harriet dropped her head and closed her eyes. Several minutes passed before she again made eye contact.

"Ben, the woman is from our hometown. I focused all my energy on the face, and in the process I lost contact with the spirit world. I need to learn patience, for they refuse to be rushed."

Ben had heard this story many times, always on the brink of discovery, but never quite getting there. He knew not to ask if she could take another look; once the spirit world had given, it gave no more on the same subject.

Sarah had him somewhat convinced a serial killer was living among them. But he was more confused than ever: a woman responsible, how could that be? That would also make her responsible for Timmy's murder. She would have had to know of Cindy's recovery. Lights were being turned on in all directions. The killer was in attendance when Ben made the announcement at church of Cindy's return to society. But that wasn't all: Ben generously gave her his departure date; he delivered Cindy's death sentence. The executioner left her hometown, jumped a plane, killed Cindy, and then returned. It sounded ludicrous but completely feasible.

Harriet just gave Ben a reason to focus on something other than the babies' things; she would be the one to finish what had barely been started.

He excused himself, making his way into a small room off the kitchen that served as his office. Ben had had but one request: when he and Harriet married he would have a space he could call his own, this coming from years of being his own man. The marriage gift from her was a keyed lock. No one would have a duplicate. This was his home away from home; a cluttered mess of papers greeting him as they paved the way to his private desk. He admired his haphazard handiwork. The stuffed file cabinets containing years of forgotten police business stared him in the eye. Yes indeed, this was Ben's sanctuary. He allowed no one, not even Robert, a peek.

Ben reached into his top desk drawer to extract a pencil and a tablet of paper; he would piece together all the so-called accidents that had transpired in the last few years. He listed them in chronological order:

1. Timmy Fossold
2. Zac Parker
3. Silva Felders
4. The Parker Family
5. Doc and his wife
6. Mr. Hewlett

Willie was the only absolute case of homicide. And if there was a connection between him and the others, what could it be? Ben was wearing down the lead of the pencil from the constant tapping on the lone sheet of paper, his brain working harder than it ever had.

A knock on the door drew his attention. Harriet leaned towards the locked door, her mouth almost touching when she spoke.

"Ben, Robert stopped by. Is it okay if I show him to your office?"

Talk about moving fast... Ben opened the door, stepped through it and relocked it so quickly Harriet had to jump aside to let him rush past. Her voice trailed after him.

"Good grief, Ben, if the doctor could see you now, he would chain you to your bed. I don't think this is what he meant by rest."

"I don't need Robert nosing around my personal papers. Besides, if he came in, I would have to go out—that's how limited the space is."

Harriet could not believe the stupidity of those words. Surely Ben had not forgotten the confinement of the trailer he once called home. He was showing a different side of himself. Was he as unhappy as she was? Did they rush into marriage because of the pregnancy?

Harriet felt trapped; if she did not get away soon she was sure their marriage would not last. She was getting restless; her lover refused to exit her mind. If she did not see him and feel his lips and hands upon her soon, she was sure she would go out of her mind. But having Ben underfoot prevented her from calling him; she would have to wait until she was on the road.

Robert made himself comfortable in Ben's recliner, helping himself to a handful of cashews — Ben's favorite munchies — from a bowl that always occupied a space on the end table.

Ben pulled up Harriet's chair, a Chippendale she had purchased at the antique shop in town long before Simon took ownership. He placed himself close by Robert; he wanted his full attention.

"Robert, I pray your visit is not to see if they are still hanging?" Ben could not help himself; he had to laugh at his own joke. The laughter soon ended, and Ben's demeanor turned serious.

"Robert, I will be returning to work by week's end. In the meantime I need for you to do some research. I need the name of every woman that resides in our town. Harriet had a vision as to the person responsible for the death of Cindy. She is firm in her belief it was a woman and that she lives in our hometown. Now you know she is seldom wrong, so we must work together and bring this killer to justice. I need your help in this, I can't do it alone. Are you with me?"

"Ben, from what you've told me, Cindy hasn't lived here for years and yet the killer from our hometown traveled to Chicago and slaughtered her. Do you realize how preposterous that sounds?"

"I know, I know, but bear with me while I lay out the facts." Ben outlined the deaths starting with Timmy while noting the hard part, finding the motive that would link all of them together. Ben was overly excited; he hadn't felt this good in a long, long time. He could see his glory day rising up before him; he could almost feel the pats on his back, the congratulations ringing in his ears.

Robert jolted Ben back from the fantasy world he sought to live in.

"Ben, I think while the doctor was in the process of removing your baby maker, he also clipped away your rational thoughts, leaving you sterile from top to bottom." He was hoping to bring forth a chuckle while trying to make light of a stupid suggestion. Ben's brain was in thinking mode, giving no thought to his balls; leave it to Robert to revisit that experience.

"Robert, I don't need you to remind me of the loss to my manhood, and if you think putting a serial killer behind bars this late in the game is farfetched, then step aside; I will do the leg work myself."

"God, Ben, give it a rest. If you're playing on my sympathy in regards to your surgery, you have it, but everything else is bullshit when it comes to your attitude."

Ben, like Harriet, needed to get out of the house, get back to the insanity of his job; anything was better than staying home arguing with his wife. In a small way, he was glad she was leaving; he could turn back the clock and recapture his bachelor days.

Ben apologized and Robert accepted. He would get on the list immediately; he would continue to be Ben's partner.

Harriet took Ben's treasured mementoes and stored them with her documents while admiring the placement of the babies' items. Everything was arranged side by side in threes. The clothing was taken to the laundry room; she would remove all the tags and wash the clothes when she returned from her very short visit with her friend. The majority of her time will be devoted to her lover. She could not wait to see the look on Marnie's face when she told her of Phillip's return.

Ben was seated at the kitchen table tapping his index finger to his tongue as he turned the pages in the yellow book, searching for an agency dealing with nannies. Harriet approached him from behind. When she spoke, her words caught him by surprise. She intended to put her arms around him; instead something of a different nature took over.

"Ben, do you think we made a mistake getting married?"

Her thoughts echoed forth, words made vocal so quickly, it was if someone else had possession of them. It was too late for a recall. Ben's tear ducts responded before he could utter a word. He turned in his chair; her scent seizing his attention. But he was quick with a verbal answer.

"Never, but apparently you are having second thoughts."

"Ben, I can't believe I just said that. I have no idea where that came from. Please forgive such nonsense. I love you. I pray the days I spend away will straighten out the mess I seem to be making of my life and yours."

Ben had cause to be worried; if Harriet did not find the source of her problems, he could be facing an eviction.

He turned his attention back to the yellow book. Worrying about tomorrow was as disturbing as the thought of dying, both of which he had no control over. Harriet continued to stand alongside him, but when she received no further response to her comment, she went about her business. Ben was sulking again; his attitude towards his wife sucked. He decided to give up his search for now and give his thoughts a rest.

Harriet could feel the flow of energy ebbing away like the day, and they still hadn't eaten dinner.

She had some beef stew left over from the day before; that would have to do. The table was set, the food steaming in the bowls when she announced dinner was ready.

She was placing some dinner rolls onto the table when Ben approached her. He took her face into his hands, gently kissing the lips that were always eager to feel the depth of his kiss, and now those lips refused to part. What more could he do, wear out his knees begging for forgiveness? What exactly had he done? If complaining about pain caused such a rift between them, what would happen if something really serious came their way?

Ben was done apologizing; it was her turn. He turned away from the cool, or rather cold, response. He took his folded napkin and placed it upon his lap; he would eat and retire to bed.

Tomorrow is another day.

CHAPTER THREE

The day started off on the extreme side of cold, the sun taking a peek and trying hard to show itself.

Harriet's four packed bags were waiting by the front door. Her cashmere black wrap with attached neck scarf and her favorite hat, a beret, lay across her Chippendale chair. She was ready, more than ready, her mind full of Phillip. She had awakened earlier than usual and when her thoughts registered the day, she smiled that one-dimpled smile. She gave Ben a hug and a brief kiss to his neck, and then bounced off the bed. A quick refreshing shower would help give a boost to her energy level.

Ben felt the moist kiss, but did not dare turn towards her; he was afraid if he showed the least bit of interest, she would again rebuff him. Was he to continue living his life tiptoeing around his wife, only making love when her body demanded satisfaction? Would he be treated as a service animal? He had to ask himself if he would be content with such an arrangement. Harriet had proved time after time she was far worse than he when it came to sex. She behaved like a bitch in heat, always on the prowl, and like the animal he was he gave and gave. He would not suffer long before she attacked him. Yes, he would force himself to accept her terms.

They ate a simple breakfast: Cheerios with low-fat milk, accompanied by coffee. Conversation consisted of small talk, making the atmosphere pleasant and happy.

Ben caught Harriet glancing at her watch; he knew it was her way of letting him know it was time to go. Nearly everything was ready. The babies were no longer breast dependant, and Harriet had called the NICU the night before to let them know she would be a no-show for at least a week. She assured the nurse that the babies' daddy would visit daily and possibly their brother Marc. So Harriet knew her babies would be taken care of, still she could not leave in good conscience until her home was in pristine order, bed made, dishes stacked in the dishwasher, floors swept, dusting done and carpets vacuumed.

Ben watched her in action. She would have been a great partner for Robert, the two of them bumping into one another in their quest to be the best of the best.

Ben would be the first to admit he was clean about his person, but messy when it came to housework, but he was who he was, take him or leave him. Surely this wasn't the reason for Harriet's displeasure with him. She had spent many a night in his trailer, and never once did she make a comment on his non-cleaning habits. No, there had to be more to it. All he could do was play the wait-and-see game.

It was time for Harriet to say good-bye to her husband. They stood holding each other, lips not yet making contact. Ben was feeling great; his pain had subsided. He was having a hard time releasing her. He pushed away slightly.

"Do you mind if I kiss you good-bye?" He asked, his tear ducts ready to do what they were good at.

Harriet could feel his hurt. They had never known separation; her unexpected breakdown did not enter into the picture. She reached up, taking his face into her hands, her lips locked tightly onto his, her body pressed tightly against his. He moaned with relief. Her kiss was deep and long, and there was no mistaking his arousal. Harriet wanted to please him; would it really hurt if she did so?

"Ben, I'm desperate for you to make love to me. Do you think you could try? We can always stop if it makes you uncomfortable. I can't think of a better send-off, can you?"

It did not take much persuasion. With joined efforts her coat fell to the floor, their lips clung tightly as they each helped remove the other's clothing. A line began to form starting at the front door and continuing down the hallway into their bedroom. Ben yanked at the bedspread to give them access to the sheet, never once taking his lips from hers.

Harriet was ready to receive her husband. What was her intention? Oh, yeah: to please him. Who was she kidding? She could not get enough of him; her moans soon turned into a mounting scream of satisfaction. Of course, Ben brought her to orgasm, but Phillip propelled her to unbelievable heights of extreme ecstasy that would continue for several minutes.

The intensity of that gratification left her unable to move or talk. Ben was a sampler; Phillip was the whole enchilada.

She was now in a hurry; Ben had reminded her what she was missing. A quickie shower was all that was needed. Harriet followed the path of the discarded clothes, stepping into them in the reverse order of disposal. She was now ready for the road, her suitcases having been secured in the truck of her car earlier. Having pacified her husband with her body, she now felt justified to carry on an adulterous liaison with her lover.

She appeared calm as she walked to her car. Once inside, a smile played on her lips as she visualized the reception she would get from her lover. Ben waved her off, secure in the knowledge he had given her what she could not do without. She would look forward to coming back to more of the same.

The heater finally kicked on. Harriet hated the winter. The cold, ice and snow she could do without. She kept her eyes focused for the road signs. Any gas station would do. She was eager to call Phillip and tell him of her intentions. Her heart was taking on far more beats from the mere thought of him when she almost missed the first off-ramp.

The receptionist answered on the second ring.

"Chadsworth and Chadsworth. May I help you?"

"Yes, would you please connect me with Phillip Chadsworth?"

"May I ask who is calling?"

"You need only to tell him his past has returned."

The receptionist recognized the distinctive voice; it was the same woman who refused to acknowledge who she was the last time.

Phillip gripped the receiver. Three words defined his longing: "I've been waiting." There was no denying what the other felt. They would reclaim what was forcibly taken years ago.

Harriet began to weep upon hearing the sound of his voice. Words of unmistakable meaning poured forth.

"Phillip, in two hours I will be in Chicago to meet up with a friend I haven't seen in years. My husband is under the assumption I will be spending a full week with her, but it will be less than four hours; she has to depart out of Chicago no later than 4:30 p.m. Phillip, you are my love and the pain of missing you is unbearable. I need to see you. Do you think you can steal away for a week to be with me?"

"Name the place and I will be there."

"Ritz-Carlton suite 3011. Please hurry."

"Nothing will hold me back. Whether it is a blizzard or ice storm, I will walk or crawl if necessary."

His words tugged on her heart. God in His goodness gave to her a guarantee of true love, and she will not turn her back on His wisdom. Harriet was now on the road racing towards the gift God so graciously gave her. She will soon learn to live a double life and love every second; guilt will never be put upon her. The blame of shame should be tattooed on those that governed her life, starting with Mother Superior, followed by the rapist and ending with a jailbird/bigamist. She will take back what is rightfully hers.

Harriet pulled to the front of the Ritz-Carlton Hotel. One valet was ready to take her car keys while another removed her luggage. The Ritz in all its elegance could not hold a candle to the Chadsworth estate. But she had to give a high five to the hotel; she was dazzled by Chicago's finest.

She signed in and while accepting her key card mentioned to the receptionist she would like a bottle of their finest champagne along with strawberries delivered to her suite as soon as possible. The luggage was taken care of when she applied her signature to the registry. She looked around the grand lounge searching for her friend. The reception area was overflowing with guests; she made eye contact with many women but with no recognition.

Doubt began to set in. Would Marnie know her after twenty years? Of course she would; Marnie was standing no more than fifteen feet away when the years faded, taking them to their beginning. The tapping sounds from Sarah's and Marnie's high-heeled shoes on the marble flooring grabbed the attention of many. But there was no one in their line of vision other than each other as they raced forward, their arms reaching and holding. The flow of happy tears streaked their flawless complexions. They would pull away to look at each other, then resume their tight embrace…time and again this happened, until they became aware of the many eyes that were trained on them. It was time to escape.

Hand in hand they rode the elevator to Jena's room. Several women with their significant others focused their attention on the friends' clutched hands and showed their revulsion. Marnie gave Jena a glance. Jena read her thoughts: *Let's give them something to talk about.* Jena moved in front of Marnie and began to caress her face. Marnie leaned forward. Her lips were ready to accept Jena's kiss when the elevator opened. All bodies contained within pushed forward.

If the women were not so fired up to make a quick exit, they just might have noticed a couple of their husbands winking their approval. It's a proven fact that of the organs given men, the least used is the brain when it comes to sex.

Left alone in the elevator, Jena and Marnie burst out laughing. Their ride continued, taking them to the most elaborate and finest suite available. Jena would be treated by staff as a person of nobility.

As requested, the chilled champagne with a stemmed crystal bowl of strawberries was waiting, complemented with a spectacular arrangement of flowers. A bouquet of red roses and white lilies with a whisper of greenery was set in a tall crystal vase atop a lace-covered table. It was meant to express yuletide joy for the holidays. Other displays of fresh flowers expressing good wishes were scattered about the adjoining rooms.

Together Jena and Marnie flung their coats and hats on a navy club chair just off the foyer. Jena promptly went for the champagne bottle; she filled their glasses to the rim. Years back while under the employment of the

Chadsworths, she had mastered the art of popping the cap. They settled down on a multi-colored mint green brocade sofa; pillows tucked behind their backs, shoes kicked off, while the bubbles played on their lips and tongues. So many years to catch up on, but not enough hours in which to do so, but they would do their best.

The conversation went back and forth. Marnie still clung to single life, while Jena had again subjected herself to sharing a life with yet another man, and in the process triplets were added to the household. She told of her son Clayton seeking her out and their grand reunion, thanks given to Marnie. Their talk was nonstop, often interrupted by laughter. Jena was the first to end the years of makeup when her tone turned serious.

"Marnie, I have done something that could cause you to think ill of me. But I need to confide in someone and you are the only one I can trust."

"Honey, have you not read your Bible: 'Judge not, lest you be judged'? Nothing you say or do could ever sever our friendship; we are bound together for all eternity."

Jena moved closer, looking about the room as if someone could hear what she was about to say.

"Phillip has re-entered my life and taken back what was rightfully his, my heart. What can I do? I love him. I made a vow to never again

marry after Trevor, and yet I married Ben."
Tears collected and began to fall; she needed to
find forgiveness for what she was about to
embark on.

Marnie reached over and gathered Jena close,
tissues within reach; she blotted the tears as they
fell. Several minutes passed. When the intensity
of the tears diminished, Marnie spoke.

"I can't begin to imagine the shock of seeing
the father of your firstborn show up at your
doorstop after so many years. How can you not
have feelings?"

Jena stared at her trusted friend, confused.
Then it dawned on her that she had never
shared with her the horror of the rape. Marnie
would now know, with nothing held back; the
gruesome details would be told in their entirety.

When the past presented itself, it was far
easier the second time around. It was being told
as if read from a sheet of paper, feelings null and
void.

Marnie was now the one using the Kleenex
while hugging her best friend fiercely. When she
was able, her voice trembled with emotion.

"Oh honey, my heart bleeds with the injustice
of what has been done to you. Why didn't you
tell me? Maybe somehow I could have
helped…at the least I could have been someone
in your corner to get through the worst of days.
Never would you have suffered alone."

"Marnie, I'm a breath away from fifty. I want to have what was taken from me. Is that so wrong? I truly thought I loved Ben; everything was perfect until a couple weeks ago when Phillip pulled up to my home. The passion of that long-ago love swept over me like a thunderstorm at its max. No words were spoken. I took him to my bed, the bed I share with my husband. Just how repulsive is that?" The tears made themselves available once again.

"Oh honey, there are no words to release you from the torment you are feeling. Each of us has to make our own decisions and live by them. All I know is, from the beginning of your young life, you were dealt several hands that caused you to lose everything you loved. If I were in your position, I would listen to my heart. Pick up the pieces of your traumatized life and reconnect them. Until you do, you will never have peace of mind."

They both wept when all was said. Marnie prayed for forgiveness for telling her best friend to commit the most heinous of sins. Jena was thankful for the go-ahead to bed down with someone other than her husband. After all, what are friends for?

It was time to say good-bye; Marnie had a plane to catch. They hugged while making promises to see each other, the same kind they'd made years ago.

Marnie shut the door behind her; she knew Jena would begin pacing the floor waiting on her lover. Marnie felt the pangs of her lost love and was envious. Jena had to ready herself to receive her lover. She had several seductive teddies, each very different from the other.

She remembered the day she ordered them...

It was getting more difficult to stay in focus on what should matter in her life. Harriet was unhappy and it showed. She was using the babies' rocker more often than not, as if rocking would ease her frustration with life when she heard the mail truck pull into her driveway. She could hear the rattle of the lid from the door slot as the mail dropped into the foyer. She had been up since dawn doing what was now a habit, fixing Ben his breakfast before he set off for work. A peck on his cheek was all she was capable of giving. She raised her weary body to retrieve the correspondence. (When depression rules your life, both your body and mind feel its effects.)

She gathered what appeared to be a catalog along with a wastebasket full of junk mail. The paper-covered catalog was addressed to "occupant" from Frederick's of Hollywood. She never received any catalogs—much to her satisfaction, for they were a waste of her time. But for some reason she could not wait to tear off the wrapping of this particular booklet.

The Chippendale instead of the rocker was now occupied as she turned the pages. There was the royal blue satin teddy that barely covered anything. The black fringed one guaranteed to delight the wearer and the viewer, and the sheer pink lace number left nothing to the imagination. But the teddy of all teddies was a very naughty red glitter garment with an attached garter belt, and finally the white fishnet exposing all the goodies.

She opened the small drawer from the table sitting beside her chair, fingers searching for a pen; never did she take her eyes off the catalog. She was trembling with excitement as she began checking off the ones that caused her to blush. That day gave her something to look forward to, the arrival of a new life. She would say a nightly prayer hoping someday to wear them.

That day was now. Jena was eager with the thought of playing the role of a hooker. She would be seductive in her approach; Phillip would drool at the sight of her. But before she allowed him to take her, he would crawl to her. He would never want or desire another when she finished with him. She no longer was the mother of five; she was a cat on the prowl for her game.

CHAPTER FOUR

The receiver found its way to the base of the telephone with a trembling hand. Phillip sat in silence, his hands clasped together, thanking God for returning his Jena. He would be given the privilege of spending a full week with her; how much more blessed could he get? But what would he tell his boy? Should he be honest? How would his boy feel knowing his father/brother would be bedding down with his mother? It would be better not to say anything, lest a curse should befall him. But Phillip still had a dilemma: How could he explain a week away from the office? While he was deep in thought, a knock sounded at the glass door.

Destiny was hard at work.

Clay poked his head inside the now slightly opened door.

"Got time for a coffee break?"

"Time is all I have. Business couldn't get any slower, although sometimes it is a relief."

Clay replied matter-of-factly, "It's the holidays, happens every year."

Phillip, in easy reach of the coffee maker, opened the cabinet with the stored coffee cups and helped himself to a couple mugs. He began pouring the always available coffee, gaining additional time to figure out a plan of action. Clay took the offered cup of his preferred black coffee while settling down into a mahogany leather barrel chair; his father joined him in its mate. Phillip was lost in thought as he sipped the steaming cup of coffee until his boy spoke, breaking his concentration.

"With the holidays fast approaching, I'm concerned that Sloan is headed toward a deep depression. I found her rummaging through the attic when she came across our stored Christmas items. The first thing she unwrapped was Grandmother's favorite five-generation tree topper.

"Remember the angel, Father? The angel with her head tilted downward, wings spread wide, the tips curled to embrace a family of children. Sloan stared long and hard at it, until it got the best of her. She clutched the angel to her chest and fell to her knees. Her wrenching sobs tore at my heart, and yet I did not go to her. Instead I crept back like a wimp and retreated down the stairs, leaving her to wallow in her own grief.

"There was no doubt she was grieving for the loss of her family, but how could she bare her soul after telling me a totally different story? And if I told her I knew of her family, she would most certainly question why I never spoke of it. She began the lying process and I followed suit."

Clay dropped his shaking head, refusing to cry over combined deceit, but he quickly regained his composure.

"Father, I would like to take her away, somewhere far from here. I would like for it to be a minimum of two weeks. It would be sort of an early Christmas present. What do you think?"

Was not another angel working her wings?

"I think you should call her and leave immediately. Well, don't just sit there—get going. I don't want to see or hear from either of you for a minimum of fourteen days. Enjoy."

Clay did as told. Other than calling Sloan, he would wait until he had her in his arms.

Phillip also had to get a move on; he had yet to call his pilot. He would leave all the arrangements to the pilot. He noticed his boy talking to his personal receptionist, in all likelihood telling her of his intentions. The door to the exit swung closed after his departure.

Phillip was now free to assist his mistress in the sins of her adultery. He too had no qualms; he was taking back what was rightfully his.

CHAPTER FIVE

Several knocks gave way to frenzy. Jena threw the door open. Phillip crushed her body to his; her legs positioned themselves around his back, squeezing tightly. Her right hand left his back just long enough to close the door. They were alone in their sins. Their lips clung tightly, giving way to moans. He carried her to the bed, gently laying her down. He began to disrobe her, never taking his eyes off her face when she stopped him.

"Oh, my darling, you must be patient. I have something that is sure to please you."

Jena gave him that smile that was never forgotten. He was aroused, but he would have to wait. She scooted off the bed, touching him in his most sensitive area. Leaning toward him, she seductively whispered,

"I'll be right back."

The red glitter teddy with the garter belt felt the fire within as it slid onto her body. The cat was ready to make her move.

Phillip glued his eyes to the door by which Jena exited. He did not need or want any surprises; his only desire was for her. He gasped, his heart started to pound, his breath quickened. If he tried to stand he would surely fall. Jena was framed in the doorway, and her hands began a workout, sliding up and down her body. She gave a look that promised she would give him more than he thought possible. He could barely breathe waiting in anticipation. She was adding a bit of intrigue as the scent of her fragrance flowed throughout the room, setting the mood for what was to come.

He had never seen such a provocative creature in his entire life, and he had been with many women. He was savoring the delicious moment. He knew, she knew, what she was doing to him—it was deliberate—but he would show her he could do as much to her as she to him. The cat cornered her prey, there was no resistance. The wages of sin screamed out time after time, the wanton desires of the flesh would never again be denied. Phillip proved over and over he was more than enough man to satisfy Jena's hunger.

All her teddies accomplished what they were designed to do: leave her man drooling for more and more. Phillip and Jena exhausted all their energy, taking them far beyond anything they could ever imagine; they had met their match.

While not making love, they squeezed in as much about their life as possible.

"I wish I had been there when you told Clay about his beloved Ali and the horror of what his grandfather had done. It had to have crushed his heart."

"There is nothing you could have done to lessen his grief. This is something he has to work through on his own. The power of healing comes from our Lord, though I doubt Clay will ever get over the loss of Ali."

Jena nodded, understanding. She then asked if he remembered an associate of his father's, Charles Mannigan.

"Of course I remember Charlie. He was one of Father's greatest architects. I don't think anyone since his death has come close to his remarkable talent. But how in the world did you know him? He was never a guest in our home."

Jena pulled free from the comfort of Phillip's arms, assuming a sitting position; she could not wipe the tears fast enough. She asked for the when and how of Charlie's death. Phillip was taken aback; he never expected that type of reaction. He would soon learn in great detail how much Charlie gave of himself to come to Jena's rescue. Remorse was high on Phillip's list when he chose the easy way out and continues to the present day.

"What can I say other than I am so sorry? I had no idea my father made Charlie the villain in taking you away. Though I can see why he chose him; Charlie never refused anyone his services if someone needed his help. I just can't visualize Charlie doing something so vile. There had to be more to it, but what I'll never know. And if there is any blame for his death then let it fall on my shoulders, for I was the reason behind the grave injustice that befell you. He was a stranger and yet he was there for you when I wasn't. Can you ever forgive me?"

Jena kissed away his manly tears.

"Oh, my darling, it is I that should be asking for forgiveness for telling you that Clay was your son. I lived a constant battle with bitter feelings leaving no room for love. It was when I gave birth to Marc that I chose to close that chapter of my life. Our time is now, Phillip, no more regrets. All I need to know is how my sweet Charlie died."

"Honey, he died in a horrifying car accident. His car flipped several times at a steep winding curve at Skinkers Road. The car exploded—he never had a chance. I remember someone saying his rate of speed was calculated at ninety miles per hour.

"To this day it baffles me how this could have happened; Charlie knew that road like the back of his hand. It was a road he traveled day in and day out. He was a cautious man; he would never take chances that could possibly endanger another life. And because of this I remember asking my father to follow up with an investigation to see if there was something wrong with his brakes."

It was at this point Phillip gave pause.

"Now that I think about it, Father's attitude was not what I expected. Charlie was his best friend and yet he waved it off as if Charlie was a stranger. Why, after all these years, am I remembering these details? I can still see my father flailing his arms about screaming obscenities, telling me to keep my damn mouth shut, that Charlie got what was coming to him."

Tears again found their way into Phillip's eyes and he began to choke on his words.

"I was at the office the day Charlie returned to work after a lengthy stay away. I remember saying hello, but I received no response. He went straight for my father's office. Nothing seemed out of the ordinary until he walked out, never to return. Something had to have transpired between them. What I have no idea. All I know is Charlie died the following day…

"Oh my God…how stupid am I not to have put together the pieces? This is no coincidence; my father without doubt had a hand in Charlie's death. That was why there was never an investigation. I wonder how many people benefitted from his death; hopefully their lives are suffering because of it. The evil just never stops. How could my father live with himself?"

This time Jena could not comfort him, for she too was distressed by that revelation. And Phillip could not escape from thinking the horrible truth that he was his father's son; would he too be like him?

He will soon become a believer in the power of psychics.

"You are not your father; never will you be like him."

Phillip felt as if his thoughts had been invaded. How could this be? He looked at Jena, bewildered.

"Yes, Phillip, I read your thoughts, but don't look so frightened. It doesn't happen all the time, so relax. This ability to see and hear things is something I was born with. In the beginning I thought it was a curse. I could ignore the voices by concentrating on something else, but the visions would linger, leaving me weak and confused. It was only once I was on my own that I realized these powers could help me to survive in an unkind world, and with Charlie's help I succeeded."

What more could either of them say? Charlie was gone, and thankfully so were the evil doings of Phillip's father. The time was fast approaching for them to say their good-byes.

Phillip was the first to speak, grief obvious.

"Jena, I don't think I can let you go."

She was also beginning to feel the stress associated with separation. She began to weep.

"Oh Phillip, just the thought of leaving you is making me sick at my stomach. I am so miserable in my marriage to Ben, but what can I do?"

Phillip had the answer. "You could divorce him and marry me."

That comment brought forth a flood of tears. The *if* and the *but* words entered the picture. *If* she does this, she would have everything she ever wanted *but* she would lose the respect of not only her husband and her son Marc, but the entire community she had grown to love. And what kind of mother takes her babies away from their father? Jena was tired of thinking about others; did she not have a right to be happy? She would take the bull by the horns. She made her decision; there will be no turning back.

"Yes, my darling, I will marry you."

CHAPTER SIX

Sloan was indeed on the verge of sinking into a deep depression; she missed her papa and mama. She had never felt such unhappiness. She retraced her memory, trying to remember the last words spoken to each member of her family; it was impossible, making the pain even more excruciating. She had everything she desired and yet that was not enough. She wanted to feel the arms of her papa and mama.

A company that decorates homes for the holidays was called in and with instructions from Clay rescued Christmas items from the attic, and with a detailed pencil drawing laid out before them, they tackled the tedious job of bringing Christmas into the home. Sloan watched the workers and complimented them on a job well done. They were just about to finish putting the finishing touches on the twenty-foot-tall tree in the grand room when she told them she would take responsibility for the tree topper. The workers did as told, leaving the twenty-foot ladder in place for later removal.

Sloan watched in awe as the lights flashed on. What should have brought forth a feeling of warmth and joy instead brought a torment of tears that forced her to her knees, the angel clutched to her breast as before.

She loved Clay, but the pain she was left to endure was like a hangman's knot cutting off her air supply. She would gladly return to her former life if given the chance. The worst of it was having no photographs; Sloan was afraid that with each passing day the faces she loved would gradually fade into nothingness. She screamed out to God for such an injustice.

"What did they ever do to You? You were their heart. They put You first in all things and yet You struck them down."

Clay found her sobbing, the angel absorbing the wetness of her fallen tears. He sank to the floor, taking her into his arms; drained of energy, she gave no resistance.

Sloan prayed God would forgive her for breaking her vow, but she could no longer honor Lydia's request. She had to tell her husband, but before she could, he spoke out.

"What's with the tears? If it's the holidays that are getting you down, I have a pleasant surprise. I am going to take you away to anywhere you wish to go. Two weeks of nothing but us. What do you think?"

The tears were still wet upon her face and that of the angel when she spoke. "Clay, I can't continue to live my life that started with a lie."

He felt the hand of God striking him down. Can someone's heart actually stop beating? He thought his had. What kind of lie was she talking of? Did she find out he was her uncle or has she known all along? He needed to sit with the forthcoming confession, his. He tried to find the right words.

"Sloan, I know I haven't been completely..." *Honest* would not be heard.

She threw up her hands, stopping him.

"It's over, Clay. All lies stop this day." She could not control her weeping.

There it was, the truth of their incest was about to come pouring out of her mouth. He had no defense; they would no longer be a *we*.

"I promised your grandmother never to reveal the truth about my family, but it's destroying all I was taught to believe in, including the most important thing, 'to thine own self be true.'"

Clay listened intently as she told him how in the beginning she lied to him about her family, and how his grandmother had the foresight to see she was holding something back.

"We were deep in conversation about everyday things when she began to bombard me with questions about my family. She appeared anxious, not at all like herself. It was when I spoke of my mama she fell silent. She no longer focused her attention on me; she went away, somewhere where I couldn't reach her. The silence was deafening, and then it gave way to hysterical screams. There was nothing I could say or do to ease her agony. It was apparent something out of a person's worst nightmare was holding her captive. What triggered this definitely had something to do with my family. I just wish I knew what it was.

"Oh Clay, I made such a mess of my life and now I went back on my word and betrayed a woman I loved and respected. How appalling is that?"

Sloan never waited for a response; she continued trying to explain why she did what she did.

Clay left her rambling, as his thoughts turned to his beloved grandmother. His grandmother would never again feel the warmth of her baby girl Alexandria but was given the greatest of gifts, meeting and holding her baby's baby. She was given the privilege of a granddaughter but also the realization that Sloan was her grandson's cousin. Clay was thankful his grandmother never knew of the rape of Jena and that he was not Sloan's cousin, but her uncle. His grandmother spent her entire life protecting him from the horrors of the life she was forced to live, never righting the wrong. She suffered greatly from the sins of her past, and while she lay dying she confessed to him those sins, freeing herself. In the end she committed the most grievous of sins, allowing him to indulge in incest.

He was unaware tears coated his cheeks until Sloan, assuming his tears were for her, used her fingertips to gently wipe them away. Clay's arms reached for her as he agonized over the tragic loss his grandmother was forced to suffer while enduring the horrific pain of cancer. He shook himself free from trying to imagine her grief. It was far easier to turn his thoughts to his wife.

"Oh babe, I wish I could find the words that would put an end to your pain and suffering, but I cannot. All I can say is how deeply saddened I am for the loss of your family. Even if you had told me in the beginning, nothing I would have said would have helped; the holidays remind us of the things that are important.

"But we need to put the tragedy of their deaths to rest and focus on the memories that brought joy to your life. You were taught as well as I to believe in the afterlife; you must hold tight to that belief. Right this moment your parents are looking down, excited and happy that you found someone to love you as much, if not more than they, and babe, I do. If you let me help we can eradicate the demons that are hell-bent on destroying your life. What do you say?"

Clay provided the comforting words she needed to hear. Sloan knew he was right; her family would want her to continue on.

She rose unassisted from the floor and gave him the answer he wanted to hear and to where she wanted to spend their time away.

"All I ask is for you to take me away from the bright lights of this Christmas; somewhere where the sun always shines, giving warmth to my body, if not my soul."

Clay's confession would not be heard.

Clay always had use of the several estates bequeathed to his father. He chose one of his favorites, a lavish beachfront mansion on the island of Oahu, Hawaii. That trip will be exactly what she needs, although not what he expected.

CHAPTER SEVEN

Ben felt lucky. The first interview proved to be a success. Her name was Brittany Hightower, she was forty-six, married, and had been a nanny for twenty years. She was an ordinary-looking woman but with a super personality. Ben took an instant like to her—she was a keeper. Brittany could work the day shift from 8:00 a.m. till 4:00 p.m. They negotiated on the pay, and she left accepting what she considered a reasonable salary.

He never considered that finding a caretaker for the night shift would be as next to impossible as it proved to be. Before the sixteenth prospective nanny took the offered chair, she sweetly stated that she prayed it wasn't a waste of Ben's time, but she would prefer to work nights. If he had springs attached to his legs, he would have sprung from his seated position, possibly tossing both applicant and chair to the floor. Thanking her was not enough; Ben felt like hugging her. His feeling could best be described as stepping into another way of life, similar to being told he had just won the lottery.

Although many applicants did not fit Ben's definition of a nanny, it made no difference; the majority ran for the door when shown a picture of the three newborns. How could he blame them? He himself had heavy doubts about whether he could cope with triplets, and they were his.

Ben smiled during the entire interview while Emily Anders gave the requested references and basic information. She would be the first to stand eye to eye with the mistress of the house. Her hairstyle was no-fuss: long dark brown hair tied back in a ponytail. She had no need for makeup; her complexion was flawless. Ben approved of her looks; it sent a signal that she was not into herself, but solely committed to those in her care. But she did have something going for her, and it was her lips. They were lips that told of a longing to be kissed, and kissed a lot. Emily was no dog by a long shot, but it was when she told him she was thirty-five and had never been married that he thought he heard the ringing of wedding bells.

She could be a front runner for Robert. Well, the only runner, but what the hell? Ben could do the introductions and let the heavens take care of the rest, for he knew it would surely take a miracle.

Just as she rose from her seated position, Ben took over Cupid's role and threw the arrow.

"I pray you won't take this the wrong way, and you can call me crazy, but would you be interested in meeting my deputy? He's waited a long time for someone like you."

Emily's face beamed bright. "I would love to meet him."

Was a miracle in the works?

In less than six days Hannah, Taylor and Nicholas will show their vocal cords are as strong as the best of them.

Harriet was to return at any given time. Ben sweated the outcome. A short blast on the horn got his attention. He pulled the drape aside, peering out the front room window. It was his wife's red Chevy Malibu. His heart started to pound as he tore into the hall closet to retrieve his coat, gloves and stocking cap. A predictable snowstorm was making its appearance; the purity of the white flakes will not be compared to Harriet's dark mood.

Ben ran across the snow-covered driveway, leaving behind the imprint of his size-thirteen shoes. The temperatures were dropping to an intolerable degree. Harriet had the trunk of the car open; her suitcases were quickly becoming snow-coated to match the surrounding area. Ben took the last of the luggage from her hand, while leaning over to give her a welcome home kiss.

"Good God, Ben, can't you wait until I get indoors? I'm freezing." Harriet wished at that moment the words that fell from her lips had changed direction. He did not deserve her flippant attitude.

Ben looked rather stupid standing with a suitcase in midair as if frozen in time while the heavy flakes crystallized on his face.

Harriet was not about to debate why she said what she said while standing in a virtual blizzard. She reached behind him and took a suitcase in each hand, followed by a blatant statement. "I'm going in; don't forget to shut the trunk."

Harriet kept peering through the draperies. She was getting a bit concerned when Ben continued to stand outside in that same position. Not willing to let him freeze to death while she stood by and watched, Harriet was about to don her coat and gloves and coax him inside when thankfully Robert pulled up behind her car.

She turned her back on them; she had her mind on many things, Phillip heading the list. She forced herself to get her priorities in order. Her babies were coming home in a few days. She had their laundry to take care of, not to mention the clothing she'd worn during her week away and the teddies that Phillip had deliberately taken his time peeling from her body. She began to hurt from the need to feel his body joining hers. She had no choice: she would use Ben; she refused to suffer.

Robert trudged through the rapidly growing mountain of snow.

"I see Harriet made it home safe, thank God. This is turning into a real mess. Here, let me help you before someone mistakes you for the abominable snowman."

Ben did not acknowledge Robert until he began to tug on the suitcase. Ben shoved his disappointment and anger aside; he had to get his act together.

"Yeah, I hear you. Let's make more tracks."

Ben gave up the right to the suitcase and followed Robert. With the door ajar, Robert proceeded to take off his hi-top boots, while Ben continued to heap on more snow, all the while shaking his head. Robert, now hopping on one foot, was having a hell of a time trying to stay on the foyer rug while attempting to remove his right shoe. Ben lost his patience and shoved him aside.

"Damn, Robert, get with it. We're not heating the outdoors."

Robert, with his foot still in hand, fell against the doorframe. He turned his head in Ben's direction.

"Well, pardon the hell out of me. I'm not one to leave a sloppy mess. I think your wife has enough to take care of without cleaning up after non-family members."

If Harriet had not shown contempt for Ben's kiss, Ben would not have made such a big deal about Robert's obsession.

"I'm sorry, Robert; I had a really bad day. I don't know how you put up with me."

"It's easy, you're my best friend."

Ben smiled at the comment, thinking how Robert really was a great guy. Then the image of Emily came to mind; he could not wait to tell his deputy about her.

Ben could hear the washing machine running. Harriet never took a break; well, almost never until this past week. His mind was whirling like the machine. Should he put to rest her smart-ass comment or question her about her negativity? If he continued along that line, it would in all likelihood end up in an argument. He decided to act as a well-behaved child: speak when spoken to.

Ben stomped his feet a couple of times. No way would he be another Robert; his shoes would remain on. While Ben's nearly frozen hand struggled to grasp the handle of the lone suitcase, Robert was pleading for a rag. How could Ben forget such a vital part of Robert's very existence? Mr. Clean has to prove he would do what no ordinary man would think of doing.

"I'm right on it; be back in a flash."

Ben stood at the opening to the laundry room watching the woman he loved passionately go about her normal routine as if nothing were wrong. She had her back to him, clipping tags from the babies' garments, one load already on the delicate spin cycle, four more to go, baskets stuffed with outfits the babies would soon wear. The neighbors had been more than generous; it was sad the marriage vows did not come with a guarantee like the gifts did.

Ben refused to show his weak side; he called back the makings of a tear. He could wait, she could not. She would come to him out of desperation looking for sexual gratification.

He turned, making his way into their bedroom. He was about to set the last suitcase with the others when he thought he could lend a hand; Robert and his rag could wait.

Ben unzipped the smallest of the three, exposing its contents. His hands began to shake when he removed a white fishnet teddy; the overhead light beamed brightly, revealing the obscene nightie held together with what looked like bits of string. His eyes traveled down, peering onto what was a colorful collection of never-before-seen sexual nightwear.

He continued to examine each piece. *Disgusting* was the word he would use to describe the trash that was now clutched in his hand. This was not the woman he married; something evil had taken up residence in his home. If the man bedding down with his wife had no respect for a married woman, he would learn to respect the fist. Ben quickly replaced the garments, intending not to reveal what he'd discovered until he could come up with a solution to the colossal problem facing him.

Robert was still sitting on the floor patiently waiting for the solution to his problem. He caught the tossed rags, followed with a comment from Ben.

"When you've taken care of your mess, come over and take a seat. I have something I know will put a smile on your lips."

Robert gave his acknowledgment but without eye contact. He was on hands and knees wiping and wiping, putting a shine where none before ever existed. Ben thought it possible he missed his calling.

Robert finished, quite pleased with the outcome. "I'll just take these rags and put them in the washroom, okay?"

Ben nodded. Robert knew the layout of Ben and Harriet's house as well as his own.

He tossed the wet rags into a bucket sitting near the entrance to the washroom. Harriet's back was to him. She apparently was lost in thought and gave no acknowledgment to the sound the rags made when they hit the bottom of the pail. Robert noticed a travel bag she was picking through. She held an item to her face — was it getting a sniff test to see if it had been worn? It was none of his business. Robert was not about to say hello; it would look like he was invading Harriet's privacy.

Robert took a seat facing his friend and work partner. "Okay, I'm ready for that smile. Lay it on me."

Ben really enjoyed Robert's company, fetish and all.

"While Harriet was taking a break from life, I was given the task to employ some idle hands and put them to work. Robert, I met the woman that will steal your heart and seal your fate. Her name is Emily Anders; she is one of the nannies I hired to help in the care of the babies."

Was Robert's look one of surprise or relief or both? And where did Ben come off giving Emily away, when everyone before ran for an exit? Did Ben have a plan now that money was no longer an issue? Was it Ben's intention to heap an ungodly amount of cash on Emily, then lead her to the altar and force her hand into Robert's, and call it a wedding gift?

Robert took to pacing the floor. Did he already feel like the nervous groom? Was he ready to count his blessings before they were given? Shame on Ben for giving hope where none may be.

The deputy stopped walking the floor and took to shaking Ben's hand, thanking him over and over.

Harriet stepped into the room and noted the jubilance; she presented that bewitching smile.

"Did I miss something?"

Ben found relief when Robert removed his hand, acknowledging Harriet's presence. Ben turned in his wife's direction, focusing on her smile. He felt like crying.

"Ben found a woman that is interested in meeting me. If we're compatible, maybe we'll get married."

Harriet looked at her husband while still retaining her smile. His attention was now on Robert. Upon her arrival home, she had opened her mouth and put her foot in it; Ben would ignore her until she apologized.

"Oh, and how did he manage that? He was home all week. She would have had to come knocking on our door." Again she glanced at Ben. This time she got his attention.

He said, "That's exactly what happened. While you were off enjoying yourself, I was looking for someone to take care of my babies." Had he a spear, he could not have hurt her any worse.

Harriet was taken aback, but she was harsh with her comment. "I can't believe you just said that. When did they stop being *our* babies?"

"The second you walked out that door and turned your back on us."

Robert would never have believed what was taking place had he not been a witness. He continued to turn his head in the direction of whoever had the floor.

Harriet was instantly on Ben's cruel reply. "Okay, I get it; I should never have jumped your ass over a kiss. That's what it's about, isn't it? If you're asking for an apology you got it, but don't you dare tell me I don't care about my babies."

Ben was now standing; it appeared to be a faceoff with his opponent.

Robert was not about to stay around for the finish. The coat and hat he'd removed earlier once again felt the warmth of their owner's body. His hurried "see you later" was ignored.

Ben continued with his brutal attack.

"You've been home for better than an hour and yet you failed to mention anything in regards to the babies. Is that normal for a caring mom? I don't think so. I'm sorry, but I'm damn tired of playing Mr. Nice Guy. Maybe what you need is another man, because it's apparent I can no longer take care of your needs."

There, he said it, he got it out in the open. Now she could either own up to the fact of her affair or she could give him his walking papers.

Instead, reality jumped aboard. Harriet sank to her knees. There would be no controlling the tears. Her head was so filled with Phillip, there was no thinking room for anyone or anything. Deep down in a place she kept hidden was the undeniable love for a man who was always there to comfort her when the horror of her past continued to resurface. Ben never questioned her prior life; he was there for her, he was her rock. The kind of love she was searching for, she already had. She'd thought Phillip was the answer to a better tomorrow, but now realized she was already living those kinds of days. All because of a guy named Ben. Phillip was her past, Ben her future.

Harriet crawled across the carpet sobbing as she made her way toward her husband. She prayed he would forgive her.

"Oh my God, Ben…what have I done to you and our babies? I've crossed over a road I should never have taken and I am so sorry, but you must believe me when I say I truly love you. I know now I need professional help to get back to where I belong, and that's with you and our babies. Please tell me you will stand by me during this process. I don't think I can do this alone."

Ben reached down, pulling her to himself.

"Hush, my sweetheart, no more tears. Never will you stand alone. I am with you always." Banished from his thoughts was her infidelity." Love is forgiveness unspoken.

CHAPTER EIGHT

This was the last day Sloan and Clay would enjoy the benefits of swimming off the Pacific coastline. Their two weeks turned into three with Phillip's blessing. They were wrapped tight, the splendor of making love long past, as well as the beginning of a new day. Sloan had been awake for some time while Clay was still in the sleeping mode. She traced the outline of his face. He had given to her all that the heavens allow, while she gave nothing in return. She could give him something if she did not have to deal with his use of condoms. Although he did not always use one, more often than not he did. If it was his intention to have a child, the condoms would be unnecessary.

She gently shook him watching as his eyelids began to flutter and then open. He rubbed his eyes awake and yawned.

"What's up, babe? Can't you sleep?"

If she hesitated she would never say what was in her heart.

"Clay, I want a baby."

Talk about a fast wake-up call; Clay's attention instantly reached its peak.

"What?"

Sloan wanted to reach out and pull the words back. It was apparent by Clay's demeanor he was not happy. She could rely on her mouth to get her in trouble, but if she showed a weak side he would forever be in charge.

"I should have wished upon a star, I would have gotten a better response."

Clay was not stupid; he knew this day would eventually show its face. He had to be careful with his choice of words, lest he end their vacation not speaking.

"I did it again, didn't I, throwing out words before thinking of their impact. Babe, I didn't mean it the way it sounded, harsh and unfeeling. Of course, someday kids will be in our future, and when the time is right, we'll make it happen. But for now I'm greedy, I want you all to myself. Will you please allow me this privilege?"

What could she say? He had the control. From that day forward, Clay's thinking tool when in use will never be without its wrap of protection.

Sloan held her tears, careful not to show her disappointment. She had learned early on that tears made all things possible, but for some reason she knew not to push with this request.

She was now anxious to return home. They were to attend a New Year's Eve party at Garth and Krista's home in two days. Krista would be the one to offer support and possible guidance as to a solution for what she considered a problem in the baby department.

After Sloan's agreement, Clay returned to sleep. She cuddled close, putting her thoughts to rest; she will think about tomorrow when tomorrow arrives.

Party time at Garth and Krista's arrived. When Sloan presented herself to her husband wearing a strapless body-hugging gold mesh Roberto Cavalli gown, Clay stood as if a dignitary had walked into the room. He would live his life always on guard; he loved and hated the attention Sloan drew, mindful that at any time someone could take her away.

"I worry that someday I will need the use of an oxygen tank; you never fail to take my breath away. Come here." He took her face into his hands and gently licked her moist lips. Further encouragement was not needed; she quickly responded. He pulled back, reminding her they were late for the party, but assuring her by night's end her desires would be met.

A valet service was hired for the evening to park the cars while several maids were in charge of the guests' outerwear. Clay in all his glory escorted his wife. The ballroom was three steps lower than the main floor. Those in early attendance were given the benefit of seeing and later gossiping about the apparel of the late arrivals. When the butler announced Clay and Sloan's names all eyes turned in their direction. The women's eyelids dropped to a squint, an obvious sign of hatred for a woman who never failed to capture the attention of her counterparts.

Krista and Garth greeted their very late guests. Sloan greeted Krista with a kiss to her cheek and an apology; Garth was ready for the same. Sloan pulled away, waving as if to acknowledge someone else. He grinned at her; he knew, she knew. Sloan labeled him as a cad.

Sloan pulled Krista aside. "I need to talk to you when you get a minute — it's important."

"Now's as good a time as any; the majority of the guests have arrived. I need a break anyway; I'm beginning to feel the effects of too much drink." Krista looked around. This would not be an easy escape; the men were already making use of their walking shoes in their direction.

"Come with me. The only place to find privacy will be my dressing room." Shoving the animals out of the way was proving to be almost impossible until Krista announced she was about to expose the contents of her stomach. Needless to say, the best of them have not the guts to view upchuck.

They took a seat on the vanity bench; Krista took a hold of Sloan's hands. "Okay, honey, what's up? Is there something going on I should be concerned about?"

Sloan got to the point of what she considered a problem. "I want to have a baby and Clay said he's not ready to share. Does that sound normal to you? I have a feeling there's more to it, but what I have no idea. Should I give him a deadline or just wait it out? I don't want to be a nag, and yet if I say nothing the wait could turn into years. You're my best friend — what would you do if you were me?"

Krista came to the rescue with what she considered good advice. "Honey, you have been married what...five months? That's not enough time for any man to get used to the idea of being married, let alone being told to ready himself for daddyhood. Besides, it's not as if your biological clock is ticking; you're barely out of puberty."

Krista thought that would lighten the subject and bring forth a laugh, but she thought wrong. Sloan began to cry.

"Oh honey, I'm sorry. Sometimes I say things meant to amuse and instead it backfires."

Sloan reached for a tissue to wipe the tears as they fell. "Krista, I'm not crying over what you said. The tears are a show of relief for not making Clay out to be some sort of ogre. For that I thank you."

"Okay then, no more gloom; let's enjoy what's left of the old year before we begin taking our frustrations out in the New Year. Besides, I don't dare leave Garth alone. He uses drinking as an excuse to put his hands and lips where they don't belong, although tonight I plan on keeping him on a short leash; the only lips he'll wet will be mine."

They left the dressing room arm in arm, laughing.

Krista was a special friend; Sloan hated knowing Krista's husband cheated every chance he got. Clay had told her of Garth's adulterous affairs should he ever proposition her. She did not have the heart to tell him of the inappropriate places Garth managed to touch without being seen; had she done so, she would have been a witness to Garth's murder.

Before the countdown to welcome in the New Year the women began their search. They had the right to show dislike; their husbands, like the animals they were, stood in groups near Clay's prey, drooling for a taste. But Clay was wise; this could be the only opportunity his friends and acquaintances would have to place their lips on his wife, but it would not happen in his lifetime. He glanced at his watch. Ten minutes and the bells would sound; it was time to exit.

He reached for his wife's arm. "It's time to leave. Stay close."

Sloan was trying to protest as he pulled her along. She turned her head towards Krista, signaling an apology with her shoulders.

Everyone was keyed up, the noise level nearing its peak.

Krista shouted out, "Tomorrow we'll do lunch. I'll call you."

Sloan nodded.

They managed to escape only because Clay told those that attempted to stop them to back off. The valet driver pulled their limo to a stop. Clay was driving tonight; Gus never worked holidays. Just as their car door was about to close, the all-time favorite "Auld Lang Syne" rang out.

Sloan felt the effects of the first day of the New Year, but not from drink. Clay, it seemed, could not get enough of her; red marks resembling carpet burns had left their calling card. Between her legs it felt as if the skin had been removed. Feeling like a tree minus its bark, she could barely move, but she welcomed the pain for the extreme pleasure it brought forth.

She would not be having lunch with Krista.

CHAPTER NINE

Robert, the gentlemen he is, did not question his boss about what transpired in their home when Ben returned to work with a smile.

Harriet was true to her word. She received treatment for post-partum depression and during this process she scripted a Dear John letter to her lover. She never once regretted her decision. (Well, maybe a time or two.)

The babies grew at an alarming rate, leaving behind their diapers and pacifiers and joining the ranks of little people. Their disruption of an otherwise quiet household gave Ben and Harriet a joy, although sometimes they were left with headaches.

Robert and Emily did meet, and behold a miracle did take place; they fell in love and married. Ben no longer questioned the saying "for every man there is a woman."

Norman was gifted Ben's trailer and he was found to be quite handy. His hands possessed the skills of a master carpenter, first with architectural design, and then with application attaching a wrap-around porch to his home. He was finally given respect and praise; now everyone recognized his face. In short order, his hands were put to good use, leaving no time to maintain the cabins. Reluctantly he gave notice. His boss took over the chores, for no one answered his help-wanted ad; it was a hard lesson to learn that Norman was a diamond in the rough. With Ben's help Norman hung a sign on his front porch: "Master Carpenter For Hire." Norman came into his own; he was now in the bucks, making more money than the average Joe.

Dr. August Rolan came out of the closet and moved in with Henry White the coroner. He attached a for-sale sign on his home, the renovated house of the late Dr. Harrison.

And yes, Robert with down payment in hand, purchased that house for his wife Emily and their soon-to-be-extended family. Their four-year wait for a baby was about to end when their daughter presented herself to the world.

Marc graduated from college and with an identity change (unknown to his mother) he chose Chicago for his first serious place of employment. He needed a resume for when he would make New York his home and workplace.

Sunni was already established in her business and was quite comfortable in her Manhattan apartment.

Many of God's blessings were moving along.

Ben knew it was time to put an end to pursuing the killer of the town's residents. In the beginning he was hyped up when he remembered Silva on her last day of life, waving that stupid red folder. A folder that contained all her good deeds was unaccountable. It proved Sarah was right; the killer takes something that belongs to each victim.

And Robert did an excellent job gathering the names of the town's female occupants, but with each interrogation Ben's giddy-up wound down; his rainbow was now an illusion.

Ben removed himself from his desk chair and made his way out the front door. Robert was busy sweeping the debris from the porch of the station. He would eventually make his way down the stairs.

Ben pulled up a chair before saying what was on his mind. "Robert, I've decided I've wasted enough of the state's money on a case that is going nowhere. I'm calling it quits; it's time to turn in my badge and gun. I'm going to use what little bit of energy I have left on my wife and kids. But before I leave, I'm going to put in a recommendation that you take over my position."

Robert was stunned; he also took a chair, cleanup put aside for the moment.

"Ben, I'll believe it when I see you walking around town in civilian clothing and not before. Besides, if I were to be made sheriff I would have to give up my cleaning practices and assume the role of a desk hugger." Laughter would finish the day.

Ben placed the call to his superior to give his two-week notice and recommend Robert as his replacement. He was already feeling the pangs of departure. In Harriet's case this would have been just what the doctor ordered, but years back. The nannies were long gone; the stress of settling fights was wearing thin. Relief would show itself in short order; school was right around the corner. And now Ben decides to retire. Is there something wrong with this picture?

Harriet had just put Hannah, Taylor and Nicholas down for a brief nap. Taking care of triplets kept her moving at a constant pace; she all but dragged the three off to bed. She settled in Ben's recliner chair waiting on a kettle of water to whistle. A cup of tea always seemed to mellow her out. The hot tea with sugar and lemon did the trick.

She thought back to the conversation she and Marc had two years after his graduation...

The kids were outside playing on a jungle gym safely enclosed in a fenced-in yard. She and Marc were seated in lounge chairs watching their antics. Their conversation centered on the kids, then it quickly ended when Marc took his mother's hand into his. A serious topic was about to emerge.

"Mom, I need to say something that will break your heart, but it needs to be said."

Those words came back to haunt Harriet, forcing her to remember the letter written to her lover so long ago. Those words broke her heart then, and now her son was about to do the same. She could do nothing but listen, tears sitting on her eyelids ready for the onslaught.

"You know I love you, but it's time to move on. You and Ben have your hands full; you don't need me underfoot every weekend. The owner of the rental room seldom sees me, other than to collect my hard-earned money. It's such a waste; I can find better use than to give it away. Besides, it's time to make a name for myself and Chicago is not the place to do that. I've decided the Big Apple is the place to make this happen."

Harriet was stunned with his choice. Why New York? Did his planned move include meeting his brother?

Marc was honing in on his psychic abilities, though he would not own up to it.

"My intention is to secure a position in Clay's firm without him knowing I am his brother."

Harriet's mouth dropped open, ready to question how he intended to do that.

His window of seeing the other's thoughts was beginning to surface.

"Mother, I see I have upset you, and that was not my intention. But a new life awaits me, and with that comes change. I applied to Social Security for a name change along with the necessary changes at the DMV immediately following my graduation. I kept this from you until I was ready to make my move, and now the only thing missing is your blessing."

Harriet could feel the shame of his intentions.

"Oh Marc, this is so wrong. I lived in a house of lies and liars; you saw what it did to me and the end results. Why would you subject yourself to the same kind of life?"

"Mom, I played out many different scenarios until my head began to ache. If I were to tell him I was his brother he'd feel obligated to hire me. I intend to prove I am as good as or better than all of them. When I gain the reputation I feel I deserve, Clay will then know my true identity. Mom, I need for you to stand behind me on this decision."

Harriet hung her head. She could not convince him. He will have to experience on his own the pain that follows liars. She gave him her blessing.

CHAPTER TEN

Phillip was seated at his office desk deep in thought. The letter written five years past was clutched in his hand. He'd read it so many times he could recite it by heart.

My darling Phillip,

Where do I start? How do I tell you something that is sure to break your heart—and yet it needs to be said. I was wrong to bring you back into my life, to offer you something I have no right to give. Ben is my life, as well as our babies. I cannot separate one without the other. We lost out, my darling, and we cannot go back and reclaim that which was taken. The splendor of our time together has shown its ugly side by demanding our good-byes, but locked inside my heart, tears reign.

I will forever remain your Jena.

He wiped the tears; will they ever end? In one way, he was thankful. How would he have told his boy that his mother was to be his bride? And what would he have said to her when she learned that Sloan was not only alive and well, but was also the wife of her son? She would think lies were his way of life. No, it's better it ended like it did; he and his boy could continue living the life of deceit safely.

Phillip tucked Jena's scented letter in his breast pocket; never did he not have it close to his heart. He traveled back, recalling his week away with the woman he called his wildcat. It brought a smile to his face. While lost in the moment, a knock on his glass door forced him to put aside the erotic memory.

Clay stuck his head in the door apologizing for his intrusion.

"You must have had your head in the clouds; I noticed a smile on your face. Anyone I know?"

How Phillip wished he could tell his boy of his short-lived love affair, but it was not to be.

"Come in, my boy, have a seat. Must you have all the heavenly moments? Am I not entitled to a few myself?"

"In your case, Heaven continues to wait. Come on, give — what was that smile all about?"

His conscience whispered in his ear, *Phillip, you can't back down now; you need to keep the tradition of lies flourishing. You have to admit you are getting quite good at it.*

"Reminiscing about your wedding always brings a smile to my face. But I have a foreboding there's trouble brewing in Happy Land."

Clay was shocked his father had noticed; he thought he was hiding his discontent quite well. His response had a sharp edge. "Five years is a long time without some disagreements. It's minor shit, but we'll work it out without any interference from outside parties, and that includes you."

Phillip had hit a raw nerve. Did his boy think of him as a meddling fool? Something was taking the bliss out of what was an extraordinary relationship. His boy was changing right before his eyes and he could do nothing to stop it. He did not press the issue any further; Clay made it quite clear it was none of his business. And yes, for the very first time his boy crushed his heart.

Clay saw what he had done and tried to set it right. He was deeply apologetic.

"Father, there is no excuse for sounding off like I did. I thought I was hiding my feelings quite well, forgetting how we could always tap into the other's feelings. Something like this helps to remind me of our special connection. And you are absolutely right; I am having to deal with a situation that is out of control. And the worst of it is, there is no solution."

Phillip was beside himself; anything that affected his boy affected him. "Do you want to talk about it?"

Clay was more than willing to unload, his father the only source. "Sloan and I can no longer communicate without a bit of sarcasm thrown in. I've tried to find our way back, but it's proving to be impossible. I'm to the point of giving up."

Phillip felt the pressure of trying to extract the motive behind Clay's behavior. "There has to be a reason this is happening. If you're keeping something from me as not to upset me, you're too late. I'm here to help — will you let me?"

Clay too was feeling the pressure, but his was much worse. Will his father agree with him that to include a baby in his and Sloan's future would be disastrous? There was only one way to find out.

"Years ago Sloan asked if she could have a baby. I told her I wasn't ready to share her, that I needed more time. She agreed reluctantly, but as the years come and go the desire for a baby has become an obsession leading to our present day.

"Father, you know as well as I, we cannot have a child. I refuse to put an end to our lives together, and that is exactly what would happen if we were to have a baby born with birth defects, and the possibilities on a scale of one to ten are in the high range. The only acceptable excuse I could possibly give is to tell her I'm sterile, and knowing her as well as I do I'm sure she would ask for proof. So Father, if you have a solution to this epic problem besides a snip job, now is the time to share."

Did Phillip dare think of a future generation? Of course he did; that nagging thought invaded his dreams on a regular basis. His boy was right: there could never be children. No one in their right mind would purposely give birth to a handicapped child. Was there a solution? Not in his lifetime. Clay would pray for a miracle that Sloan will change her mind.

Not in her lifetime.

CHAPTER ELEVEN

Changes took place over the years at the Chadsworth Mansion. Sloan took it upon herself to free up her home from servants on the weekends, giving her the opportunity to experiment with her own style of cooking. The cleaning she would leave to the servants; after all, she would not dare expose her manicured nails to such a chore.

There was no disputing that money now had a stronghold on her way of living. Clay gave her free rein over the estate; she could also go and come at her leisure. But he would go only so far in keeping the peace, as Sloan would soon come to find out. She shunned the services of Gus, their personal chauffer; Clay would again be his passenger. She now had in her possession her driver's license, which led to the purchase of a black Jaguar, reminding her of the good times spent with Sunni.

Krista now owned the title of best friend. They would shop till they dropped, this done on a whim when Sloan could not stand to be in the house one minute longer. Krista, with purse in hand, was always ready to oblige. Sloan bought things that were of no use; she spent money as if it grew on trees. In Clay's case, he owned the forest. She was filling a void in her life, all because Clay refused to give her what she desperately longed for.

She was spending more and more time in bed without him. Today she forced herself to rise. The night before she had checked the calendar of events. Today was a free day, and she would check out their apartment, which she did on a monthly basis.

Clay was up and out the door before she had a chance to say good-bye. He was always cordial, treating her more like a roommate, but only until he could no longer take the pain of doing without. Sloan searched her memory, trying to recall the last time they made love with the sole intention of pleasing one another and not because the body craved God's ultimate gift of pleasure.

The servants were tiptoeing around making sure not to disturb the mistress of the house until they heard the sound of her footsteps. She was dressed in a pale yellow Anne Bowen pantsuit; her choice of footwear for pounding the pavement was a pair of low-heeled brown

Guccis. Krista was ready and waiting for a pickup.

Sloan addressed Truman Black, the butler, as he held the door open for her to exit. His resume brought him inside the mansion shortly after she and Clay married. He was Caucasian, forty-seven years of age, and married with no children. He was as short as he was round, and had a head full of dark hair many men would lack as their years gave way to grey and thinning. Truman would live out his lifetime in their employ.

The Jaguar brought to the front was ready and waiting. Sloan seemed to be in a hurry as she ran down the steps. The tires squealed as she sped out of the driveway.

Krista was sitting on the steps of her all-too-perfect mansion. Garth, a real estate investor, was in a close race claiming the rights to his own forest of money trees. Money, though, was not what drew Krista and Sloan together; they had developed a bond not unlike that of identical twins.

Krista started running, flapping her hand, always excited with the appearance of her friend. If she were any faster she could have leaped into the car, making the door handle a non-essential item.

"Tell me quickly, what's on the agenda besides raising our husbands' eyebrows when they see our charges?"

Through the laughter they hugged. What would Sloan ever do without her friend to pass the time of day?

Sloan said, "It's that time of the month; I need to go make sure the apartment is still intact. The white glove treatment is getting old, but as I've been told by the master of the house, if this is such a big deal we can sell. How can I turn my back on the one place that was the beginning of my life, the start of my tomorrows? How does one walk away without losing a part of themselves?"

Krista replied, "Honey, you know what your problem is? You put too much emphasis on life in general. It's a thing, it doesn't have a heart. Trust me, you can live without it."

"That's just it, I can't, and it does have a heart: mine."

What more could Krista say? In a way Sloan was right; when Sloan gives, she gives it her all.

They sped along. The drive would take less than an hour; they were in no hurry. In the city, Sloan was lucky, more than lucky, to find a space to park her car very near the apartment. She and Krista ran up the steps, and the doorman who replaced the buzzer during the day tipped his hat while opening the main door to the building. Over time the doorman came to know who occupied the overpriced apartments.

As they entered, the elevator was in use, its door about to close.

Sloan yelled out, "Hold the elevator."

The woman inside the elevator was about to act as if she had not heard the request, until a chill swept over her; she reached out a slender hand with an array of rings on four fingers and pressed the hold button. Sloan looked the young woman in the eyes and thanked her. Krista was talking nonstop when the young woman, the only other occupant and operator of the door continued to press the hold button. The woman directed her attention to Sloan.

"My God, I can't believe it. I thought you were dead—all these years and no word. How could you?" Sunni started to cry, first out of relief and then out of anger pushing forward.

"How could you do this to me? You were, are my best friend—friends don't do what you did. I doubt I can forgive you for putting me through continuous years of hellish pain."

Krista gave her mouth a rest, while Sloan gave hers a try. "I'm sorry; I think you have me confused with someone else."

Sunni got the impression Sloan did not want to be found out; then she remembered her own make-over. Years back she decided on a change, one that would better suit her. Her long dark hair was cut away to but a couple of inches bleached white and spiked. She had double piercings in her lightened eyebrows, a circle of earrings on one ear and a single piercing in her lips, which were painted the color of charcoal. She wore what appeared to be a man's grey tailored suit. She put her arms out to welcome back her best friend.

Sloan could not back up any further. Krista was about to step in front of her best friend as if to protect her, when Sunni made her announcement. "Honey, it's me, Sunni..."

If there was somewhere to sit, Sloan surely would have taken a seat. She could not believe the creature standing in front of her was her long-ago friend. Why in God's name would she make herself so outrageously ugly—or did she see herself as beautiful? Sloan accepted Sunni's arms, although awkwardly; this woman would definitely not fit in Sloan's circle. Was Sloan turning snobbish? Call it as you see it, she would be ashamed to be seen in Sunni's presence.

But sooner rather than later Sunni would be a welcomed guest in Sloan's home. She had acquired a name for herself, and not because of her outlandish looks; she, like Sloan, was the talk of New York, although for different reasons. She climbed the ladder of success and earned the right to sit at any and all tables. Her talent won and continued to win many awards.

Sloan spoke before thinking of what the impact of her words would do.

"Well, it is certainly nice seeing you again, but my friend and I really have to get a move on."

Was Sunni being given the brush off? And what was that added bit about Sloan's friend, was she Sunni's replacement? Rage reeled inside, but she excelled in keeping her feelings hidden.

"Oh, you can't get rid of me that easy. Whatever you have planned can wait, this day calls for a celebration. Please, will you allow me to take you both to lunch? We have so much to catch up on...okay?"

What could Sloan say? She had been out-and-out rude to someone who always looked out for her. Now she would show courtesy by accepting. The elevator that day would not be in use. Introductions were made, while idle conversation followed them out of the door and onto the sidewalk, whereby Sloan and Sunni discovered they owned apartments in the same building; the odds of this happening were astronomical.

Sloan offered to take her car, but Sunni declined. She had a chauffeured limousine waiting. Sloan looked at the limo and then at Sunni. She was trying to link the two together; it was not a fit.

Within minutes they were welcomed into the finest restaurant in Manhattan, Ducasse's. Sloan and Krista looked at one another. Only the very wealthy could afford such a place; this was their favorite restaurant to dine.

The maître d' took Sunni's hands into his. "Miss Harrison, what a pleasure it is to see you; it's been a while. May I show you to your favorite table?"

"Yes, but today I have friends joining me."

He then gave his attention to the couple standing somewhat away from Sunni. Krista and Sloan were embarrassed to be seen with her.

"Well, well, it looks as if all my favorite people will be dining together. What a pleasant surprise." The maître d' proceeded to lead them to what was known as Sunni's table; she paid high bucks to always have her table available.

As Sloan and Krista followed, Sunni was stopped several times. "Miss Harrison, you look fabulous. You must call me."

Others who felt they were on a more personal level also had their say. "Sunni darling, please call me. My appointment book hasn't seen your name for a while."

And yet another voice was heard. "Darling Sunni, what do I have to do to get you to call me?" Kisses were being blown in all directions.

Sloan could not understand what was happening; not once was she hit on or acknowledged, something she considered annoying, but expected.

Once they were seated, Sloan couldn't hold back. "Okay, give. What is going on?"

"I did it, Sloan, I conquered New York. There isn't anywhere I can't go where I'm not recognized. But I couldn't have done it without you."

Sloan was puzzled. "I still don't get it."

"Did I not promise that I would take care of you, and that you would want for nothing?"

Krista noticed Sloan's expression as one of confusion. Surely Sloan was reading into what she was hearing, or was she? Krista was a witness to an open display of affection, one that a man has for a woman, only this was no man. Sunni was a lesbian in love with her best friend. Were they involved years ago? Did Sloan give in to the temptation with the promise of wealth? Knowing the poverty Sloan endured, Krista believed she might have crossed over to the other side. Krista stood. She refused to be a party to possibly hand holding or beyond.

Sloan was drawn away from Sunni's words when Krista made an announcement. "I think I will leave you two to catch up on old times."

Sloan started to protest as she too rose from her chair.

Krista staged a show of consideration. "No, no, please don't worry about me. I will hail a taxi." She could tell Sloan was unsure of what to do. "Honey, it's no big deal. I'll call you later, okay?"

Sloan was agreeable.

Did Krista just notice a sigh of relief from her best friend, or was her imagination working overtime? All she knew was she had to get out of there; maybe she would call and maybe not.

Krista, with all her goodness and light, drew the line when it came to the gay movement. Maybe she would have thought differently had her mother not run off with her lesbian lover, leaving her father despondent and crying in his pillow night after night and forgetting he had a fourteen-year-old daughter. He stopped working, preferring to wallow in his misery until he could no longer take it.

He was found in the early morning light, his once handsome face completely blown away. Evidence showed a.367 magnum revolver was used to end his life. The gun had been placed inside his mouth. Blood and brain matter covered his bed sheets and headboard, with the excess splattered about the ceiling and walls. Experienced in the handling of guns, Krista's father knew that his weapon of choice meant he could never be revived. In the final analysis with gun residue on his hand and his fingerprints found on the gun, there was no reason to doubt he died by his own hand.

Sloan was now intrigued, but one has to wonder, if Sunni had not been treated as someone in high standing, would Sloan have tried to escape as she did with Marc?

Brunch soon turned into lunch, conversation never at a standstill. Sunni covered all the aspects of her life since the disappearance of Sloan, ending with the death of her parents. Sloan's tears assured Sunni that her performance exceeded her expectations. Sloan loved the Doc and his wife almost as much as her papa and mama had. Sunni offered Kleenex taken from her steel-grey low-slung handbag. There was a lull in their conversation, forcing Sloan to remember her personal tragedy, a memory she tried hard to keep at bay.

Sunni thankfully brought Sloan back to the present; she pushed for her to come clean about her disappearance, pumping her with questions.

"All that glitter on your hand must have a man's name attached. I was hoping you would have saved yourself for me."

Shocked beyond words, Sloan felt the rush of blood playing across her face. Sunni wished she had not said what she said; Sloan was not ready to accept her declaration of love. In time, she would come around; Sunni was not reading into something that was not evident years back.

"God, Sloan, you should see your face. Red is definitely not your color. What happened to the girl I thought I knew? When you left did you also leave behind your sense of humor?"

Sloan was embarrassed thinking her friend hid in a closet. Sunni was and still is her best friend; she was entitled to know all that took place up to and after her disappearance. When Sloan finished, Sunni was stunned. The woman she wanted in her bed did not need a ladder to climb, she was already there. She wondered what it would take to bring Sloan to her side.

Her ability as an actress resurfaced.

"Well, leave it to you to put fiction to fact when it comes to the story of Cinderella. I'm really happy for you, honey."

Sunni was reeking with hatred for someone she'd never met. Sloan's husband will plead for mercy when the night caller pays him a visit. She put aside her thoughts of murder for another day; she had much to impress her lover.

"I want to show you something. It will blow your mind."

Sloan could be considered a hip-hugger, clinging to Sunni like a small child. She would soon enter a totally different world, one of the working class and finding a kind of fulfillment her home could not provide.

Before the chauffer pulled the limo to a complete stop, Sunni was out holding her arms upward. Ni's House of Design spoke volumes: it was half a block of announcing that Sunni had arrived and was here to stay. Yes, she was bragging, and Sloan accepted what the eye could see.

Sunni opened the door to her studio, followed with a statement. "You are my guest, have at it."

Sloan entered slowly. The magnificently displayed studio was a work of a genius. She could not contain herself, she took off running. There would not be a single thing she did not touch.

She captured the attention of Sunni's ten employees. Five carpenters and four electricians were added but never did they feel the sting of a less than a forty-hour weekly paycheck. Computers, telephones and fax machines were in constant use; several prospective clients were walking about viewing the showrooms separated by partitions. Walls and tables were covered with sample books of paint colors, wall coverings, fabric patterns, carpeting and furniture. Sunni traveled the world with blood money, buying and then selling those products to be used in her clients' homes. She no longer had use for a ladder; she had made it to the top.

Sunni followed Sloan inside, but she settled down onto a custom-made chair. She enjoyed watching her lover rush about.

Sunni's yearly net income was fast approaching the ten-million-dollar mark. She climbed the ladder, that was true, but never would she have had that kind of success without the smear of blood that coated her hands. Had she known her parents' worth, she would have done them in much sooner; Sloan would then be riding high on her backside. But the word *never* was not intended for her use. Sloan's wedding rings were somewhat of a hindrance, but one that could be taken care of in good time. Sunni smiled with that thought and the smile lingered when she thought of the others who'd died by her hand. *Vengeance is mine; no one makes my woman cry and lives to tell about it.*

Sunni smiled as the memories of the killings replayed...

Timmy was the first to start the flow of Sloan's tears with his ugly reference to Sloan's baby brother's nickname of ReRe, and to top it off, how Sloan's papa loved him more than Sloan. And because Sloan believed this to be true, Sunni had to make Zack cease to exist. Sloan could then reclaim first place in her papa's heart. Sloan ran home after his dreadful remarks, tears flying in the wind. Sunni repeated Sloan's words, how she too hated Timmy and she would no longer be his playmate. But Sunni shortly returned, this time with some of her mother's medication placed in a small vial hidden in the pocket of her shorts. She told Timmy she was sorry for yelling at him, that she still wanted to be his friend and that Sloan was just a big cry baby.

They continued to play, until she suggested making Kool-Aid, but only with his sitter Cindy's permission. She pleaded with Cindy to allow her to make it unchaperoned. She remembered Cindy's comment while giving

Sunni a hug: "Okay, sweetie, I guess you're old enough."

And with that Cindy took Timmy by his hand into the playroom. Sunni had already crushed the tablets; now she added them to Cindy's drink. While Sunni and Timmy giggled and played games, Sunni kept her eye on Cindy. When the signs of drowsiness became evident, Cindy left Timmy to lie down upon the couch. Sunni went to her and knelt near her face. She lifted the sitter's eyelids to see if she could focus; she could not. She whispered in Cindy's ear, telling her what she had done.

"You have just been drugged with a deadly combination of sleeping pills and valium. You will never again rise up to meet the day, and your precious Timmy will soon be joining you. Toodle-oo."

Cindy tried to respond but was unable to form words. She mumbled something incoherent and then slid into unconsciousness.

Timmy, unaware of what had taken place and with Sunni's tempting suggestion, went off with her to the swimming hole.

It was much harder to kill Timmy; after all, he was her first, and she was only ten years old. She struggled with a large rock while he splashed in the water. Its weight hindered the force of the first blow, allowing Timmy to turn and face his attacker. Blood ran in streams, coating his eyes while turning his lips a ruby red. He tried to speak but Sunni was swift to silence him. She struck him repeatedly until his mouth moved no more.

She pushed his body as far out into the water as possible until her feet could no longer feel the bottom of the lake.

Baby Zachary, or ReRe, the only name he responded to, was next. Sunni knew the layout of Sloan's house as well as her own, so she had no difficulty finding the bedroom of the "little man," as Saul proudly addressed his boy. Sunni did have a concern, though, with the sounds the back door created, but there was no way to prevent this, so she just plunged ahead hoping everyone was dead to the world.

Evil stood over Saul's little man. The small child's lips were in constant motion as if sucking on his mother's tit. There was no hesitation, Sunni's hand pressed tightly over ReRe's tiny nose and mouth, while the other secured his head from behind. The intense struggle proved Saul's little man would have been a fighter. Why she positioned his body facedown with his legs tucked under his tummy will probably never be known.

And there was Silva and her nasty mouth, upsetting Sloan's mama, thereby making Sloan cry. That experience brought an unexpected thrill, heightening Sunni's desire to kill again.

But Mr. Hewlett was the one that caused Sloan more grief than all of them, but he was also a thorn in Sunni's side with his assumption there would be a man in her life smiling over her fortune.

She enacted the worst possible punishment upon Willie's body.

Sunni called him, apologizing for treating him so badly on the day he delivered the news of her windfall. "I would like to meet with you in one of your hideaways to show you just how sorry I am."

She lowered her voice to a seductive tone. "Would you like for me to ride you like a horse while naked, Willie?"

Of course he would. She told him the time and the date. He assured her they would have nothing but the very best of the cabins. Did he say the very best? The cabins were all identical; Willie would not know the best unless his bedding companion chose another place and she did the paying.

The night was as black as coal dust, the sky empty of stars. The shopping district was at rest, as well the townspeople. Sunni entered Cabin 14. A glimmer of light was provided from the adjoining bathroom.

Willie boy, naked with a stupid grin plastered on his face, shook his head in the direction of his privates, as if to say, "Look what I have for you." Just the thought of being with a man brought bile to Sunni's throat.

She got down to business, hiking up her skirt to straddle him. She knew this would excite him, he was more than ready.

"No, no, you must have patience. What I have for you will be equal to none, but first I must blindfold you," she told him.

He complied on condition she disrobe. Sunni could taste the beginnings of vomit; it played on her tonsils. She could just slit his throat and be done with it, but that would not give her the satisfaction she so desperately hungered for. The joy in the kill was what it was all about.

She now stood in front of him slowly removing each piece of clothing and tossing it in Willie's direction. He grabbed hold, burying his face into each item. He screamed out for her to do what she wanted, he could not wait a second longer. A man's handkerchief was then tied around his head; he would see nothing until the final act. Nylons were used to tie his hands and feet to the bed posts. Willie always fantasized about being held captive, but never did he believe it would happen; he was beginning to feel a height of pleasure never before experienced.

After several minutes passed and nothing could be felt, he began to grow impatient. He was growing tired of Sunni's antics; he wanted to be free of the restraints. His yell of protest caught in midair was silenced by a band of tape, although she was kind enough to remove his eyepiece.

She had a few final words. "You should never have told Sloan her family was worthless."

Willie began shaking his head uncontrollably. He was unable to speak; beads of sweat told of his fear. He caught a glimpse of the scalpel as the blade swept up and then downward, removing his penis with one swipe. Mr. William Hewlett's running days were over.

Sunni hated to leave those vivid memories, but watching Sloan's reaction to her studio was something she never wanted to forget. It was time for Sloan to join her, she wanted her input. She yelled out for Sloan's attention, and Sloan danced over to her friend, giddy for her success.

"When I told you of my desire to design a studio that no one could duplicate, you went to work and created a masterpiece. You won the highest achievement award in our senior year for that drawing, do you not remember? Look around, honey, your canvas has been brought to life, giving my studio a heart. Do you not feel it?"

Sloan began to cry. "Oh Sunni, what have I done to you?"

Sunni should have put her talent to work as an actress; she accomplished what she intended, playing on Sloan's heart, knowing she was a sucker for sentimentality.

But her greatest performance followed the death of Sloan's family...

Before she doused the Parkers' house with gasoline she checked to make sure Sloan was indeed where Chrissie said she would be, sleeping outside by the barn.

Remembering that night brought a renewed sense of pleasure. The pies she baked for the Parkers' consumption loaded with every kind of pill available did indeed work their magic; why two of Sloan's sisters were aroused from what should have been a dead sleep will remain a mystery. And while the townspeople's tears washed the roads, Sunni's show of mega tears would have convinced God Almighty, had he been present, that they were genuine.

Sunni pushed past that memory, drawing Sloan into an embrace while relishing in her scent.

"Hush, no more tears. We are together, and that is all that matters."

Sloan realized she missed the comfort Sunni always managed to give.

Sunni wished she could freeze the moment or go back in time and undo the mass killing of her best friend's family. But that wish quickly ended when the rush of Saul's words blasted her memory: *We must separate Sloan and Sunni.* And she hated her father for agreeing. By their own words they brought about their execution, and fearing Beth would carry out Saul's wishes, she had to join him, and what would the kids do without their parents? And because she considered her parents a couple, when one departs, the other must follow.

When Sunni's parents dropped her off at the airport to return to school, she cancelled her flight and returned home, although she waited until the light of the day turned into the blackest of nights. She drove a rented car, a black compact Nissan, into the town's shopping district that was shuttered for the night; the parking lot was empty of cars. She drove slowly to her parents' house, keeping an eye out for the roamers unable to sleep, but the only thing moving that night was the night caller.

Sunni parked deep in the fields behind her parents' house, fields left to nature's care. She crept inside. Her parents never locked their door; they had no fear of the unknown. A palm-size flashlight gave the necessary beam of light to add two more mementos to her growing collection. She was puzzled to see a number of her mother's suitcases sitting by the entrance. She opened a small travel bag, surprised to find a jumbled mess of jewelry with no semblance of order. She did not have time to analyze what was going on; she was on a mission of destruction.

She took the first piece she touched, a simple jade ring. Her father's office provided what she could possibly use in the future, a tool of his trade stored inside his medical bag. Had Sunni taken the time to give her parents a final look, she would have found them sleeping for the first time in separate rooms.

The burners on the gas range were turned to the on position, flames extinguished, leaving fumes to accumulate. She waited several minutes for the fumes to amass. She leaned a couple of open gasoline cans on a two-by-four then gave each a nudge, spilling the contents. An inquiry was sure to take place. The authorities would assume the cans had been stacked on the wood and somehow became dislodged, thus causing an explosion.

The fumes were doing their job; Sunni began to cough. She was standing at the exit of the garage that would take her back through the fields she'd come from. She struck the match, which she prayed would take her parents' lives. Then Sunni ran before the flames licked at her ass. Explosion after explosion caught her off guard; she barely made it out alive. It was like nothing she expected: the earth shook and fireballs ascended into the sky, lighting the paths the townspeople would walk and weep.

The smile she carried with each victory, deepened. She knew she had stayed too long when she heard the sirens of the fire trucks blasting through a town she would no longer call home.

Ben was the lucky one. Had it not been for Sloan's disappearance with his promise to keep Sunni updated should news come forth, he would have been her next victim for failing to keep an eye on her Jaguar.

Sloan interrupted Sunni's pleasure trip. They were now seated in her private office. Strict instructions were given that they were not to be disturbed or someone's head would roll. The employees did not doubt the threat. The two old friends were enjoying a glass of iced tea, but Sloan was having difficulty getting past the thoughts of her family. Sunni's presence brought that memory to the surface. She could not hold back the tears, praying she would not upset Sunni by forcing her to also relive her own tragedy.

"Sunni, do you ever think about the day your parents died, that maybe, if you had done something different, they would still be alive?"

Sunni's performance was still at work.

She took Sloan's hands into her own.

"Honey, I was away at school. Nothing could have changed that. For years, I lived in a prison of hate, throwing away my beliefs, refusing to forgive God. But eventually, I realized without Him in my life, I had no life. Honey, don't you see? We are living in His timetable; He decides who stays and who goes.

"You know what your problem is? You have too much time on your hands. You need something to keep your mind occupied, and I think I have the solution. How about you and I tying the knot in a business partnership?"

For the first time Sunni prayed, thinking if she repented her ghastly sins and promised to sin no more, God would lend his hand. God did listen, but He would provide no help, for she was about to embark on yet another killing spree.

Sloan was crestfallen. Here was an opportunity to escape the walls of the house that were closing in, but it could never be.

"If only I could, but Clay would never permit it. I'm sorry, Sunni."

"There's only one thing you need to be sorry for, and that is allowing a man to rule your life. You used to have guts and grit; you gave meaning to the rights of women. Whatever hold your husband has over you, you need to break away or you will never come into your own."

Sloan was always eager to accept advice from her peers, if it worked in her favor, and this time was no exception.

"You are absolutely right. But first I'll be the passive wife. I'll ask his permission, and if he refuses I'll ask for a divorce, which will cause him to sit up and realize I'm someone to reckon with."

Sunni could not keep her hands to herself; she hugged her woman tightly with a final comment. "Honey, I'm depending on you. Whatever happens, do not let your old man sway you from your decision. You must stay firm."

Sloan removed herself from Sunni's embrace, promising not to back down. She was now in a hurry to get home with the news. Sunni, her renewed best friend, paved a path to share in the limelight, and Sloan would be damned if she allowed Clay to stand in her way.

CHAPTER TWELVE

Marc Anderson was now Chase Anthony with a totally different look. He was no longer the boy Sloan left behind. He could give Clay fierce competition in the looks department. He was a man pursued by every woman up and down the streets of New York, phone numbers tucked into the palm of his hand as he strolled the streets. He purchased only the finest in men's apparel, shoes and accessories; money no longer was an issue. His prior salary would make any man proud of his accomplishments.

His mother's desire to purchase an apartment for him was declined. He was not ready to have a place of his own. He moved into a Quality Inn minutes from Clay's architectural firm by way of the subway. His truck was returned to his mother, and Ben took over ownership of it.

Chase would impress his brother Clay and Clay's father Phillip not only with his debonair manner, but with a talent not unlike that of Charles Mannigan. In the coming months some of the now older co-workers Charlie had taken under his wing would come to believe Chase was Charlie reincarnated.

Chase's time had come. He swung through the double glass doors of his brother's establishment. His eyes rested on the face of a beautiful blond receptionist. A telephone resting on her shoulder fell onto the desk; the caller not only heard but felt the blast. The greeter was not herself; she spoke before thinking.

"Hi. My name is Shawna. Are you married?" When those words actually passed through her ears, she dropped her head, embarrassed.

Chase quickly put her at ease. "It looks as if we locked into each other's thoughts. I was just about to ask you the same question." He introduced himself and told her what she wanted to hear: he was available. They would end up being bed partners, but his heart could not be shared.

Phillip was working at his drafting table when Shawna buzzed him; he would do the job interviews, freeing up Clay's time. Shawna directed Chase, pointing her finger towards Phillip's office.

Chase whispered, "Wish me luck."

She smiled, swimming in his blue eyes. "You got it."

Phillip put aside his work and took to his desk. A gentle knock announced Chase's presence. Phillip welcomed him into his office, accepting his hand while introductions were made. Chase stared at the man who was the first to win the heart of his mother, wondering if there was still a spark burning. His thoughts were interrupted when Phillip, after viewing his portfolio dating back two years, stated he was more than impressed with Chase's work.

"We've had an opening for some time waiting for the right person to fill a position that has been vacated. It looks like you're our man. Welcome."

Phillip extended his hand. Chase, showing his appreciation, clasped it with both hands. It was at that moment Phillip noticed his boy about to pass his door. He swung around his desk, apologizing to his new employee.

"Excuse me; I want you to meet my boy."

When Chase heard those words he abruptly turned. He was about to meet his brother for the first time; his heart pounded.

Phillip stepped outside his office door, said a few words then turned back inside, his arm around his boy's shoulder.

"Clay, I would like for you to meet Chase Anthony, someone I believe will have a powerful influence in our workplace."

In time, that power will extend into their lives.

Both brothers took steps towards one another, hands extended; an electrical shock from the newly installed carpet took them by surprise. Laughter followed with Clay's response, "Now that's what I call a handshake."

Chase was stunned when he recognized the man standing before him, but he held his tongue. He was about to take Clay back to their encounter years ago, two bodies knocking the other off his feet, but a voice within told him to keep that information to himself. He listened.

Only after the introductions did Chase also realize that neither Phillip nor Clay was aware that they were not father and son. He had some questions for his mother.

In a matter of minutes the three of them, chairs drawn close, were engaged in deep conversation detailing the aspects of Chase's new position.

Chase will endure the worst kind of pain given man, when he comes face-to-face with his long-lost love, only to lose her again.

CHAPTER THIRTEEN

Sloan's tires screeched to a halt in front of the steel gates. She keyed in the code then once again squealed her tires; parking she would leave up to her butler. She rushed through the front door, her long-strapped handbag held secure when she took to the stairs. The heat of the day took its toll on her hair, as well as her body. She would welcome a bath. She refused to approach Clay without looking her very best; that would give her some much-needed confidence when the word *work* tumbled out of her mouth.

Clay was in a great mood. He had finally found a replacement for one of his best architects, who decided to give up the drawing board in favor of the golf club. When he entered the front door Sloan was adding water to a flower arrangement, flowers she personally cut from a garden she tilled, planting seeds one by one. Her patience paid off with each growing season. She achieved what her mother failed to accomplish; she did this in her honor. Clay stared at what he considered his personal property with a single thought: *If only she knew her desire for a child is shared, to have a son to carry on my name, nothing could compare.*

Sloan could feel his presence, smell his fragrance. She too had a thought: *God, if you hear me, show me the way to bring us back to what we had in the beginning. I love him so very much.*

They were certainly on the same path, but traveling in opposite directions.

Clay, his usual brass self, broke his concentration and forged ahead. "I'm going to take a shower. I'll eat later." He headed towards the stairs, but was stopped by words he'd never given a thought to.

"Clay, I've been offered a job. Well, not exactly a job, but a partnership with a well-known designer. I'm sure you've heard of her, Sunni Harrison of Ni's House of Design. Well, it turns out the owner is not only from my hometown, but was my childhood friend. Can you believe it?"

Clay's world was set to collapse if he did not take command.

"Do you honestly believe I will permit you to work? You must think you live in Disneyland where fantasies are created."

Sloan could display anger when it was called for, and this was one of those times.

"I'm sorry, I was under the impression I was living in a fantasy world, one that you created. Apparently that only applies if you have your hand in it. Well, I'm here to tell you I don't need your world; I can start my own by accepting Sunni's offer."

Clay was shocked; did she mean she would be moving out? Did he go too far in trying to keep her under his control?

"Sloan, sometimes I move my lips before I think. By all means, if work is your pleasure, then go for it. Now if you'll excuse me, I'll see to my shower."

She had put him in his place; Clay was a man defeated, and Sloan should have been happy. Why then did she wipe away the start of tears when he turned his back?

Sunni was sitting at her desk wondering if Sloan would accept the partnership, when the phone began to ring; she was getting quite good at picking up on the first ring.

Sloan got to the point. "When do I start?"

Weeks turned into months, but the job was not what Sloan expected. Sunni followed her around like flies to shit. She had turned into a leech, sucking out the small amount of life Sloan had left. Sloan was caught daydreaming, her thoughts on Krista, when Sunni tapped her desk.

"You seem lost in thought. Care to tell me what or who pulled you away, or is it a secret?"

Sloan answered truthfully, "I was just trying to remember the last time Krista and I got together."

Sunni began tossing some papers she was carrying into a bin to be shredded, acting as if business was on her mind when she nonchalantly asked, "And when was that?"

"It seems like ages; I was just about to give her a call. Anything on your mind?"

"Let's put that call off for a while, what I have to say is much more important. How would you like to go on a business trip/vacation to Venice, Italy?"

Sloan's spirits lifted. Maybe this could be a turning point in her so-called career. Traveling would be better than sitting behind a desk, but would Clay agree?

Dinner was being eaten in silence. Sloan dreaded bringing up the subject, but she pushed forward.

"Clay, I have to go away on a business trip for a few days. I should be back by Friday at the latest. I hope this doesn't interfere with any of your plans?"

She was about to add, "I will miss you," but before she could, Clay stood abruptly, his chair no longer upright, the dinner napkin now a companion of the floor. He leaned over, his hands now on the table and with graces that fell to the wayside, he blatantly stated, "I am so sick of your bullshit; you never once mentioned that traveling was involved. But you know what? I really could care less. You do what you have to do, and I'll do what I have to do."

Sloan was caught off guard. What did he mean by that? Was he about to turn the tables? Did she carry her act of bravado too far? If she backed down now she would never have a foothold on anything. She would forge ahead, praying it was the right decision.

While Sloan was making her plans, Clay was making his. He would bed down with his company's receptionist, Shawna, who, unbeknownst to him, was also his brother's playmate.

CHAPTER FOURTEEN

The flight from New York to Venice, Italy, was long and exhausting. Sunni, it seemed, could not keep her hands to herself, excitement her excuse. But Sloan was tired of her handholding; she could not wait to land.

Reservations were made at Bauer II Palazzo, a hotel best suited for those whose pockets never emptied. Their suite with a panoramic view faced the Grand Canal. Sunni, the considerate lover she would be, surprised Sloan with a shuttle ride to Bauer Palladio, the sister hotel and spa. It was the perfect place to unwind after a tiresome flight and to enjoy the benefits of a massage and beauty treatment. Sloan tried to refuse at first, but Sunni like always was persuasive. After experiencing the delights of the spa, Sloan decided she would never again object; heaven could not be better. But like all good things the day came to an end, and she was ready to feel the comforts of a bed.

Sunni was the one to open the door to their

suite, her excitement building. Sloan was no longer surprised with her surroundings; she had grown accustomed to the life of the rich and famous. Bed coverings were turned down; suitcases sitting close by were ready to be unpacked.

Sloan kicked off her shoes and dropped into the nearest chair, her arms dangling off it sides.

Sunni had thought ahead. At the spa, she'd waited until Sloan was out of earshot before calling the hotel and placing an order. The order was meant to entice her lover and put her in the mood for a taste of what it's like to be with a woman. It was waiting to welcome them.

"Well, honey, I think a glass of champagne and some strawberries are in order, a perfect blend to finish off a perfect day. What do you think?"

Sloan loved the taste of champagne, she could not refuse; besides, it would help her unwind and possibly induce sleep.

"While you're pouring, I'll get out of my clothes." Sloan strolled out of the room pulling her suitcase behind her. Sunni was greatly disappointed, having hoped they would share the same bed.

But Sunni was prepared. Before their trip she'd visited the doctor with complaints of severe insomnia and the considerate doctor had prescribed a combination of Amytal and Tuinal. Thicken anyone's wallet and you are guaranteed any request. She planned to wait until Sloan was pie-eyed before she emptied a packet of the two drugs, now in powder form, into Sloan's glass. The combination of these drugs was guaranteed to put the recipient out for a minimum of six hours. She would have her woman tonight; she had waited long enough.

Sunni made love through the night, her hands and mouth never at rest until Sloan began to show signs of moaning with undeniable pleasure. She stopped before bringing Sloan to an orgasm, preferring to continue this sort of foreplay while she herself had multiple orgasms. She would have been more satisfied had Sloan been an active participant, but she was thrilled with what she had to take.

Sloan began to hold herself, moaning and twisting around the bed; her eyelids began to flutter. Dawn was a blink away. Sunni had played too long, failing to notice that time was no longer a friend, but she was always a step ahead. She slid back into her nightgown as she rushed to her own bed. Her acting skills would soon be put to a challenge.

Sloan's lack of fulfillment shook her awake. She was embarrassed with what she thought was an erotic dream. Hurting with desire, she turned her thoughts to her husband: *Where is Clay when I need him?* She rolled over to check the time on her watch. Amazed at the coolness of the sheet against her skin, she looked down and was shocked to find she was naked. She shivered. Something was trying to work its way into her memory. *Was someone in my room during the night? Was I taken advantage of, or worse yet, was I raped?* She felt moistness between her legs. She shot out of bed.

Sunni gave the appearance of being in a deep sleep when Sloan pounced onto her bed.

"Sunni, Sunni, wake up. You must call the police. Oh God in Heaven, I think I was raped." Sloan sought the comfort of Sunni's arms as her hysteria turned into weeping.

Sunni was ready with a great story.

"Honey, you must have had a nightmare. The security here is the best. There is no way someone could have gotten into our suite without a key. And besides, I'm a light sleeper, I would have heard something."

But Sloan was not buying this story. She continued to feel violated.

"Okay, I can see that didn't go so well, so why don't you just go ahead and tell me why you think you were raped."

"I awoke from what I thought was a sexual dream to find myself naked; my nightwear was lying on the floor. Someone had to have removed it; I never sleep in the nude." There was no need for Sunni to know Sloan's sleeping habits with her husband.

Sunni burst out laughing, and then apologized when Sloan became upset.

"Is that what this is about, your stupid nightie? Honey, look at me. Before we allowed ourselves to get wasted, we readied ourselves for bed. Then as the night wore on the liquor began to take its toll. You complained that the apartment was stifling, and without further thought you staggered into your bedroom, tossed your teddy onto the floor and then staggered back to continue drinking. I should have called it a night; I'm really sorry for causing you such stress."

Sloan felt like a fool. Sunni's explanation was more than plausible.

"You must think there's something seriously wrong with me."

"No, honey, I do not. But I'll say one thing for you, you sure do have a wild imagination, or is it wishful thinking?"

Sloan threw out her fist, playfully giving Sunni a punch, acknowledging the joke. Sunni in turn gave a shove to the naked Sloan, telling her to get a move on. They had a schedule to keep with their distributors, and it would be a long day.

The business part of the trip was successful, and the remaining three days were left to sightseeing. The list was long: the Renaissance, St. Mark's Square, the Bridge of Signs, Piazza San Marco, Academy of Fine Arts, Rialto Market, Arsenale, Ca'Pesaro, Palazzo Ducale, and the finale night, a gondola ride through the Grand Canal shared with no one.

Sloan thanked Sunni over and over for a trip never to be forgotten, while trying to forget the lingering thoughts of someone having their way with her.

But soon a terrifying memory she thought was a thing of the past would return to make her nights a living hell, putting aside the abuse of her body to be recalled for another time.

CHAPTER FIFTEEN

Clay could not have felt any worse if he'd had a migraine. He knew Shawna had a thing for him for years—she was easy prey, but that did not make it right. He now had another sin to add to his growing list. Shawna was one of the nicest people you would ever want to meet. She did not deserve to be used for his sinful act.

He called her into his office the following day; he had to apologize.

"Shawna, I am so sorry. I crossed the line. You can be assured it will never happen again. Do you think you can forgive me?"

Shawna dropped her head, having just been told she was a one-night stand. She could not find the words Clay wanted to hear; all she could do was nod. But what he did not know was, her letter of resignation would be facing him when he returned to work the following day.

Shawna had been warming her bed with Chase when she pulled Clay in. From the beginning of their courtship she and Chase accepted the fact they had little in common, but it would have been extremely difficult to give up the kind of lovemaking he had introduced her to. So out of kindness Chase offered himself to her when she could no longer go without. But after the tryst with her boss, Chase would have had an additional companion in her bed: guilt. She could no longer continue with this masquerade: someone was bound to get hurt, and the way it was looking, she would be the one.

Clay was sitting in his study looking over Shawna's letter of resignation. What he deserved from her was a bullet, not a letter. He told no one of the letter, but shortly after, Shawna gathered her belongings, telling those in hearing range she had found another job. Within minutes she was gone. A temp would take over her position. And now the weekend was facing him; he and Sloan would be alone. The servants had long ago been set free to enjoy their own weekends.

He was lost in thought, pondering his fate should Sloan find out he had done the unforgivable, when he heard her call out.

"I'm home."

Clay rushed to the window, wondering who was behind the wheel when his wife was dropped off. He was thinking that she too had

had a fling but her lover did not have the gall to show his face. He was losing it. Guilt had attached itself to him, and the only way to find relief was to confess. But the nagging question haunted him: *What if she leaves me, or worse, she throws me out of my own house, suitcases to follow? But there is a slim possibility she will forgive me.* But the way things were going in their relationship, Clay had about a teaspoon of faith riding on forgiveness. But some clemency should be shown; he does have a conscience, for without that there would be no guilt.

Do you not hear a "hooray" for those with a conscience?

Sloan received no response. Did she really think she would hear one? Clay's study door was ajar; there was no need for a knock. He had returned to his chair when she strolled into the room. Her appearance as always grabbed his breath, refusing to let go. The thought of suicide entered the room almost at the exact moment as his wife. His internal organs were screaming with pain, while he struggled with a single thought: *How could I have betrayed her?*

She had her own thoughts. *How could I have gone off to do my own thing with no regard for my husband? I need to apologize and tell him my place is by his side, not off trying to conquer the working world.*

Clay's eyes may have been focused on the papers lying before him, but his thoughts were of his wife. He desperately wanted to take her in his arms, telling her how much he loved and missed her, while she listened to his confession of adultery…but of course, that was not about to happen.

"Clay, if I could have a minute of your time, I need to say something."

He was thoughtful enough to give her his attention, although with a somber look.

"I was thinking about quitting my job. I miss being at home." But before she could add, "I miss being here when you get home from work," he cut her off.

"Your conscience must be riddled with guilt, as well it should be." When those words found their way from his mouth, Clay knew the word *apology* may as well be eliminated from the dictionary. He could not have done more damage had he run her down with his car.

Sloan refused to give in to the temptation of arguing; she would agree with anything he had to say.

"You are absolutely right."

She turned to exit when he again spoke out.

"Sloan, while you were off enjoying yourself, I assumed your position making arrangements for a dinner party to honor an architect that has proven over several months he has what it takes to be the lead man in our company. I would like for this to be a couples dinner, but the honoree is single. Do you think Sunni would be willing to be his companion for the evening?"

"If she doesn't have other plans, I'm sure she'll be happy to join in. Would it be too much to ask who our invited guests will be?"

"You'll find the list sitting on your writing desk along with the date and time." Clay turned his attention to the papers in front of him; his wife was dismissed.

She left the way she came in, although with a different attitude. When Clay reaches for her under the cover of night, she will refuse.

CHAPTER SIXTEEN

The party was in full gear, with twenty-four couples in attendance. They were now waiting on the honoree. Beauty flourished throughout the ballroom. Every wealthy man had a glamorous woman — either a mistress or a wife — on his arm. But none of them compared to their hostess.

Sloan was dressed in a strapless ivory Christian Dior gown with multiple strands of diamonds around her neck. Neither the gown nor the diamonds drew attention away from the woman wearing them. She wore her shimmering dark hair straight and parted in the center, this now her signature.

Sunni attached herself to her lover, although Sloan focused her attention on Krista. Krista gladly accepted. When the days of not returning Sloan's calls stretched into weeks, and then months, Krista relented; she missed her best friend terribly. She was there to mend what was broken.

Sloan, totally lost in her working world, never gave a thought to what Krista was doing with her life, until Krista tapped her on the shoulder, pushing Sunni aside. The unmistakable love that only the best of friends share brought shared tears.

Sunni could not continue to watch the scene before her. About to explode with anger, she excused herself, the marble bathroom now her sanctuary. Locked inside she found her release; the walls did not give under the pressure of pounding fists. To Sunni, the behavior of her lover and Krista told of them sharing the same bed. Inside a sick mind there is no room for understanding true friendship. The night caller would be quite busy in the months ahead.

Clay stood with a few of his friends but was not engaged in their conversation. Instead he glanced about the room searching for the honoree.

He spotted Chase shaking hands with his father and his father's female companion for the evening. Chase had arrived just in time: dinner was to be served in less than fifteen minutes. Clay walked over, anxious for Chase to meet his wife; introduction to the actual guests would be made at the dinner table. Phillip understood Clay's eagerness; he and his female friend excused themselves to mingle with the guests. Clay took Chase by his arm and then leaned towards him as if he were about to whisper a secret. "It's time for you to meet the woman that controls the rhythm of my heart."

Clay approached Sloan from her backside, Krista was facing her. The two friends were deep in conversation, aglow with happiness over their reconnection. Sunni was standing close to Sloan's side and showing signs of what Clay perceived as boredom. But he knew that look would soon be swept away; any woman would appreciate Chase's companionship.

Clay drew his wife to him, and she lovingly responded, portraying the perfect adoring wife.

"Babe, I would like for you to meet the man who made this party possible."

Sloan turned to face the man who had loved her his entire life. Chase took a step back, stunned. He wished somehow he had been forewarned; then maybe he could have conducted himself a little better. But as it was, he fumbled with his words when making her acquaintance.

Sloan was puzzled by his actions. This was to be the company's lead man? Was she missing something? Not until she was seated across from him at the dinner table would she recognize him as someone from her childhood. Dinner was announced on schedule and the guests quickly found their place cards. Clay was placed at the head of the very long table, with his father Phillip at the opposite end. Chase with his appointed date Sunni sat to Clay's right. Chase was facing Sloan, the woman who for more than two decades had carved her name into his heart.

Conversation continued nonstop until Clay tapped his glass and all in attendance turned in his direction. His speech was well received. Chase, a bit embarrassed when asked to stand, relaxed with a broad smile when all stood to applaud.

Sloan could not take her eyes off the man before her. She could not deny what she was feeling: an ache of desire that would not go away until she had this man in her bed. Chase noticed her eyeing him and nodded to her ever so slyly and she knew that he knew she wanted him. Chase received a confirmation from her that all was not lost. Sloan dropped her head, ashamed. Was he reading her mind?

Chase did in fact read her mind; his mother's ability transcended. He intended to win her back, brother or not.

Sunni was laying it on, playing up to her designated partner, and Chase obliged. Each had the intention of making Sloan jealous. Sunni was elated that it was working; Sloan could not take her eyes off of them.

Yes, it was true; Sloan did have her eyes on them, but out of disbelief that Chase would find Sunni to his liking. Of course, she was happy for her friend, but shocked to feel a pain of such magnitude; it somewhat resembled the loss of her family.

Chase glanced in her direction and winked. She caught his meaning: *I'm playing with you. Sunni means nothing to me.* She tried to turn away, but his eyes, not unlike those that belonged to someone from her past, refused to let go. Chase/Marc was here to claim what was rightfully his. Sloan abruptly stood; her chair met no resistance. She excused herself, although no one gave notice but the man she had run from years before, and from whom she no longer wished to escape.

She forced herself to remain calm as she prepared to leave the dining area. Clay took her hand. Sensing something was wrong, he was truly concerned.

"Are you not feeling well?" he asked, not realizing he was giving her an out.

"I'm really sorry, Clay. I hate to ruin your evening, but I have a miserable headache. Would you mind giving my regrets?"

He continued to be considerate. "Should I go with you? I really don't mind."

Sloan looked into the face of the man who for several years had looked at her with contempt, though she'd never understood why. Now that man had vanished and in his place was the man she has always loved, yet her heart was racing with thoughts of another.

"Thank you. I appreciate your thoughtfulness, but someone really should stay with the guests." She leaned towards him, warming his lips with her moist kiss, whispering a promise of what lay ahead when the evening came to an end.

He too whispered engaging words. "If you no longer suffer with a headache, I plan on holding you to that promise. I love you, babe."

"I love you more." She held back the tears of joy, relishing in the moment, all the while praying Clay would come to her as he was now, not as he had been before.

Chase waited a decent amount of time after dinner before he excused himself for the evening. He removed himself from the dining chair and turned towards Clay.

"I really hate to run, but it's a long drive back to the hotel."

Before he could finish, Clay offered him a guest room for the night.

"I will not take no for an answer."

Chase felt destiny giving him a hand. He gladly accepted. For years he had shunned the powers given to him by his mother; this was the first time he'd held himself open to receive what Sloan was telling him.

Excuse yourself from the table — no one will dare ask why — take the elevator to the top floor then turn left. The first door you come to is where I will be waiting. Don't worry, we will be safe.

He directed his attention towards Sunni; he had to get a move on before Sloan thought he changed his mind. He leaned close and whispered what every girl longs to hear if someone is truly interested: "I'll be right back. Hold my chair."

Sunni watched as he made his exit.

Chase could have removed himself permanently; Sunni could have cared less after Clay told his guests the reason behind Sloan's departure. But Sunni showed a good side, dripping with sweetness and very apologetic to her host.

"I'm really sorry, Clay, but I have to call it a night; I have an early morning call that cannot be put off. I had a wonderful evening. Thank you for the invite."

Chase, when he did return to his chair, would be more than happy to learn of Sunni's departure.

Sloan could not help herself; she desired two men with the possibility of loving them both. She tried to justify her actions: Chase/Marc in all honesty should have been the first to share her bed.

Chase opened the first door on the left and there she was, just as she said she would be. This was his moment, although it must be brief because Clay and Sunni were waiting.

After he told Sloan of Clay's offer of a stay-over, there was no need to rush through what his heart demanded to be said. Sloan would find him; she knew the rooms that were used when guests stayed. They now had plenty of time; she would come to him when she felt it was safe.

The party lingered well past midnight. When the guests noticed their host yawn, they began to say their goodnights, a consideration given even by those no longer able to stand without the assistance of their partner. Clay was anxious to close and lock the door—was not his wife waiting to fulfill her promise?

There was no way she would refuse his lovemaking, if he came to her as he was when they first met. Sloan ached for what followed after hours of lovemaking: his arms holding her close, whispering endearing words of love and how much she meant to him. It had been too many years since those words were spoken. Will she hear them tonight before she trots off to possibly bed down with her yet unknown husband's brother?

Clay entered their bedroom and walked to the side of her bed. The lamp was turned low, but she was awake. He knelt at the bedside, gently caressing her forehead, and then asked the all-important question. "Have you found relief from your headache?"

Sloan was beyond happy; he was still the person she left at the dining table. "Yes, I have. Thank you for asking."

He cupped her face into his hands, gently pressing his lips to hers. His next comment was tender. "Would you like to take a shower with me?" He was already making love to her with his words and yet he was unaware.

This was the man she fell in love with, the man she promised to love till death do them part. What was it that changed him back?

"Clay, there is something going on that has me baffled. You've taken on a personality not unlike that of Dr. Jekyll and Mr. Hyde. What's with the sudden change?"

"I never realized how far apart we've drifted, until I noticed how Chase and Sunni hit it off; it was obvious they were really into each other. I think they're a good match. Anyway, it reminded me of us in the beginning. I want that back. Are you willing to give us another chance?"

Before she could answer, she ran his comment through her mind: *Chase and Sunni are a good match? Is he blind?* Never could she find two people who were so unsuited.

Sloan did not voice her opinion, but she did tell him what he wanted to hear. "Oh yes, my darling, yes. We'll start anew, and maybe this time around you'll reconsider having a baby."

When Clay heard those words, he was up and out of the room.

Sloan screamed after him, tears rolling down her face like rain in a thunderstorm. "Clay, please don't do this!"

She turned over, burying her face in the down-filled pillow; there would be no lovemaking or the feeling of contentment that followed. They would not find their way back.

After Chase and Sloan had made their plans, Sunni began making hers. She will arrange another vacation, only this time it will be for several weeks, time enough for Sloan to experience the wonders of making love with another woman.

CHAPTER SEVENTEEN

Sloan knew Clay was not about to return; when things did not go his way, he made his bed in his study. She would seek out Marc. She selected a sheer nightgown that was guaranteed to bring arousal; it was one of Clay's favorites. She held the gown up and off the floor as she made her way to what was a haven for a stay-over.

From afar, she noticed a bright light guiding her towards what she hoped would be her first act of adultery. She would show Clay: she would find another to warm her bed. She whispered through the slight opening. "Marc, are you awake?"

The door swung open, and Marc had her in his arms.

"Do you have any idea how long I've waited for this?"

She searched out his mouth; the moistness of his lips caused her to sigh and sway. The way he held her head and moved his lips, she knew he was a man sure to bring pleasure. She could not get any closer without climbing into his clothing. She began to tug at his pants, but instead of obliging, he pulled away.

"I'm sorry, this is wrong. You belong to another; I do not have the right."

Sloan was stunned; never had she expected this.

"I thought you wanted me. What a fool I am. I should never have come to you."

He reached out as she turned away, ready to run again. She felt anger, but the humiliation was much worse.

"Sloan, look at me. You know the depth of my feelings. I just got carried away; I should never have kissed you. I am desperate to make love to you, but not this way."

He again drew her to him.

"If we are meant to be, it will happen. Until then, I can only love you at a distance."

What could she say or do? Getting on her hands and knees to beg would be useless; Marc's morals spoke loudly. But what if fate looked away—would that mean she would have him in her bed?

He took her by the hand and led her to a settee, where they began what would be a lengthy conversation.

Sloan was the first to speak. "Why the name change? Are you in hiding?"

She should laugh at the absurdity of that question. His mother's influence taught him to always walk the straight and narrow; never would he allow disgrace to enter into their lives.

"I have an explanation, but the timing is not right for disclosure. I thought my identity would be exposed when I found out Sunni was our Sunni. Thank God she did not recognize me. Now it's up to you. Can you keep this to yourself for a while? I promise there is nothing sinister behind my actions. You just have to trust me. Can you do that?"

Sloan nodded. Who was she to question the "why"? She too did not reveal all there was to know when she first met Clay.

Their conversation went from questions to answers. But nothing could have stopped the roar of laughter when Chase brought up Sunni's makeup change: "And to think she thought I was the weird one."

When the night began to ease into the light of day, Chase told her he was not going to stay around, and that she should try to get some sleep. Sloan regretfully returned to her room. As she'd expected, Clay had not been there.

She fell into a deep sleep, entering a place that she'd thought was long gone:

The fog was thick; the only way to get through was to use her hands to shove it aside. Sloan pushed forward; fear would not hold her back. The mist began to clear, but before she could feel a sense of well-being, someone blocked her path. She turned, ready to run, but a wall of tears, her tears, blocked the path to freedom. She screamed for assistance, pleading for someone to help other than the fast-approaching figure.

A disfigured hand with twisted fingers pushed through the wall then directed her to follow. She opened her mouth to scream out her objection until the hand pressed firmly onto her mouth: *"You must be quiet, or you will not see."* She obeyed. The hand pulled her along gently, until the pace turned into a running marathon.

She collapsed. Sweat beads formed on her forehead and upper lip; she wiped them away only to find her hands covered in blood. A piercing scream was hanging on the tip of her tongue, ready to be released, but again it was silenced by the hand.

From inside the draped garment the hand extracted a blanket: ReRe's favorite, the one the coroner used to wrap his tiny remains. This time nothing was held back; her screams blasted the murkiness. This time the figure hiding within the cloak allowed her time to grieve. Then she was again pulled along, this time to be placed in front of a screen door, the back door to her home. She was instructed to go inside. She tugged on the door and was met by the same sound she heard the night of her baby brother's horrible death. She found herself standing over his crib silently watching as a hand covered ReRe's tiny mouth, preventing him from taking another breath. But before she could again discharge the mounting scream, the hooded figure leaned close, touching her ear with his grey cracked lips: *"Beware. It is someone you know."*

The intensity of Sloan's screams brought Clay to her side. Although he'd walked away several hours ago, he would never forsake her if she needed him. He often displayed an angry side, but many times he would forget, and his true feelings would float to the surface.

He gathered her in his arms, trying to calm her fears. "It's okay babe, it was just a dream, it can't hurt you."

Sloan clung to him until her weeping came to an end. She welcomed his warmth and understanding, something that was hard to come by.

"Clay, it was not just a dream. Someone was trying to tell me that my baby brother did not die from natural causes as thought; he was brutally murdered."

"Oh, babe, you were just a child when he died. Besides, that would mean someone from your hometown, a neighbor or a friend, was the assassin. There's a lot of hate going on, but for someone to take the life of a wee baby, that person would have to be a psycho. Do you not see how ludicrous that would be? You need to let it go; it was just a horrible nightmare."

She tried to look at it from his perspective; it was not working. She was too tired to get into a deep discussion. She pretended to accept his explanation.

"You're probably right; it just seemed so real."

After Clay left her to return hopefully to a peaceful sleep, Sloan wrestled with the "why." Why would she revisit that horror from her childhood? She remembered vividly the evil that was watching her at the "hole" when she ran for her life screaming. Marc was there to catch her when she slumped into unconsciousness. Only this time it was Clay at her side, and he was not as understanding as Marc had been.

She tossed and turned trying to understand, then like a flash she sat up. The "why" could not be denied: Marc and Sunni's return prompted the awful memories to resurface. This recent dream was nearly the same with a few added details. Then why did her dream not reveal the villain? Was it her responsibility to find him?

She must call Ben to tell him of her dream, praying his schedule was still the same and that this was his alternate weekend to work. Sloan took to the floor running, not walking, to the telephone. She wondered if memory would fail in recalling the police station's number.

The ringing of the phone sounded distant, although she knew that was impossible.

"Deputy Foley here. How may I help you?"

Sloan was taken aback. Surely Deputy Robert had not quit. She lingered with that thought when the deputy asked if she was still there.

"I'm sorry. I was hoping to speak with Sheriff Ben. Is he around?"

"You're a little late, missy. He retired—over two or three years back if I recall. Can I be of any assistance?"

She gave no reply. The receiver was returned to its cradle. If Ben was no longer on the police force, what more could she do? Telling her story to someone other than Ben would only make that person think Sloan lived in a world not yet discovered. She was left with the thought that maybe Clay was right; maybe it was just a bad dream.

Sloan strolled back to the comforts of the bed, praying for a bit of sleep. This time she would not allow the black-cloaked figure to return. She would think of no one but Marc.

They agreed to meet on a weekly basis. The apartment that once gave meaning to her life, and now was abandoned, would be shared with Marc. She would see him on the sly, a friendly kiss here, some handholding there, but if he thought they would never be intimate, he had a lot to learn about her.

The weekend finally came to an end, and Monday was not looking any better. Sunni was informed Sloan was not feeling well. Sloan hoped she could make it in by tomorrow; if not, she would call.

Still full of rage, Sunni was contemplating the fate of Krista and Clay, when one of the staff approached her pointing to a gentleman that requested her attention. She recognized him from the dinner party. How could she not? Whenever she directed her attention away from her lover, she would find him eyeing her. All men disgusted her and now she was faced with what she perceived as someone who was looking for something she was not willing to give.

She held out her hand.

"You were at the Chadworths' dinner party. I'm sorry we were not introduced. My name is Sunni Harrison, and yours…"

After he gave his name, he told of his intention.

"I had no idea you were the one that cornered the market on interior design. I would like to hire you to do a renovation on my wife's private getaway."

He started to laugh.

"You have no need to worry, you will not travel far. Krista's sanctuary is two hundred feet behind our house. She told me years ago she needed her own space, and who was I to argue?

There are times I stay away for days — of course that is strictly business."

Sunni looked him in the eye with a grin. Garth laughed.

"So, okay, I fool around — what man doesn't? — but that doesn't mean I don't love my wife. You see, what I have is an uncontrollable itch that can only be scratched by the hands of someone other than my wife."

Sunni moved a little closer. She wanted him to feel her breath upon his face.

"I will tell no one of your hunger, for I too have special needs."

What he thought was an understanding, was in fact a way to blackmail him. She needed to know Clay's habits, and the best source was his closest friend, Garth.

Krista, the foolish woman she was, had divulged how her husband and Clay had weathered the good times and the bad from elementary school till the present, and how if they could, they would occupy the same skin. Krista's comment brought forth laughter. In the end, Garth would be Clay's worst enemy.

Sunni was ecstatic. The man standing before her could now solve two of her major problems; the first would be the elimination of Krista. Sunni led Garth to her private office. He told her he wanted this to be a gift for their tenth anniversary; the deadline was three months.

"I will not disappoint you, but you must realize that from time to time a number of things could come up that will need your approval. If that happens would you be agreeable to come to my residence to settle any problem should it arise?"

"Absolutely."

Sunni will have no need for excuses after Garth's first visit to her residence. From the beginning he will understand her persistent problem, and he will be more than willing to go along with her ideas. He will be introduced to a different kind of sex not unlike sadomasochism. He will fall under her control, never again to enjoy what others perceive as normal sex.

Krista never refused her husband's generosity — that would break his heart — but when told of the impending gift and the designer doing the renovation she balked; just the thought of Sunni entering her retreat upset her greatly. Instead of going into detail of her dislike, she simply told Garth she was not ready to give up her haven for that length of time. He would not take no for an answer. She would feel a heavy burden if unable to visit her getaway, but the next best thing would be the ocean's ridge and its sandy beach; this would have to do until the renovation was finished.

Sunni has no intention of doing a transformation on Krista's refuge. When she does enter her property, it will be to put an end to over a year-long problem.

Sloan did return to work the following day. She was there to give her notice, telling Sunni she wanted nothing more than to become a mother, and working did nothing to help her and Clay's already deteriorating marriage.

Sunni accepted her resignation, pretending to understand. She asked if she could take Sloan on one last vacation before she gave her life to motherhood. Sloan shook her head; one vacation away from Clay was enough to last her a lifetime.

Sunni again felt rage. If in the past year she had gained knowledge of the habits of the intended victims they would have already been dead and buried and facing their worst nightmare, the interior of a cramped coffin.

But when the days turned into weeks and then months with no information, she lost the confidence to end the life of another. With age comes wisdom. The thought of being caught was uppermost in her mind. This time she was not dealing with small-time hicks who could not find their way around a playground had a child led them. The only way the serial killer that preyed on the folks in her hometown would ever be found was if the assassin turned himself in.

The deaths of Clay and Krista would have the authorities breathing down everyone's neck,

Sunni included. This would not be an easy undertaking; it would take precise planning. She was thankful Garth turned up when he did; she would be forever grateful. But a thought did cross her mind: if Sloan had not given her resignation and removed herself from Sunni's side, maybe, just maybe, Sunni would have reconsidered not removing Clay and Krista from hers.

But as it is, Krista's days are numbered as well as Clay's. Their deaths will rock the foundation that Manhattan was built on.

CHAPTER EIGHTEEN

Chase drove slowly to his hotel; he could not believe the mess he's gotten himself into. Had he been truthful from the beginning, Clay would have known Sloan was his neighbor. As it was, because of his deceit, he had put her in an uncomfortable situation, forcing her to go along with his lie. And God surely must have had a hand in saving him from himself. The temptation of taking his brother's wife to his bed was overpowering. That in itself was difficult, but the fact that Phillip and Clay referred to one another as father and son has been gnawing at him from his first day of employment. He respected his mother's decision to keep Clay's birth father from public knowledge, but he felt his brother had the right to know his biological father. He would pay his mother a visit, but for now Sloan was high on his list of priorities, so that visit would have to wait.

Several days had passed since Sloan's departure from Sunni's design company. Sunni sat in her private office going over and over the best method of ending Krista's life; it must be quick and quiet. The opportunity arose when Garth informed her she could have access to Krista's private sanctuary for she was planning on spending the day on their beach. Because Sunni had not thought through the means of doing away with Krista, she told Garth it would have to be another day; she had to drop in on a client whose home was near completion.

She was to the point of being brain dead, nothing was being processed, then like a bolt of lightning it struck. What little girl in her growing-up years, or a boy for that matter, does not have a tinker box full of what she or he believes is of value. Sunni had such a box, and cluttered inside with other nonsense was a thick circle of baling wire she'd clipped from a bolt that was used for baling hay. The baling wire sat on her parents' property for years before it was finally hauled away.

Sunni did not waste any more time, she told her staff she would be gone for most of the day. No one questioned her comings or goings; business took her away several times a day.

She did not hesitate when she pulled into the Casines' driveway. She was ready to key in the code given to her by Garth during one of his sexual tortures when she noticed the gates were wide open. Their house was much closer to the road than that of the Chadsworths. Garth had drawn a diagram, should Sunni need it. Three driving paths led onto the property: one to the golf range, another to the beach, and the main road to their home. Sunni pulled onto the winding road leading to Garth's private golf course; it would not be in use today, as he was off on one of his business trips. Several trees and bushes followed the path, providing cover for her car.

After parking, Sunni climbed out and proceeded on foot, staying within the confines of the heavily wooded area. It was then she noticed three trucks with two shredders and a forklift. But all was quiet. The workers appeared to be on a lunch break. Branches removed from some of the surrounding trees and bushes were placed in a large pile in front of the shredder. She decided to wait until they again went about trimming trees and shaping many of the overgrown shrubs. She almost laughed out loud but caught herself. This was too perfect: any one of the workers could very well be accused of the slaying of Krista. Also in her favor, Sunni had a client a short distance from the Casines' residence. She would pay her a visit, for when she was questioned, as she knew she would be, this would give the detectives an accounting of her time away from the office. In addition, as always, a change of clothes was stored in the trunk of her car should a victim's blood leave its mark.

She worked her away around to the path leading to Garth and Krista's privately owned beach. From her viewpoint all that was visible was a very large umbrella. Sunni prayed Krista had not changed her mind about spending time on the beach. She kept to the woods as far as she was able without being seen. She had less than two hundred feet to be exposed but she had to wait it out; four men from the trimming crew were conversing, two of them facing in her direction. After a few minutes they turned away to resume what they had started. Sunni took off running like the police were already in pursuit. She collapsed against the side of the house breathing heavily, not from the running, but from the fear of being seen. After several minutes of waiting, she considered herself safe.

Krista was lying on an extra-large striped beach towel, a book by her side, sunglasses clutched in her left hand and a bottle of suntan lotion within easy reach. She appeared to be sleeping.

Sunni strolled in front of her, flush with excitement. It had been a long time, too long, since she'd felt blood upon her hands.

"Well, well, don't you look peaceful?"

Krista was startled into a response, forcing her into a sitting position.

"God almighty, Sunni, you scared the hell out of me. I could have had a heart attack from fright. You don't approach someone from behind without making them aware of your presence. What the hell is wrong with you? And what brings you here anyway? Garth never said a word about you stopping by."

Sunni snickered.

"Come on now, do you honestly believe he tells you everything? Well, I'm here to tell you a few things about your asshole husband. He is a nauseating whore of a man. When he's not in your bed, he's in mine. You see, Krista, he hungers to be dominated, he needs to be tortured into submission—only then can he truly be satisfied."

Krista did not know how to respond to the question and refused to believe the statement that followed, although she did make a harsh comment.

"If you're here for a reason, just spit it out. I really don't have time to listen to wishful thinking."

"My, my, you have quite a mouth on you, don't you? You are really making it hard for me to be your friend, do you know that?"

Krista said nothing. Her glaring look told of her severe dislike.

Sunni laughed it off.

"Well, if you don't believe me about your scheming, adulterous bastard of a husband, then you surely won't believe me when I tell you Clay is Sloan's uncle. So much for telling it like it is. But let's put all that aside and get down to the reason for my apparently unwelcome visit. I'm no fool; I know what's been going on between you and Sloan. You're thinking that she could never love anyone other than you... well, I'm here to prove you wrong."

Krista knew all along there was something wrong with Sunni. It was now confirmed.

"If you think I would believe anything you have to say about Garth, then you're crazier than I thought. As to Clay and Sloan being related, that's babbling nonsense. Only the mind of someone heading into territory reserved for the insane could think of something so vile. As to my relationship with Sloan, I have no idea what the hell you are talking about."

"It's called love, baby, something that only I can give. She felt that love when we went away together. She told me there was no comparison when it came down to who was the best. My skills gave her pleasures that literally shook her body. She couldn't get enough, which was the reason for our long stay in Venice. So you see, I win, you lose."

"You're disgusting. I really wish I could feel sorry for you, but I can't. You wouldn't understand what she and I have if it were outlined on a sheet of paper and shoved into your face. Sloan, the thoughtful person she is, couldn't see the thorns on a rose bush, but someday, she will see you for what you are, you can trust me on that."

Krista then waved her hand, a signal of dismissal. Tanning lotion was now being put to use. During the somewhat heated discussion Sunni had taken a crouched position, she now stood reeling with anger. Her ugliness spilled into her thoughts: *How dare she take that stance with me?*

Sunni gave the appearance of walking away, while her hand searched in her cargo shorts for the necessary tools: a pair of leather gloves and a spool of wire. She thought of the scalpel that had removed Willie boy's penis, but a single slash to Krista's throat would not give her that much-needed dose of excitement.

Krista directed her attention on the application of lotion to her legs. The umbrella was tossed aside and with the swiftness of a hawk, Sunni had the wire twisted around her neck, catching Krista off guard. The instinct to tug at the thing that was beginning to cut off her air supply was as great as that of the attacker. But the cream that coated Krista's hands prevented her from grabbing hold. She jerked and twisted in an effort to free herself from who she now knew was her and Sloan's enemy.

The ooze of blood was about to turn into a gush, Sunni's hands working the wire tighter and tighter with a force that would bring

Samson to his knees. A rage such as hers brought about an adrenalin rush that gave strength where none would otherwise exist. The blood ran. Krista's chest felt its warmth as it pooled onto her lap, sneaking its way between her legs and onto the striped beach towel. Her life struggle was at its end, but with her last breath and thought, she forgave her mother for deserting her and her father.

It took less than one minute to nearly decapitate the beautiful Krista and even less to throw her towel, glasses, book and lotion onto the surface of the ocean, her body to follow. The umbrella was returned to its prior position, keeping the blood that seeped into the sand protected from the sun's harmful rays.

Sunni strolled back to her car in high spirits, never giving another thought to exposure, confident she would remain unseen. Shoved into the pocket of her black shorts was Krista's wedding ring valued at $500,000. The leather gloves coated with Krista's blood would be washed and stored for future use.

Garth will soon be laid to rest beside his wife, the guilt of infidelity.

CHAPTER NINETEEN

Clay was going over some blueprints when the phone sounded. His ear was met with hysterical screams releasing an agony unlike anything he had ever heard. He sank into his desk chair, his heart taking on more beats than acceptable. He did not want to hear what the person on the other end had to say. But with all bad news, someone other than the recipient has to be told, and now he was the chosen one. The screams dwindled down and were replaced by sobbing. Clay thought he recognized the caller from the sounds emitted.

"Garth, is that you?"

"Oh God, Clay, what am I to do? The cops are all over the place. They think I did it, but you know I would never hurt her. I loved her. Do you think I should get a lawyer? Oh God, it is my fault—I should be shot, or better still, I should be castrated. Oh God, I am so sorry. Please forgive me."

Clay was hearing the ravings of a man who

was on the verge of confessing. Confessing to what?

"Garth, you need to get a hold of yourself. I can't help you if you don't help yourself. You need to tell me what happened. Talk to me."

Garth was making a sincere effort to get his crying under control, to tell his friend about his loss.

"It's Krista, Clay. She was found at the ocean's edge strangled. Oh God, Clay, you've got to help me, the pain is unbearable. Help me, Clay, please help me."

"I'm on my way. Hang in there. I love you, buddy."

Garth uttered the same. He knew he could always count on Clay, but he never knew he would expect Clay to hold his hand to get him through the funeral.

Clay dropped the receiver and took off running to his father's office; his running once again will be tested. He did not knock as was his custom, and when he entered he stumbled through his words.

"I just received a call from Garth. Krista was murdered! I must go to him, he needs me."

Phillip did not miss the pooling of his boy's tears.

"Oh, my God in heaven, this is unbelievable. Can I help in any way? Would you like for me to go with you?"

"No, Father. I think that would be a bad idea. Garth said the place is swarming with cops. I doubt they'll let me pass. But I do have a request: if by chance Sloan were to call, please do not tell her of this. This is something I have to handle with extreme care, or I could be visiting a sanatorium. But Father, if you know of some magic words that would ease Sloan's pain when I tell her that her best friend was murdered, please tell them to me?"

Phillip wiped away the start of many tears, shaking his head in his boy's direction. Clay was on his own.

Clay called for the delivery of a rental car; he did not need his chauffer hanging around if he was given access to Garth's property. At present the fewer people knowing about this the better; it would hit the newsstand soon enough.

The road leading to Garth's home was quiet. Two police officers were assigned guard duty at the gates of the Casine estate, standing as if ready to salute. Clay pulled his car to a stop directly in front of them. As he climbed out to say a few words, the cops' hands were already in the "hold it, buster" position.

He spoke quickly, before he was told to haul ass.

"My name is Joseph Clayton Chadsworth of Chadsworth and Chadsworth Architectural Firm. My card, sir. The gentleman of that house is my closest friend. He called for my assistance." Did they stand in his way? What do you think?

He was allowed to drive his rental car onto the property, keeping the outer road clear for passing motorists.

Clay could sympathize with Garth; it looked like every cop in New York had descended onto his property. This was bedlam at its worst.

Garth did not see Clay's approach; he was sitting on the steps of his estate with his head in his hands. He was weeping for more than the loss of his wife: just the day before, she found out that they were expecting their first child. Krista had decided her biological clock was about to run out; ten years of waiting to see if she and Garth were compatible gave her the go-ahead. They were planning on a party to announce their surprise, but they could not hold back the news from their dearest and closest friends, Clay and Sloan. They were to be told that evening while having dinner at their favorite restaurant, Ducasse's.

Garth traveled back into yesterday, remembering Krista's reaction when the doctor called:

He was sitting at the dining room table having a cup of coffee while reading the newspaper when the telephone rang. Krista had been antsy all morning, informing one of several maids she would take all calls. She refused to take her hand from the receiver; she would not allow it to ring a second time. The phone did not complete its full ring before Krista, forgetting to say her name, shouted into the receiver, "Am I?" The telephone took flight as she bounced about the room.

"Yes, yes! We are going to have a baby! Oh Garth, we are going to be a mommy and a daddy. God has looked favorably in our direction. I am so happy. Thank you for being such a wonderful husband."

Krista would never experience the joy of holding her baby; Garth would not be a daddy. His tears could not be contained; he was not the husband Krista thought him to be. He loathed what he had become. He was to blame for their death and nothing would convince him otherwise.

Clay joined Garth on the steps, placing his arm around his friend's shoulders, offering comfort and sympathy.

"I'm here, buddy."

Garth left yesterday behind and fell into his best friend's arms.

"I killed her, Clay; I killed my wife and our baby."

Clay's reflexes were amazing; his hand smashed against Garth's mouth, silencing his lip movement, praying no one heard the words that could convict him.

He could no longer be sympathetic; his friend was definitely not thinking straight, especially if he thought they had a baby. Keeping his hand over Garth's mouth, Clay got into his face.

"As soon as I get home, I will notify your lawyer. In the meantime, you are not to say another word. You need to calm your ass down. Do you hear me?"

The harshness of Clay's words forced Garth into reality. He nodded.

They continued to sit; Garth's hand entwined into Clay's, the substance for drawing strength. They were lost in thoughts of their wives, one gone, the other a possibility.

When it was apparent Garth was somewhat in control, Clay told him he had to leave before someone leaked the tragic news to Sloan.

Garth apologized for only thinking of himself.

"Of course, you have to go. My concern should now be with you. I pray Krista's death doesn't destroy what is left of your fragile relationship."

"It's sad to say, but if anything, it should bring us closer, but only time will tell. I'll get back with you as soon as I can."

They stood, and Garth reluctantly released Clay's strength; they would see each other one more time.

Clay hated to walk away from his friend at the worst time in his life, but he had no choice; his wife must come first. He drove slowly, dreading what lay ahead. He keyed the code into the black box allowing him access to his gated home. He pulled up to the entrance and noticed Sloan in her private flower garden. She was being careful in her choosing. The flowers had to be perfect to grace their dining table. Clay shook his head. *How can I tell her she no longer has a best friend?* He felt a tear as it rolled onto his cheek.

Sloan felt a presence nearby forcing her to turn around. Clay exited the car. His walk was staggered and he seemed unable to hold his head upright. She knew instantly that something was dreadfully wrong. He was home way too early and was driving an unfamiliar car; his appearance alone was a dead giveaway. She dropped her too perfect flowers lying neatly in a row in their handled straw basket and ran towards him. Before she could say a word, he grabbed onto her, pulling her head to his chest. He tried, but he could not hold back the tears.

She pulled away, her own tears making an appearance. She reached up, taking his face into her hands.

"Clay, what is it? Is it Phillip? Has something happened to him?"

Before he could answer, he turned away and dropped to his knees sobbing. She began shaking him, trying to accept what she now knew to be true. Her beloved Phillip, Clay's father, was no longer with them. There was no other explanation for his behavior. She would find out the how and when later. This was her husband's father, and no loss could be greater.

She took her place beside him, praying for help that she could give him the comfort he would need in the days ahead.

"My darling, I am so sorry, I too loved him."

Cay kept shaking his head trying to make her understand. He could not hold back; at any given second someone could call, or worse, drive over.

He pulled away from her embrace. It was his turn to offer comfort, but at arm's length. Without direct eye contact she would never accept what he was about to tell her.

"Oh babe, it's not Phillip, it's Krista. I am so, so sorry."

Sloan could feel herself falling, but Clay held on. Screams of anguish and obscenities at her God along with a string of words stretched far into the heavens.

"How dare You take the only friend I ever truly loved. Was not my family enough? Is it your intention that I live my life in pain and sorrow? The God I was taught to believe in has forsaken me. I will live out my life with hate in my heart. You deserve no better."

She managed to pull away from Clay's hold only to collapse onto the hard surface of the driveway. She clawed at her fallen tears as they seeped into the dry concrete; a show of blood began to appear from her torn fingernails. She was weeping for someone that was not meant to be in her world.

There was nothing Clay could do. If Sloan turned her back on God, what kind of punishment was in store for him? He lay beside her ignoring the discomfort. He too was feeling the effects of Krista's death; Garth and Krista were like the brother and sister he never had. Her death would weigh heavily on his heart.

The screams did not go unheard by the household help. The concerned servants, many already crying over their mistress's distress, ran to them, asking their boss if they should call the family doctor.

Clay shooed them away with unkind words.

"Her needs are being taken care of, do you not see?" Clay was sorry the minute the words left his mouth; he would apologize when he got his life back on track. He and Sloan lay there for some time until she fell into a troubled sleep.

Clay would carry her into their bedroom. It will be a long time before she reaches for him.

CHAPTER TWENTY

How true the saying "bad news travels fast." Krista's beautiful face graced the cover of every newspaper, magazine and tabloid. With the news of her death the whole of New York bowed their heads and wept. Children clung to their mothers, not quite understanding why their friend would no longer be visiting with them. Krista was known for her dedication to the poor children of New York and was often seen standing in front of a rented van with hired hands, distributing food baskets in the poorest sectors of the city. She never failed to hug the children, while giving each a goody bag tied with a ribbon. The tears of the children will outlive Krista's short life.

The investigation was in full force. Everyone in close contact with Krista was hung out to dry. Garth was high on the list of possible suspects, unable to account for his time because he either could not or would not remember. It was a slow and tedious undertaking; hundreds of people were interviewed and released, and Sunni was one of them. When all was said and done, one has to wonder why those in authority did not notice the difference in the skin coloring where Krista's wedding ring would be worn. Had they, they would have realized Garth was not the one responsible. New York cops, aren't they the greatest?

The burial was put on hold at Garth's request. He instructed those in charge that he would make the decision when her body would be laid to rest; until such time they were to let him be.

Clay knew he was suffering, but keeping Krista's body locked away in cold storage would not bring her back. It was time for a visit.

Garth's sixty-year-old butler, Jack, answered the door. The bloodshot eyes on his six-foot frame told of his grief.

"Mr. Clay, you are blessing in disguise. I pray you will not be offended with voicing my concern, but Mr. Garth needs help; he hasn't opened his bedroom door for days. I fear for his health."

Clay patted him on his shoulder, giving assurance. "Prepare something light. We will be dining together."

"Bless you, sir. I'm right on it."

The sounds of "Amazing Grace" brought tears to all those in attendance. Garth stood to the right of Clay and Sloan; Phillip and Chase were to his left. Sunni sat a couple of rows back; she would not be sitting in the reserved area. She could not very well ask for special seating; Sloan was off the deep end. But if Clay took it upon himself to invite Chase, why then did she not get the same treatment? Were she and Clay not considered a couple at every social gathering? She kept her fury under control; after all, she would soon have Sloan all to herself.

Of those in attendance many were dressed in different shades of black, a show of respect. Sloan outdid them all, dressed entirely in black, from the lace veil that concealed her face, to her full-length, long-sleeved dress, to her black shoes and nylons. She was suffering inside tremendously, but that also extended outwardly. She would pick at her torn nails, bringing about excruciating pain, and yet she continued. Clay took notice, but with each attempt to grasp her hand, she would slap his away.

The convoy of cars, led by a motorcade of police officers, extended ten city blocks. Phillip and Clay had bonded with Chase from the beginning. If asked, they could offer no explanation other than the fact that they enjoyed his company. Their feelings could extend as far as accepting him as another son/brother; they were that well-suited to one another. And as a father or brother would do, his place was beside them as they drove to the burial site. Not a word was spoken. What was there to talk about, the weather?

Minutes passed into a half hour. The seven hundred and fifty people in attendance circled the area to hear what the family priest had to say. A microphone held steady within his hands was ready to blare out words of the obvious, but with newfound information.

"How tragic are the circumstances that brought us all here today, made even more tragic by the discovery that our beautiful Krista and her husband Garth were expecting their first child..."

Sloan kept her head bowed during the services in the church and continued in this manner on the drive to the cemetery, but the shocking news that her best friend was to have a baby drove a spike through her heart. The tears she had managed to hide from public view were now on display as she tore her veil away, exposing her swollen face. At the moment of revelation, she and Clay turned towards one another, his mouth ajar in disbelief. Garth had told it like it was, but he had not been listening.

But he would listen to what Sloan had to say, pushing them further apart. But would he be as attentive as the mourners pushing their way forward to hear what she had to say? Sad is the day when others feast on the misery of another.

Sloan could not help herself. *How dare Clay keep Krista's pregnancy from me?* She moved as close to Clay as she could before speaking.

"Why did you not tell me? Were you afraid you would have to follow suit? Well fear not, never again will you share my bed."

Just as she was about to turn and walk away an explosion pounded the air. Men and women alike began to run for cover. Many fell to the ground weeping, thinking their lives were about to come to an end. You could not mistake a discharge from a powerful weapon.

Garth stood for a second before he met the surface of the grass. No longer did he need to draw strength from his friend's hand. The force of the gunshot to his right temple blew half of his face in Clay's direction, coating the back of his head and jacket with massive bits of brain matter. The spray of blood blew in all directions. Sloan, splashed with the remains, screamed for someone to call an ambulance.

Police standing nearby pushed their way through the marathon of runners, careful not to step on those hugging the grassy surface. The priest, with the Bible clutched to his chest, eyes turned upward, started praying for the safety of those in attendance.

To complicate what could only be described as chaos, a hysterical woman came tearing through the people, stumbling over those still down on the ground. She was a small woman, possibly five feet, with her clothes in disarray and her long dark hair tangled into knots. She was a dead woman walking; her body language told of her distress. Screams of torment poured from her lips, forcing those other than Clay and Sloan to take notice.

Phillip rushed to Garth and felt for a nonexistent pulse. He was torn between comforting his son and daughter-in-law or looking out for the welfare of the woman staggering towards Krista's coffin. Sloan clung to Clay, offering her support, but the woman with no significant other had no one to lean on; she was alone in her grief. Phillip decided she needed his attention much more, while wondering who she was. It did not take long to find out.

Krista's mother fell onto her daughter's coffin screaming her name over and over, tearing at the bouquets, looking for the latches that kept her baby locked away. A deafening silence followed her outburst, but she was not finished.

"Oh, God in heaven, is your anger so great that to punish me, you take my baby? I know I did wrong. You entrusted her care unto me and I let you down, but God, she too suffered. If you must avenge, take me, give my daughter another chance…please, God, please."

She clung to the coffin, hands now stroking where her daughter rested, but her devastating tears would come to an end, for God forgives those who show repentance. He allowed her daughter to once again be by her side. She felt the comforting warmth of her baby's arms; she was cleansed of her wrongdoing. A brilliant light surrounded those that showed compassion. Those who were left standing tried to comprehend what was taking place; they were forced to bow their heads, shielding their eyes from the intense glare. Never had they experienced such an overwhelming feeling of tranquility.

They would talk of this for years, never truly understanding, but accepting that there is a God, for they were in His presence. Phillip needed no convincing, for he felt the hand of God when he reached for the grieving mother, drawing her to himself and offering words of encouragement.

"Everything will be all right, I promise."

Krista's mother had a ready response. "I know it will, for God has told me so."

This was not the woman who entered the cemetery; this woman had found peace. She rose with Phillip's help, thanking him. She then turned and walked away. She was leaving with her daughter at her side. God told her so.

Clay knelt beside his best friend. He too was weeping for someone who would never again share his world. Sloan no longer thought of herself; she was concerned with her husband's welfare. Although Garth made a nuisance of himself when around her, he was still Clay's best friend as she was Krista's. She took to her knees, anger set aside. She would give comfort, as Clay had when it was called for. There was no denying she loved Clay, he will always have her heart, but the desire for a baby was way stronger, continuing to drive a wedge between them.

Chase wished he could go to his brother to give him support, but felt he would be overstepping his boundaries for he had yet to identify himself. As to Sloan, his heart was heavy with sadness. He was desperate to take her in his arms, telling her he understood and felt her pain. But that would not happen today. He would have to wait until the following Saturday, their designated day of the week for spending time together.

Sunni was not a participant in God's light; she was not in His graces, although she did wonder why the people were acting as if He had ascended onto earth, prayers being hurled through the air. The priest was now lying flat upon the ground, arms outstretched, kissing the earth beneath him. The scene was straight out of an ordination.

Yes, Sunni somewhat believed there was a God. She would ask for forgiveness for her past and future sins when she lay on her death bed, but not before. She had a life to live, and by God and by damn, she would live it.

The investigation came to an abrupt end following Garth's suicide. A letter found on his person told of his confession.

It contents read as follows:

"I pray God in His mercy will forgive me for taking Krista and our baby out of the lives of everyone who loved and adored her."

When Clay heard the news he stormed into the office of the chief of police, a good friend who went by the name of Booker Washington. He was big, black and rugged, standing a few inches taller than Clay. What little grey hair remained was shaven. He did not fit his profile; he was a gentle giant through and through until duty called, and then he was no one to mess with.

Clay was livid. His friend did not interrupt him, but stood by and listened to his ranting.

"There is no way Garth killed his wife—you know this as well as I. That letter was a means of letting go of the guilt associated with adultery. He couldn't live with the fact he was with another woman the day she was murdered."

Booker was sympathetic. "Clay, did he actually tell you he was with another woman at the time of Krista's death?"

"Well, not in so many words. I mean, he didn't come right out and tell me he was getting it on with another woman, but I read the meaning behind his words."

"That's not good enough, Clay. We need evidence. Without that it's all hearsay. I'm really sorry, my friend, but you'll have to accept the findings."

"But don't you see? He will be labeled as a murderer...even worse, he will be called a baby killer. Garth doesn't deserve what is being laid on him."

"Then he should have stayed around to prove his innocence. I'm sorry, Clay, I don't mean to sound unfeeling, but the facts speak for themselves. If in the future you come across something that could help prove his innocence, then come to me and I will see about re-opening the case."

On his drive back to the office Clay thought about Booker's comment: "find proof."

Clay pictured himself standing at a podium during a charity event. The women would line up, each arguing with the others that it was she who was shaking the mattress with Garth on the day of Krista's death. Each admission would be followed with a question: "Is this not considered a charitable contribution?" Laughter would ring out, bouncing from table to table; husbands would give their wives a thumbs up. He knew these women well. Confession was not in their nature; they would go to their graves with glue attached to their lips.

Clay's hands were tied; he had done all he could do. He would suffer greatly when the newspaper hit the stands. But he turned his attention to business at hand; he had a funeral to arrange. Garth was an only child, as were his parents. His mother died in her late forties of breast cancer, his father followed a year later from complications of diabetes. It was a standing agreement that should anything happen to Garth he did not want Krista to worry over burial arrangements. If Garth were now standing here and it was not so tragic, they would laugh at the bizarre set of circumstances. Clay will forever miss his friend.

Garth's burial would be kept out of the public eye. There would be no church service. The paparazzi would have to look elsewhere for their kill. Garth's remains will lie beside his wife within a mausoleum in the black of the night. Only those who loved him the most would be in attendance: Clay, Sloan, Nico, and Sofie. And Phillip, who thought of Garth as a permanent sleep-over whenever their school closed its doors.

But as the coffin is taken away, Clay will reach over to give it a final touch. His words say it all: "Friends never say good-bye and neither will I."

CHAPTER TWENTY-ONE

Life moved ahead, as so often it does. But those in the grieving mode have no life. Clay worked and kept to himself, and Phillip let him be. Working through grief without help takes much longer to overcome the pain of loss; Sloan was one such creature. She wept continuously and only picked at her food. The weight loss was becoming evident. Her personal assistant, Jillian Bishop, became alarmed and decided to overstep her boundaries.

Clay shoved his paperwork aside when Jillian appeared out of nowhere unannounced. She was of medium height with brown hair parted to the side and cut shoulder length; blue eyes were her best feature. She could be considered pretty but that would be stretching it a bit. But she did have what many of us lack: an instinct to put the needs of others before her own. She would see that Sloan gets the help she needs; she refused to look the other way.

After Jillian had rushed through the glass door leading into Clay's office and before she boldly sounded off, he stood up, ready to boot her out. She did not have an appointment.

"I am here about your wife's unstable condition. She needs help and it's apparent you are blind to that fact. If you do not do something, I am going to report to the authorities that she is being mistreated and kept prisoner in her own home. I can lie well if I need to, so what's your poison?"

Clay had never been spoken to in such a manner.

"How dare you come into my office screaming like a banshee? This is a place of business; all other matters should be handled elsewhere. But since you took it upon yourself to show your ignorance, I too will act as such. What goes on in my house is none of your business; you were hired to help with my wife's social obligations and see to her personal requests. But because you've taken it upon yourself to change your title from 'assistant' to 'doctor,' I will change your status to unemployed. And because I don't have time to deal with threats, I will see that our doctor calls on her immediately. Good day, Miss Bishop."

If he thought Jillian would back off when he handed her her walking papers, he was mistaken—and she told him so.

"It's a sad state of affairs if you think I would overlook the welfare of your wife in favor of a paycheck. Shame on you."

She turned back around just as she was about to step out the door.

"I pray you are a man of your word. If not I will surely find out."

Clay acted as the big bad wolf, but in reality he did not know what he could say or do that would not make him look like a fool. Jillian assumed he saw what she saw, unaware that he was not allowed into his wife's bedroom.

If Clay thought his life was in shambles, Chase was standing in his shadow. It had been weeks and Sloan was a no-show on their weekly get-together. How was he to help her if she refused his calls? There will be no more time out. He will call on her at her residence.

Sunni never missed an evening sitting by Sloan's bed, holding her hand, listening to her ongoing stories of her and Krista's time together. She felt like telling Sloan to put a lid on it. She wondered what would happen if she struck her like she had when Sloan went out of control after Mr. Hewlett told her that her family's property belonged to the bank. Would the force of the blow force Sloan to face reality, or would Sunni be shown the door, never again to be seen? She could not take the chance. She would suffer through the wailing sobs. Eventually the tears will have to end, just not as swiftly as putting an end to Krista.

Chase asked for time off. Tired of living in a hotel, he wanted to check out a few listings on some property.

Clay gave him the go-ahead.

"Take as many days as you need. I'll see you whenever."

They shook hands. Clay's offer of his personal limo in the past was repeatedly turned down; he knew not to offer again. Clay's comment that followed Chase out the door made him feel worse than he already did, reminding him of the liar he had become.

"Tell the cabbie to drive carefully; the traffic is a nightmare at this time of day. We wouldn't want to find out what life would be like without you."

Chase's mother's parting words struck home: "lies are no way to live a life." He was sorry he started this charade; its weight sat heavily on his shoulders. It was time to bring everything out in the open and let the chips fall where they may, but not before he pays a visit to his mother. This visit, in comparison to the others, will cause many a tear to fall.

Chase put aside one Saturday a month for his family that was tucked away in Mason's Mill. Sloan accepted this without question; she would give anything to be able to do the same. She pleaded with Chase not to tell Harriet her whereabouts. When she felt the time was right, she would revisit her hometown. They now depended on one another to keep to themselves Chase's deception about his name, and hers that she remained missing.

Clay was another story. He had yet to visit with his mother, although he wrote regularly. His reasoning was easy to figure out. He could continue to lie about his life in letters but to face her would have made that impossible. He was sure to slip up and she would see her firstborn as the liar he'd become. It was better his mother thought of him as a continuing workaholic. And yes, he did feel the pangs of guilt and remorse. Imagine having siblings and never being there to see them take their first step or hear them call your name. His heart hurt with that thought. He chose to settle for a substitute, a case full of hidden pictures shared only with his father. His mother was kind enough to send pictures every three months or so to his office. Pictures as the children grew from infancy to toddlers, then to become little people. He would laugh over many and shed tears over others. Someday he would meet them; after all, secrets can only be buried for so long.

Chase did not hail a cab; he wanted to think about all that was about to happen, and having a cabbie yak away would not provide this. He would drive a rental car.

The time to see Sloan was now. He pulled up alongside a box anchored in a free-standing column in front of his brother's estate. He pressed the talk button and waited for a response.

"What is the nature of your business?"

Chase shook his head with a single thought: *Nothing like getting to the point.*

He recognized the voice as belonging to Clay's butler.

"Truman, this is Chase Anthony. I would like to see Mrs. Chadsworth. Would this be a problem?"

"I was told no one was permitted inside the gates, but I will make an exception in your case, Mr. Anthony."

As the gates swung open Chase's heart began to race. Truman gave his okay, but will Sloan give hers?

Truman was standing at the opened door ready to receive him.

"Mr. Anthony, it's such a pleasure to see you. So much has changed since the Casines' deaths. Mrs. Sloan refuses to leave her room. Maybe you are just the person she needs to bring her back to the living."

Chase thanked him, adding a request.

"Truman, I hate to put you in a spot, but could we keep my visit confidential? I'm supposed to be at work, but Mrs. Chadsworth has been invading my thoughts since the death of the Casines. She's refusing all calls and I thought I'd pay her a visit to see how she's coming along. I did not want to pester Clay with questions about his wife's condition, seeing as he's going through his own hell. I promise I won't stay but a few minutes."

"You are like family, Mr. Anthony. Mum's the word. Now if you will follow me, I will show you to her sitting room."

Truman tapped gently on her door. "Mrs. Sloan, Mr. Chase is here to see you. May he enter?"

Sloan granted her permission. Chase entered to find her resting in a Windsor chair, surrounded by a litter of Kleenex she dropped carelessly after each use. She could do nothing but squint through her swollen eyes, and if she were trying to lose weight, she'd more than accomplished that task.

Chase was shocked at the extent of her mourning. His thoughts turned to his brother: *What the hell is wrong with him? Did he think she could work through this on her own? Do I dare take matters into my own hands?*

He stood facing Sloan with his hands on his hips, debating whether or not to be tough. It was apparent sympathy from her family and friends was not working.

"Okay what's up with refusing my calls? If you want to get rid of me, just say it. Three months of worrying about what is going on with you is not my idea of pleasure."

"Oh Chase, I am so sorry. Do you think I wanted you to see what I've become? If I lost you too, I would surely die. The only friend I truly loved is gone and the pain of living without her is so God-awful. I wish I too would die." She pulled more Kleenex from the box and discarded them as if the floor were a wastebasket.

Without thinking Chase walked over, not to embrace or sympathize, but to put an end to her unending show of tears. He reached under her body and brought her to himself. Sloan could tell by his grip that he was up to no good. She screamed in protest while pulling at his hair.

"What in God's name are you doing?"

"I'm doing what needs to be done. You need a bath and I'm just the guy to do it."

"You're crazy. If you don't put me down, I'll scream, so help me God."

"If you scream, your mouth will be met with a bar of soap, so help me God. Now shut up."

There was nothing gentle in his treatment; he ripped at her lounging gown, tossing it onto the black marble bathroom floor. She now stood to his side naked and shivering while he twisted the knob to release water into the tub; cold was the ideal temperature. Sloan will either hate him or love him when he is finished with her.

Chase was gruff with his words as the tub filled. "Get in."

Sloan backed away, one arm tucked inside the other, defiant. "Like hell I will."

"Oh, so that's the way you want it, okay…"

Before she could say another word he again had her within his arms, but only for a brief second. The water served as a cushion when he dropped her beneath the surface. A rush of water poured over the rim of the tub. Sloan's scream was swallowed in a mouth full of water. She struggled to sit up while Chase readied himself with the necessary supplies, not only to wash her body, but her hair as well.

"I hate the two of you, Marc Anderson and Chase Anthony. What do you think about that?"

"I think it best to leave Marc out of it—he's the nice guy. Chase is the bad ass."

Sloan could not help herself; she turned her sarcasm into laughter.

Chase joined in showing a warm side. "Now doesn't laughter feel much better?"

"Yes, it does. Thank you."

"Well then, I'll let you be. Although I do have a question: Are we still on for Saturdays?"

"As always… But hold on a minute…you can't leave until you finish what you started."

Sloan stood facing him; she was definitely back to her old self, bewitching him with her wares.

He had no one to blame but himself; she was showing what he'd uncovered. He did not turn away; he wanted to see what he could not have. He would not have been human if he was not aroused. Sloan was perfection in its truest form, weight loss and all. But he had to keep it together for her sake, as well as his. He'd grown to love his brother immensely, and he would not lie down beside his brother's wife.

"Sloan, why do you keep pushing for something that you know will never be?"

"Because I never know when you'll change your mind."

He shook his head at her seductive smile. But he had a comeback, although he said it with a sly grin. "I'll continue to pray for guidance."

Chase got out of there in the nick of time, his testosterone level at its peak. He was wrung out with desire. He knew he couldn't continue seeing her if she left him feeling as he did now. He could kick himself for undressing her, for had he not, he could have kept it together; never again will he disrobe her.

CHAPTER TWENTY-TWO

Chase drove back to the office, relieved that Sloan was out of her depressive state and praying her tears would stay away. But his conscience was bothering him; he hated lying to his brother. It did cross his mind to ask if it would be okay if he paid Sloan a visit, but he feared such a request might bring about questions he would be unable to answer. Lying in itself is one thing, to be caught is another. But he could free up his conscience a bit by being halfway truthful; he would check out a few apartments before heading back to the office.

He could not believe his luck when an agent told him an apartment in the same complex as Clay and Sloan's place had just come on the market. It was listed below market value and was move-in ready, but the longer it stayed on the market the more the price would increase. The owner had relocated to another state and did not want to be responsible for two homes.

Chase immediately agreed to the asking price. He and the agent filled out the necessary papers, and Chase wrote a check for the down payment. He would receive the key as soon as his paperwork checked out. He and Sloan had been meeting on a weekly basis in her unoccupied apartment, although always in fear Clay would walk in. The only one to worry about now would be Sunni.

Sunni was obsessive when it came to Sloan. Sloan could not make a move, whether it was to sit, stand or walk, without Sunni beside her. Obsession was one thing, but Sunni carried it too extremes. But more than that, Chase was tired of her hanging on him; lip locking he managed to avoid. Thankfully, this only took place in Sloan's presence. Sunni's behavior was unlike anything he had ever seen. Although he did remember one instance when her actions were similar to that of a guy he roomed with in his last year of college. But his roomie was not one to pussyfoot around: he had a thing for Chase and he quickly made it known. For the remainder of the year the dorm room was occupied by one body, Chase.

Chase's car came to a sudden stop when he realized what he was dealing with: Sunni was a lesbian. Drivers with no time to spare pressed or pounded on their horns, heads hanging out windows yelling, "Get your ass moving!" But how could he move forward when all he could envision was Sunni with Sloan? Just the thought of her mouth on Sloan's made him want to puke. He had nothing against same-sex relationships; that was their choice. But if Sunni thought she could bring Sloan over to her side, that was something he would not abide. But now a single thought began to nag at him: Did Sloan swing both ways, or was she as blind as he was? There was only one way to find out, and that was to ask. When a guy behind him gave his bumper a tap, Chase thought it best to move on or he might be looking up at a fist.

Clay was sitting at his desk, his thoughts on Sloan. She was true to her word; her bed was no longer his bed. Three months is a long time to do without. He was beyond suffering. If she did not whistle soon, he would take to walking the streets.

Clay's thoughts were chased away when Chase leaned his head into his office.

"Well, I can officially lay claim to ownership of an apartment. And to top off the great find, it is in the same complex as yours."

Clay rushed to his side. A handshake would not do. He wrapped his yet unknown brother in a brotherly hug. Congratulations were in order; bordering on three years is a long time to put money in another's pocket. The money Chase acquired as lead man secured his future; his take-home pay afforded him anything he desired…well, almost anything. Sloan was not part of the package.

Clay was generous with his time when it came to Chase. Chase no longer was riding on Garth's coattails. He never really thought about his standing until Garth's passing. It was apparent he had what it took to be Garth's replacement as Clay's best friend. Second place was never an option, but he would gladly accept that position if Garth could be back with them. Clay would say the same.

Chase was now seated in Clay's office, each holding a cup of black coffee. They were lost in thought. Clay could not get his mind off his wife, while Chase was thinking of what he would say to his mother. The end of the day was approaching. Clay understood Chase's need to take the remainder of the week off: tying up loose ends when planning a move is not someone's idea of enjoyment.

But Clay had something that needed to be said.

"Chase, before you take off, there is something my father and I need to discuss with you. It will only take a few more minutes of your time."

Chase was left wondering as his eyes followed his brother out the door. A thought entered his mind when Clay shut the door behind him: Was he about to be demoted? He had not been giving it his all since Garth's death.

Sloan occupied his mind and his work showed his lack of interest. But the fear dissipated when Clay returned with his father's arm around his shoulder; their smiles told of job security.

Phillip turned the announcement over to his boy.

"Chase, you have more than proved your worth to the company. My father and I are offering you a partnership with the firm. All you have to do is accept."

Chase was unable to speak. Would they be so generous if they knew he lied his way into their company, even though it was with the best intentions? He would have to hold off his acceptance.

"I am truly honored, but before I accept, there are things about my personal life that need attention. Hopefully, you will allow me time to put this matter to rest."

To trespass into someone's personal life is never acceptable on any terms. Do not the majority have skeletons they like to keep shut away?

Phillip, Clay and Chase took turns shaking hands, not knowing that Phillip and Clay's shameful world was set to explode in a few months.

CHAPTER TWENTY-THREE

Sunni decided she needed a break; her nightly visits with Sloan were always filled with tears and they were wearing quite thin. She so wanted to do away with Clay, but if Sloan reacted to his death as she did to Krista's, she would not walk to the edge, she would run.

Besides, Sunni had someone else working her mind. CeCe Thorman, her biological mother, came to the forefront. A rage of hatred soared, keeping her in a foul mood. Her workforce treaded carefully when in her presence. It had been months since she'd hired a private investigator. She did not feel she could wait much longer; the urge to kill was rapidly increasing. She no longer could focus on her work; she needed to not only see blood but partake of its taste. It would be a first, but one she would surely enjoy.

Sunni was pacing the floor when her phone rang. She pounced on it and screamed into its receiver, "This had better be good."

The receptionist was quick with an answer. "You told me to ring if I heard from Mr. Gordon. He's standing beside my desk. Should I send him to your office?"

For the first time in weeks the receptionist received a joyful reply.

"Oh my God, yes, yes."

Sunni was already at the door. She all but pulled the investigator inside.

"You told me you wouldn't call on me unless you had news of the person in question. Were you able to locate her?"

He was smiling, the sign of a yes.

If Sunni's taste swung in the direction of a male, he would be the pick of the pack. Max Gordon stood an inch or two taller than Sunni. His coveted tan and dark brown hair was kissed by the sun's rays. He had amazing hazel eyes and lips that would drive a woman crazy. And if there was doubt, place him on an auction block and you would see a bidding war like no other.

But Sunni was not buying; she was still trying to acquire the greatest masterpiece of all, a piece of art called Sloan.

Max Gordon placed the folder on her desk.

"Your mother was the worst when it came to tracing her whereabouts. This woman must have hiked her way across the globe; the miles she traveled would have put many a car to pasture. But I need not go over all that; you have the information that will place you at her front door."

Sunni inserted a key into a locked cabinet and reached for a manila envelope that was stuffed with cash. A lasting comment followed.

"I have given you far more than you expected. You will never speak of this, do you understand?"

The investigator flipped the envelope open, exposing its contents. When he was through counting, he thought he had won the lottery.

He nodded and gave her added assurance. "I would remove my tongue before I will ever speak of this."

Sunni snickered.

"Out of your own mouth that punishment will come if you dare to cross me."

Max Gordon was sweating when he left, he had no doubt she would carry out that threat. He also knew she had the devil dwelling inside her.

Sunni sat down. She was trembling with delight. The long-awaited information was ready to be exposed. The folder now lay open. A five-by-seven picture was paper-clipped to a collection of documents; her mother was looking up at her. The mother who thought of Sunni as an object to be disposed of was a striking brunette with large green-blue eyes. But there was something hidden behind the charming smile; it spoke of "I'll do anything for a buck."

Sunni would soon know the amount of money she had been traded for.

A smile began to take form. She was feeling a rush of excitement to which nothing could compare. The woman who threw her to the wayside was about to be shown her past.

Sunni was on her way on what her staff thought was a regular buying trip. Never could they imagine their boss was preparing to orchestrate a blood bath for her dear old mom.

She thought through various means to end her mother's life as she drove through a number of states that would take her to her mother's hometown. Travel by air would leave a paper trail. According to the reports, for every mile her mother drove trying to escape her past, in the end she was back at her beginning.

Sunni yelled out the window, the wind whipping at her words, "If you thought you could run and hide, you thought wrong. Your worst nightmare will be no match for what lies ahead."

She was in the Sunshine State and was feeling the effects of the heat. She pulled in front of a Shell gas station. She went into the restroom as a spiked blond in a biker outfit carrying a backpack, and came out a pigtailed brunette minus her assortment of piercings. She was now wearing a black tube top beneath black bib overalls. If anyone should take notice their description would never be linked to her.

The plan for doing away with her mother was in its final stages. It was time to pay the piper. Sunni would park at a Wal-Mart and walk the couple blocks to her mother's residence.

If she ever again needed the services of an investigator, Max Gordon would be the one. He more than proved his worth. Tucked behind her mother's picture was a detailed drawing, outlining shops and streets, guiding her every step of the way. He even went so far as to draw a stick figure standing in front of a rendition of her mother's house. Normal people would think of that as a little to the extreme, bordering on weird. Sunni thought of it as paying a great deal of attention to detail. Normal was not in her makeup.

It was just past noon when Sunni strolled into the entrance of Ocean View Estates. This was not a gated community. Thoughts rushed in: *So you dumped me like a bag of garbage, only to wake up each morning smelling your neighbor's trash. There is justice after all.*

Ocean View Estates was a pitiful name for dilapidated trailers. Instead of turning back, realizing the depth of her mother's love for allowing her a chance in life, Sunni became more enraged than ever. She would have found fault no matter the situation, for nobody walked away from her without paying a price. Perhaps she would have chosen to live this way than to have all she has if only her mother had kept her.

Sunni had never seen so many unchaperoned kids clustered into one area. And out of this breeding camp, there was not one that did not need a scrub brush taken to their hide. This could be a haven for pedophiles. She took care not to walk into any undesirable substance; the dogs, like the kids, ran free. Luck was with her, but pity the child who one day will go missing. Nowhere was there an adult to be seen.

She took in her surroundings and was appalled with the view. Discarded tires, broken-down BBQ pits and metal folding chairs minus their webbing lay heaped one on top of the other. An assortment of broken toys was added to the growing mound. Beer cans hiding among the weeds were unable to expose their makers' labels. But the most disgusting were the garbage cans with their contents spilling onto the ground. The putrid odor caused bile to rise to the back of Sunni's throat. Never had she seen such filth, and yet she would have welcomed it, if only her mother had loved her enough to keep her.

Sunni's slow walk came to its end. There before her was her mother's trailer. None could compare. Several colors of paint on the exterior put a beautiful face to something that would otherwise be condemned. It was a home any kid would love to live in, but Sunni was not welcome. The small patch of land her mother was responsible for was lush and green. It was bordered with flowers and shrubs and featured a Red Knockout tree covered in roses as its focal point. Red-carpeted stairs were the welcoming mat.

How should she do this? A quick slash to the throat, or should she drag out the assassination? Yes, her father's scalpel was her weapon of choice.

She climbed the steps. The red carpet of the stairs continued right up to the front door. A polished brass knocker would be Sunni's calling card.

CHAPTER TWENTY-FOUR

The flight into Chicago seemed longer than usual, no doubt from the anxiety over whether or not Chase would receive the answers to questions that had long been haunting him. With a call ahead, a rental car was delivered and waiting on his arrival. This car was nothing impressive, just a small Nissan. He had no one he wished to impress; snobbery was really not his thing. Sometimes, he got out of his true self and then afterwards he would feel lousy. The drive to Mason's Mill with thoughts of what he would say to his mother, thankfully, kept him from thinking about the humdrum two-hour drive.

Each and every time Chase drove through his hometown he was amazed. Other than the main roads finally being paved, nothing really changed. It was as if Mason's Mill was frozen in time. Farmhouses remained weather beaten; rocking chairs never changed position nor did the people who sat in them. The roads the neighbors walked remained rutted and rocky.

Chase had to wonder whose pocket was stuffed with Silva's money; their church surely had not seen a penny of it. Shingles were missing from the roof, and the iron handrails leading up to the church's entrance were giving way to rust, while the double door was rotting at its base. The church's parking lot no longer showed the markings where the handicapped could park. Repaving and striping were always discussed at the town hall meetings, but it went no further. Sometimes the townspeople would whisper among themselves how they wished Silva was still running her diseased mouth, but only long enough to take care of the essentials. Then, of course, they would hang their heads in shame, for they were not behaving as good Christians. But the head hanging would last only until their shoed feet hit the pavement. Happiness would then return.

Chase pulled up to his mother's house. He loved her reaction when he showed up unannounced; it was if she had springs on her legs, his arms ready to catch her in midflight.

This time his mother did not answer, it was Hannah, and as usual she pushed Taylor aside. From day one Hannah demanded to be first. Taylor accepted her placement rather than upset her sister. Taylor was by far the sweetest and kindest. Hannah was a different story; she would stand in defiance if she did not get her way, hands on hips while stomping her foot. Their mother's efforts to instill discipline fell to the wayside, as Ben undermined everything Harriet tried to do. He was a marshmallow when it came to Hannah. Most parents will not admit to having favorites, but they do, and Hannah was Ben's. Why Hannah, Chase could only speculate; maybe she gave her daddy what he could not get from his wife: her undivided attention.

The help Harriet received shortly after the triplets' births seemed like the answer. But it did not release the pressure of having them on a twenty-four-hour basis. Ben did not lend support until after his retirement, and by then they were enrolled in school. Playing the father role now meant he would be underfoot, attempting to rearrange his wife's daily routine. When Harriet finished with her say, Ben never again offered his help.

Chase felt sorry for Ben's situation, but felt worse for his mom. She never truly returned to her former self after psychiatric help, but never was her sting flung his way. To interfere in what should have been marital bliss was not something he felt was his right. His mom was fast approaching the sixty-year mark, and wear and tear was evident. Only when it was time to depart did Chase venture into her thoughts, asking if anything were troubling her. Her comment was always the same: "Nothing could be better." He did not push it.

And what could he say about his brother Nick, a buddy to his daddy and a helper to his mom. He was a great kid, a brother who will make it. He too was an artist. He toted a pencil and a tablet of paper wherever his feet took him, the toilet no exception. That's dedication in its truest form. And although Nick was never one to come to the door to offer greetings, he was there to show his regret at Chase's leaving. A show of tears would hang on his eyelids until he pulled away. And without fail Chase would glance out the rearview mirror to watch his brother turn and run, knowing the flood gates had opened. Chase's love for Nick was as great as that of his mother.

The screams of "Marc! Marc!" blasted his ears. They did not call him Chase. With a double-leap, black curls bouncing, dimples exposed, they were in his arms. Taylor almost missed as Hannah gave her a last-minute shove, but this time she shoved back. They adored their big brother. Chase could not get enough of their scrubbed scent. Kisses and hugs were nonstop. What he would not give to wake up each morning to such a welcome. But never could this be. To leave his soul mate behind was unacceptable. And never would Sloan return to a place that had delivered the ultimate in tragedy.

Harriet was putting away the last of the folded laundry when the screams of joy rang out. Those sounds could only mean one thing: her son was home. She ran toward the nonstop chatter. Chase released his sisters just in time. He did not miss the moisture collected within his mother's eyes.

"Oh Marc, I've missed you so much." He held her tight, replying the same.

Nick patiently waited his turn. He did not have to wait long. Harriet stepped aside. Chase took to one knee to gather him close. Nick held tight to his pad of paper, freeing up one arm to return his brother's embrace.

Time passed quickly as the siblings updated Chase on their activities. High on the girls' list were swimming and musical instruments, which included the flute, clarinet and piano. They tried the violin, but found it not to their liking. Nick's attention was focused solely on his drawings. They were enrolled in Barrette's Academy, offering the best education and all academics. An hour's drive to and from did not deter Harriet from giving them the very best.

Finally, it was Harriet's time. She dismissed the triplets as if she were their school mum. Hannah started to protest, and then thought better. Daddy was not around to offer support.

He was off doing what he did best: play-acting as a cop without the benefits of a paycheck. His regret, as he often said, was retirement. Harriet was the first to agree.

There was something driving them apart. Sometimes Chase would get a glimpse, his psychic ability coming into play. But a force stronger than his was at work. His mother always managed to block his entry. Someday, maybe, he would see what was hidden within. Pity him, should he.

He pushed his thoughts aside; he was there for a purpose. Light conversation went back and forth as he watched his mother prepare lunch. His siblings would eat in the kitchen, while theirs would be eaten in the newly constructed sunroom. Without being told, the children knew to clean up their own mess. And they also knew that when their brother visited, their mother would be given some alone time with him. Hannah started to protest but was given a stern reprimand.

"Hannah, I wouldn't go there if I were you, unless you want to spend the remainder of the day sitting in your room."

She was brazen with her response. "Yes, M-o-t-h-e-r."

Chase gave his mom a look that said, "She needs to be taken down a notch or two." Harriet lowered her eyes, shaking her head.

Before he headed back to New York he would get Hannah aside and give her a little brotherly advice. It just might make a difference. He prayed it was only a phase she was going through. If not, heaven help those that in time have the misfortune of being her friend or partner for life.

Harriet walked ahead to arrange a white wicker glass-top table between them. Chase, a couple of steps behind, carried a red-handled tray of food. He was careful not to spill a drop from the glasses with sugarless iced tea licking at their rims. Ham and cheese stacked high on bakery buns with a side dish of potato salad and several Polish pickles was more than appealing. He was famished. They sat on thick tufted pillows with a tropical design, comfort at its finest. Conversation was on hold while they enjoyed their lunch. But hovering in the front of each bite, Chase's words were screaming to be mouthed.

Lunch was over. Plates with dinnerware and the napkins that had lain across their laps were now placed onto the tray. They would be taken away at a later time.

Harriet started the conversation. "I think the last time you were here you mentioned looking for an apartment to buy. Did you follow through?"

Just as his reply of "I did" hit the air, his mother jumped ahead.

"There is something you wish to tell me, something you've known for some time?"

Leave it to his mother to see Chase's thoughts before they were spoken.

Still seated, she leaned closely, heart in a racing pattern. She did not want to miss what was about to be laid on her. She prayed she would have enough strength to endure.

"I found Sloan. She is safe and secure."

This was not what Harriet expected; she was receiving an ominous foreboding, the coming of evil. Was she wrong? Was her talent fading along with her ability to cope without Phillip? He crowded her thoughts on a daily basis, but for now she put him out of her mind. Her son deserved all her attention.

"Oh, blessed is this day. You couldn't have made me happier had you told me the two of you are married. Oh my gosh…that's it, isn't it? You finally took her hand into yours?"

"Oh Mom, I would give anything if that were true, but apparently God didn't see me as her mate. If you'll bear with me, I have a story I wish to tell." If there was one thing Harriet had, that was patience when it came to her son.

Chase leaned forward, his hands cupped together.

"On the day that Sloan's family perished in that horrible fire she was in town to do a little shopping. We met by accident, and for the first time she was civil, which gave me confidence that I had a chance with her. We walked and talked, making our way along the graveled road leading into the shopping center. We stopped and had something to drink. It was then I professed my love for her, and told of my plans for our future. I upset her, Mom, and that was not my intention, but I felt that was my only chance to get things out in the open. It backfired. She took off running up the wooden platform of the clothing store, but I couldn't let her get away without an explanation. Unbeknownst to me, that was my first encounter with my brother; we literally ran into each other. Something happened at that moment that left me embarrassed, and it was I that ran this time."

The threatening evil was about to make itself known. Harriet prayed for time to stop, but not all prays are answered.

Chase continued without a pause. "Sloan has been with Clay since that dreadful day of the fire. And yes, I've known of this for a very long time and yet I couldn't bring myself to tell you. It's been a daily struggle to accept that she will never be my bride."

Harriet felt the mounting pressure within her lungs. The face of evil was about to show itself.

"Yes, Mom, Clay is Sloan's husband. It's apparent he was in town to pay you a visit when I bumped into him. Why did you not tell me?

And the other thing that has me puzzled is that Clay and Phillip acknowledge each other as father and son. Surely after all these years you told Phillip that Clay was not his son? Mom, you need to tell me if you're holding something back."

Harriet managed to find the strength to stand. She began to pace the length of the room and then back again. Chase never took his eyes off of her. He would give her as much time as needed; after all, he gave her a lot to explain away. But after several minutes she began to falter in her steps. He stood ready to go to her side.

"Mom, are you all right?" When she gave no response, he rushed to offer his support; she swayed in his arms, but was able to grab hold.

"Marc, I'm okay, but I must sit."

With his arms safely around her, he helped her into her chair. She was pale and trembling. He suggested calling her doctor.

"Honey, I wish the doctor could help, but he cannot."

She was searching for the right words…words that would not create such a strong impact. But reality can be ruthless.

"Clay came to see me on that God-awful day that I lost my Beth and her family. Months of searching finally brought him to my doorstep after being told by his grandmother that I did not die in childbirth as he grew up believing. I had no time to tell you of his arrival, it happened so quickly. You were off hunting when I received his phone call. After his departure, I couldn't wait to tell you, but the fiery hell that took my friend and her family fell upon me before your return. That tragic night when the Doc told me my precious Beth died, I too wanted to die. But God in His mercy sent me on a journey to help in the healing process. You see, Marc, Beth wasn't just my neighbor; she was a little girl who was entrusted into my care from the age of three to the age of nine. That was the day I was thrown out to fend for myself, that was the day the Chadsworths took my baby from me. Marc, I made a huge mistake not telling you things you had a right to know."

Harriet at that moment did not shed a tear. She was relieved, but a storm of tears was brewing.

"Marc...Beth's real name was Alexandria Paige Chadsworth. She was the sister to Phillip and Clay."

Harriet hesitated, the next flow of words could very well upset Marc; to what extent she had no idea.

Chase reached for her hands.

"Mom, why in the world would you think I would be upset with this revelation? Although I must admit I am a bit confused. I can understand Phillip being Beth/Alexandria's brother, but how does Clay come into that picture? Am I missing something?"

Harriet's hands held tight onto Marc's. Time is never on your side when the worst possible news is about to be delivered.

"Marc...Clay is the child of Phillip's father. A child conceived in rape."

Harriet never expected to hear the degrading word that burst forth from the lips of what she perceived as a perfect son.

"That low-life scum-of-the-earth bastard. I now understand why Phillip and Clay never speak of him. To talk of him would surely leave a foul taste in their mouths. If I were to be granted one wish, it would be to have him walk the earth. I would then expose him for the pervert he is. Death is too good for him."

He knelt at the foot of her chair, arms encircling her waist, head on her lap, and wept for the tribulation she was forced to endure.

Harriet stroked his hair, while continuing with the sordid details of how Clay came to be.

"I never wanted you to know of this; it was far too degrading. Now you can see the direction my deceit has taken me. But the past hangs around like a ball and chain and until you pry it loose, you can never have a life. With the birth of the babies I needed to free myself. And the only way was to face the person I wronged. I invited Phillip to my home and told him what I should have told him years ago. The news hit him hard. I took from him what his father took from me: a son. I trampled on his heart, Marc. I hurt him terribly. I am so ashamed."

There was a quivering in her voice. She began to openly cry, hands now covering her face. Chase raised his head; he was a witness to her distress. He then understood: his mother was still in love with her first love, Phillip. Chase said nothing, what could he say?

Chase knew his mother well; she needed some time alone. He exited the room saying something about using the bathroom. This would allow her time to weather the storm of tears. She had returned to her former self when he re-entered.

She continued, this time without a pause.

"Phillip promised he would tell Clay. Never did I doubt he would not. And now that I know the circumstances involved, they really had no alternative, lest his son/brother be exposed to incest. And now I am faced with the horror of Clay's predicament. You do understand what this marriage means, do you not?"

Chase shook his head; she had lost him.

"Marc...Clay is Sloan's uncle. A marriage such as theirs is against the law. Their marriage must be terminated. If it is not, Clay could be facing prison time."

Chase questioned himself: *Has "dim-witted" always been a part of my character?*

He could not believe the irony of the situation. He could now claim Sloan as his own.

His brother's rights were no longer valid. But his heart was telling him something different. Clay was his brother, one he would give his life for, his love unquestioned. He could never take from him the woman they both loved. Sacrifice will be his price to pay, the ultimate gift from a brother to a brother. But will Clay ever realize the extent of his brother's love? Life must continue as though nothing has changed, unless a solution is found.

Some of Chase's thoughts were carried over to his mother.

"Mother, you must promise never to repeat any of our conversation. It will cause more damage than you can imagine. I need time to sort through this mess. There is a way out, I just don't know what it will be."

Harriet wanted everything to be out in the open, but that meant she would have to go against Marc's wishes.

Before she could tell him her thoughts, Chase had more to say.

"There is something more that you need to know. Sloan and I meet weekly without Clay's knowledge. She and I have grown extremely close."

Harriet gasped. "Oh my gosh, you aren't...?"

There was no escaping her meaning.

"Mom, I love her. To take the woman I love to my bed without the benefit of marriage would be disrespectful. You have to understand where

I'm coming from. Sloan came to me looking for someone, preferably a man, to confide in. She has girlfriends but she needed to hear from another man his views on understanding her husband should problems arise. One such problem is Clay's stubbornness about having a baby. She wants children badly and he refuses. I can now understand why. If I can't be a husband to Sloan, then I'll take whatever she has to offer. If friendship is what will bind us, then so be it. As long as I am able to draw a breath, I will always be there for her."

Harriet went to kneel in front of him. "You make me proud to be your mother."

She will weep for Phillip. He will carry the burden of allowing sin to continue, "for a father so loved his son, he will deny him nothing." He will take the sin that ties them to his grave. Harriet's tears will once again flow for her firstborn, this time for more or less allowing him to continue to indulge in the forbidden fruit. God helps those who help themselves; not so in this case. A heavy price will be paid on Judgment Day.

But Harriet had questions of her own.

"Marc, I too am confused. How could Sloan keep Clay from knowing you are from her hometown?"

"For well over a year I was not aware she was living in New York, let alone that she was my brother's wife. We met at a dinner party in my honor. Trust me, with the name change and a change of clothes, she did not recognize me. But as the evening wore on I would catch her staring at me. Needless to say, she found me out. I managed to get her alone and asked that she not betray me. After a limited explanation for my deception, but with the understanding I would someday reveal who I am, she promised.

"And to add to the list of the unbelievable, Sunni is also a resident of New York and making quite a name for herself. They too met by chance and continued with their friendship as if they had never parted. Although Sunni was the one I was most concerned with. I knew at any given moment she could announce that I was not who I claimed to be. But as the evening wore on I realized my secret was safe."

He was nearing the end of his disclosure. He stood as if what he had left to say was just an afterthought.

"Oh, and by the way, I was offered a partnership with the firm."

He was ready for his mother's reaction. She leaped into his outstretched arms.

"Oh honey, I am so happy for you. You climbed the ladder of success without the benefit of the Chadsworth name. You did what you set out to do; you proved your worth by your own merit." This time the shedding of tears was for joy.

Ben arrived home in time for dinner as was his custom. He was in high spirits, as he always was with Marc's visits. Chase wondered what Ben's demeanor would have been had he not been there, although his mother did offer Ben her lips, and seemed genuinely happy to have him home.

Chase and Ben gave all their attention to the kids till bedtime. Then he, Ben and his mother talked until well past midnight. Then "see you in the morning" found its way. As his mother and Ben headed towards their bedroom, Ben showed his love, his arm was wrapped around his wife's waist, while his mother's head lay against his chest. Chase smiled at the sight; maybe he was wrong about Phillip.

Night did not end quickly, whereas morning was in no hurry.

Hannah was the first to enter the room Chase used for a stay-over, Nick's room. Bunking in with his sisters was not Nick's idea of fun. To find solace, he would bury himself deeply within a sleeping bag. Hannah was quick on her feet as she propelled her body onto Chase. A tangled mess of curls played on her lashes, pajamas a mismatch, Barbie hugged her upper torso, fairies fluttered up and down her legs. She was a bundle of energy, rolling over and under Chase's coverlet.

"Get up! Get up before the bed bugs bite."

Chase had to laugh.

"I think you have it wrong, sweetie. You say something similar to that when you close your eyes for the night. If I remember right, it goes something like this: Sleep tight, don't let the bed bugs bite, if they bite, squeeze them tight, and they won't bite the next night."

"Oh Marc, you are so silly. How can you squeeze bed bugs if you're sleeping?"

He never looked at it from that point of view; she just might be on to something. This little girl could light up the night if only…

"Hannah, I love you more than the whole world, the sky, the moon, the stars and the ground you walk on, but you need a lesson in respect. What I'm about to say is going to hurt your feelings, but no worse than what you do to your mother on a daily basis. You need to stop and think of the hurt you are inflicting every time you sound off. There is no greater love than a mother's love for her child. Do you understand what I mean?"

"I'm a child, so that means she loves me more than you, right?"

Chase failed. He had no choice but to tell it like it is.

"No, that is not what I meant. You must stop with your outlandish behavior. Every time you act out, it causes your mommy to be unhappy. And when she is alone, she cries over how you talk back at her. If you don't start behaving like you should, she just might pack her bags and leave you. Now do you understand?"

He got to her this time. Hannah showed she had a heart; she began to cry. She grabbed onto him, hugging him tight.

"I'm sorry, Marc, I'm really sorry. I don't want Mommy to leave. I love her."

He managed to calm her down.

"You must promise me you will never again upset her. Do you promise?"

Hannah kept nodding her head as he wiped away the tears. She was smiling and happy when she bounced out of the room.

But Chase worried he might have gone too far. Telling a little girl of eight — or as she would say, "I'm almost nine" — that her mommy might leave, was not the greatest strategy. But all he could do now was pray he did the right thing.

Harriet and the girls prepared breakfast, shooing away help from the male clan, which also included Nick. This would be a lingering breakfast.

Harriet, as was her custom, prolonged saying good-bye. But you can only put off the inevitable for so long.

Harriet and Ben, with arms wrapped around each other's waist, stood on the porch step while Chase's siblings galloped after his car, following until the rented Nissan left the end of the driveway. They sadly waved at his departure.

As expected, Nick ran back towards the house before losing sight of his brother's car. Harriet and Ben knew to step away; Nick needed his alone time.

The girls did not return to the house. Instead, they made their way towards the backyard. A playground of equipment that would stagger the imagination was waiting to entertain them. You will never hear from their lips "I want."

Harriet was about to remind the girls they were not to leave the backyard, when Ben spoke up. "I think I'll spend some quality time with them, or would you like for me to help with some of the household chores?"

"No, I can manage; the girls would love your company."

She watched him stroll towards the back until he was out of sight, then she closed the door. She had yet to informed Ben of Sloan's whereabouts and the shocking details behind her discovery.

Harriet made her way towards her bedroom, locking the door behind her. She opened the door to her rather small walk-in closet. After removing several boxes, she found what she was looking for, a Louis Vuitton carry-on she purchased with her first check from her rapist—and yes, she was being frivolous. She cradled the case close to her chest as if embracing a child. The goings-on in her firstborn's life were stored inside; letters instead of home visits lined the travel case.

She sat down upon her century-old ivory lace coverlet. The letters were tied with ribbons; each bundle represented a year. She untied the first of nine years. Surely, there would be something to suggest that someone was sharing Clay's life, but she went through letter after letter and not a hint. And yet, Harriet herself was just as bad, if not worse. Clay's siblings, other than Marc, were never told they had an older brother. She used the lame excuse that age played a factor. In the beginning they were too young to understand, and now if told, they were sure to ask questions that she wasn't prepared to answer. Maybe later, when they approach adulthood.

It was apparent Harriet never applied the motto "Never put off till tomorrow what you can do today." But with Ben it was a different story. Sloan's disappearance continues to haunt him, always making him think he could have done more.

Tonight before the anticipated lovemaking, she will tell him of Sloan's fate.

CHAPTER TWENTY-FIVE

After several raps of the brass knocker, the homeowner finally appeared at the door. Sunni gasped. The woman before her was nothing short of perfection. Large silver loop earrings could be seen through thick brunette hair that lay loosely about her shoulders. Her blue eyes would complement any lakeshore. A grey mesh top resembling a bra barely covered her ample breasts, and within the folds of her cleavage lay a cross dangling from a chain. Above a pair of low-slung white Capri pants, a silver chain hugged her small waist. Grey sandals with white stones and silver-coated toenails completed the look.

But never would eyes focus on the clothing or the accessories. Beauty was her calling card. She had been given what Sunni was denied. No one would ever say of Sunni, "She looks just like her mother." Why was she not given her mother's beauty gene? She could then claim that she had it all. Sunni could not deny she was rather plain.

Proof lay in the mirror. But soon her mother's looks would be slashed, and she too would know ugly, when shown the mirror for the last time.

"If you're selling something, I'm really not interested," was the comment Sunni received.

Sunni replied sarcastically, "No, I am not, but I do have something to give you."

With a thrust of both Sunni's hands, her mother landed on her back. The red door rattled from the force of the closure.

CeCe began pushing herself backward in an attempt to escape her attacker, while mouthing a few words.

"If it's money you're after, I have a few dollars in my wallet. I'll be more than happy to get it for you."

CeCe felt the impact of her assailant's military-style shoe. She held back from crying out in pain. She was bold in her attempt to show she had the guts to withstand any type of torture.

"Haven't you looked around? If you have, then you must be crazy; you can see I have nothing else to give you."

"Does insanity run in your family?"

CeCe was giving it her all to remove the foot from her chest while fumbling with her words.

"I have no idea what you are talking about."

"Sure you do... Wait...maybe you don't. Maybe crazy entered the gene pool when you sold me."

CeCe for a split second did not register her meaning. But just as quickly, she revisited that scene from long ago:

She could not believe what the doctor was telling her. She was more than careful, the early morning birth control pill swallowed with a sip of water. It was a habit, like going to pee the instant your feet hit the floor. As to the men she slept with, she not only provided the apparatus, but affixed the product. The first word that sprang out of her mouth was abortion, *but the good doctor would not be the butcher; she would have to look elsewhere, but she did not. She damned him then and now.*

There was no denying the creature standing over her was the beast that resided in her for nine months. CeCe bore the hideous burden only because of the windfall she hoped to acquire when she dumped the ungainly load.

She refused to buckle under the pressure.

"I don't believe you. Only the attorney that handled the adoption knew my name, and that was kept strictly confidential."

"You were misled. My adoptive mother knew, but only after I took her life did I receive that information. And now I'm here to end the life which gave me life."

Fear entered CeCe's life. But hope was not lost when a rush of adrenalin set in. She grabbed a hold of Sunni's leg and with a twist managed to shove her aside. She was up and out the front door before Sunni could comprehend what had just happened.

CeCe's escape was a breath away. She had made it to the first step when a stranglehold was placed around her neck. Only after she was pulled back did she regret not screaming out for help. Several of her sleeping partners across the road could be seen guzzling their daily intake of cheap beer. Engaged in conversation only they would understand, they took no notice of her dilemma. They would have come to her rescue, "if only."

Once CeCe was back inside, a fist pounded her face. There was no mistaking the sound: her nose was broken. CeCe's scream was caught in midair. A dusting rag lying within Sunni's reach was the tool used for silencing. A road map of blood vessels now highlighted CeCe's blue eyes; swelling was instantaneous. Blood coated her lips and dripped downward, turning her halter into a shade of scarlet. Whether from pain or from the brutal force of the fist, tears joined the flow as she struggled to free herself. But it was useless; her attacker was swift with the handcuffs and rope. Her hands were now bound and her body tied to an outdated red Chromcraft kitchen chair.

Sunni was ready to begin her mother's torture; she would give her but an hour more of life. She pulled a matching chair close so as to feel her mother's breath upon her face for the first and last time. CeCe nodded a promise not to scream if the rag was removed.

CeCe now knew the mistake she'd made in selling her baby. She should have found someone, anyone, to remove what she perceived as the greatest atrocity to descend upon a woman's body. The expectation of possibly selling the abomination that clung to the wall of her uterus gave this thing a stay of execution. And now this thing will be her executioner.

Excitement on Sunni's end was rapidly approaching the ebb tide.

"Do you have any idea what it feels like not to be wanted, to be disposed of like a bag of rubbish?"

CeCe had to think fast, somehow convince her daughter she'd been forced to give her up. She always wanted to become an actress. Now was the time to display that talent. She began to weep.

"I so wanted to keep you. I prayed nightly for God to help me provide for you. I was living on the streets begging for food when I felt myself slipping away to join forces with the pavement. I awoke in strange surroundings. A hospital emergency room is not a place a person dreams of waking up in. But had that not happened, it would have taken much longer to realize I was pregnant with you. I wept with joy. Finally, I would be given something that would give meaning to my miserable existence.

"I tried to find work, but in my raggedy attire and beginning to show, no one would hire me. I lived in shelters when there was available space. I thanked God I was there when I went into labor. The seventy-three hours of excruciating pain I welcomed, for in the end I would be given a gift like no other.

"I tried, honey; I really tried, but the weeks of living in cardboard boxes in alleys and under bridges made you continuously sick. I realized my mistake when you almost died from pneumonia on Christmas Day. It was time to say good-bye. But I refused to place you in an orphanage. I chose a lawyer that dealt strictly in adoptions and would agree to my one demand: you would leave my arms with the woman I chose to be your mother. He agreed. Your adoptive family possessed all the qualities I lacked: a home with security and a family that would love you almost as much as I. I could not have asked for anyone better. Your father a doctor, a stay-at-home mom who would be with you day and night. You would live a life like the rich and famous. This was to be my legacy to you."

Sunni could not spit the words out fast enough. "You stinking, lousy, lying, conniving bitch. Do you honestly believe my mother would not tell me the reason and the amount you demanded from them?"

Sunni got into her face. Rage was at its boiling point. Screams emitted from her mouth, as she teetered on the brink of insanity. She jerked CeCe's hair within her knotted fist.

"You will suffer long, if you do not tell me what I already know. The truth just might set you free."

Sunni's take on CeCe's reaction convinced Sunni she was on the right track. If CeCe had known Sunni's knowledge only went as far as knowing her name and that she was unmarried, CeCe would have held to her story.

CeCe's performance was unacceptable. If she lacked the skill to convince her daughter, an audience would leave before the curtain call. When she failed to give Sunni the information she demanded, silence proved to be the worse of the two evils. Sunni's fist was proving to be a wicked weapon. CeCe's distorted face was again met with a thunderbolt of a strike. This time the piercing scream would have been heard, had Sunni not had the rag ready. But a violent spew of vomit forced the cloth out. Sunni quickly untied the restraints, giving CeCe the freedom to expel the remaining vomit. She would not allow her mother to possibly die from such a simple thing as choking on her own puke.

"Are you ready to tell truth, the whole truth, so help you God?"

CeCe nodded her head; she prayed God was within hearing distance should she need His help.

"It was the truth when I told you a lawyer was involved; there is no way I could have found an affluent couple without his expertise. The fact of the matter is, I refused to be burdened with any kind of handicap, and caring for a baby is like choosing prison over freedom. Of course, abortion entered my mind until I realized the amount of money I could rake in if I found someone who was desperate enough to give me what I wanted. Your parents-to-be never balked at the amount of seventy-five thousand dollars, or I should say your mother did not; your father shook his head. He told me to peddle you elsewhere, he wasn't buying. But your mother carried the balls that day. She told him if he didn't fork over what I asked, he would be working for her when she finished with him. I would have taken way less, and I think your father knew that, but like they say, there's a sucker born every minute.

"Now that you've heard what you came here for, will you please leave? A man friend is waiting for me to join him."

But Sunni was not finished.

"You failed to mention the name of my father; even I had one of those."

One has to wonder why that statement would bring giggles to someone on death row, but then again, maybe CeCe truly thought the truth would set her free.

"Sugar, I am a confirmed nymphomaniac. If I knew the answer to that one, you can be assured he would be minus the equipment that caused it."

Sunni for the first time really looked at her mother, but with no expression other than to state a point.

"I am not your Sugar and your time is up."

CeCe never saw it coming. The scalpel slid slightly above the breast, exposing a half-inch gap. A fresh supply of blood careened downward, turning everything in its path a brilliant shade of scarlet. The Capris were about to create a new designer look. CeCe, as if in a daze, watched as the blood gush from the opening. Bewildered by its display, she wondered how this could be happening, and if it were, then why was she not feeling the aftermath of pain? And then, as if on cue, she rose, still unrestrained, and began running for her life, leaving blood in her wake as she flew from the torturous chamber.

The front door no longer provided the means for her escape. Posed like a warrior, Sunni stood rooted to the main entrance. Laughter bounced off the walls of the close quarters, braking a second to allow CeCe to hear what she had to say.

"Where do you think you're going? There is nowhere to run?"

A new blast of laughter was set to begin until Sunni heard what sounded like a door being shammed shut. *Damn, how could I have been so stupid?*

With the swiftness of a gazelle Sunni was at the back door and then down the steps. The gods were not in CeCe's favor; had she not tripped and fallen, she would have once again experienced the joys of freedom. Sunni quickly looked around. Other than the children at play in the roadway, there were no witnesses. CeCe fought hard but was no match for the evil that descended upon her.

Satisfied that she was attracting no attention, Sunni returned to the trailer. No sooner had the door closed than the slashing began. Sunni was in her element; she had turned into a killing machine. With her left arm wrapped tightly around her victim's neck, she used her right hand to slide the scalpel from the left side of CeCe's forehead downward, slicing over the bridge of her broken nose, and then into her right eye.

A spine-chilling scream ricocheted off the walls, but ended as quickly as it started as the blood pooled into CeCe's mouth. She was fighting for air; she was lingering at death's door. Sunni released her hold. CeCe hit the floor facedown. Sunni was stunned to see the exertion her mother put forth at yet another attempt to escape. She struggled to rise, trying her best to acquire more leverage to force her body forward, crawling at a snail's pace. The endeavor was pitiful. She fell onto her face several times. The only sound she could utter was a whimper, the pain was that severe. But until her last breath was extinguished, CeCe would never give up.

Sunni pulled up a chair to watch, stunned at her mother's endurance. *Maybe a swift kick to the face is what she needs.* Sunni rose from her seated position. Now standing in her mother's path that was leading nowhere, she flipped her over. Sunni was taken aback at the sight. She was accustomed to the mangled messes she brought about, but this was proving to be her finest work yet.

"My, my, you are a nauseating sight. It takes everything I have just to look at you. But who am I? What I need is a second opinion; I think the best judge of my handiwork would be the subject lying on the floor."

Sunni placed her hand to her face, cupping her chin. She then began tapping her index finger to her lips, as if in deep thought.

"Now, let's see, where would you keep a big enough mirror to view my new creation? Ah, there it is, a wall mirror, perfect." With the mirror now in both hands, she asked her mother if she were ready for the viewing.

CeCe with her lone eye managed to peer at her attacker. Only God could see her beauty. She wrestled with her words, but the sounds emitted were slurred; bloody froth bubbled. She was unable to form intelligible words.

Sunni grappled with the weight of the mirror, but managed to position it directly in front of her mother's face, dissecting a few words of an old memorable phrase.

"Mirror, mirror in my hands, who is the fairest in trailer land?"

No one good or bad should be shown the horror of what was surely caused by a deranged person. CeCe turned her face away. A single teardrop fell as she prayed for death. She could bear no more.

But Sunni was not finished. The scalpel was still wet with her mother's blood. Sunni began to dance around slicing at what she considered a diseased monster. Arms and legs were laid opened, fingers removed along with her toes. A scream was tried out but sadly fell to the wayside.

Sunni was through with her dance but not with her mother. She was thoughtful enough, though, to replace the mirror in its rightful place. She would finish with the slaughter after the use of what she considered the bondage chair. Holding onto the back of the chair, she climbed aboard. Standing erect, she glanced downward onto the face of the woman she so wanted to be loved by. Then with a single leap she jumped onto her mother's face, crushing what was left of the fragile bones. Sunni finally found the satisfaction she was seeking; never again would her mother reject her.

It was time to move on, but not before she showered. Sunni never left home without a change of clothes. She never knew when someone would give her a hard time. Preparation was the means to survival. She could smell the blood clinging to her arms. She licked the substance, surprised that it was not all that bad. The taste leaned towards metallic. As to the smell, it reminded her of something both sweet and sour.

The shower stall was small but exceptionally clean. She would take the blood-soaked clothes home to be washed.

Sunni was sure her mommy had a large plastic bag she would not mind her sweet daughter using. She would leave nothing behind.

She had one last thing to take care of: she needed her souvenir. Never had she seen someone so orderly, everything in its place. She wondered if her mother suffered from a psychological compulsive disorder. But for now that thought was pushed aside, as she was concerned with what she should take that would keep alive the memory of her dear departed mother. In the last place she searched (is that not always the way) she found something she never expected: her birth certificate.

Her mother's last words spoke the truth, her father was listed as unknown. Sunni damned her for proving she had a whore for a mother.

Other than the gore and the grisly remains of her mother, Sunni left the trailer in the exact condition in which she'd found it: pristine.

CHAPTER TWENTY-SIX

Clay could not believe the dining table was set for two when he returned home from work. Did that mean his wife was joining him? He prayed this was so; even if Sloan's attitude towards him was no different, at least he would have someone to dine with. But what would he do with himself while waiting for her to make an appearance? Finally, after he'd spent several minutes looking rather stupid leaning against the wall with his hands stuffed into his pockets, Sloan strolled into the room.

Clay almost lost control; his ability to stand was weakened. Was it possible she was more beautiful than ever, or was it because he had not seen her in several weeks? He became instantly aroused. Would he also be dining in her bed? He prayed like he'd never prayed before, he was that desperate.

The dress she chose to wear was R. Scott Frenca, a winter white knit dress that embraced her every curve. This dress was designed with one purpose in mind, and that was to bring torment and anguish to the man it was intended to be seen by. The square-cut bodice and the skirt length five inches above the knee exposed just about all her delicious equipment. Would Clay make it through dinner? He doubted it. He all but ran to her. He closed his eyes, taking in her scent as he assisted her with seating. There was silence until he sat and began unfolding his dinner napkin.

"Clay, I can't continue to live like this."

The napkin fluttered to the floor; a tear showed itself. He found his voice, but it was hard to speak.

"I should have known this was coming. You want a divorce, don't you?" He removed his handkerchief from his breast pocket. He did not try to hide his feelings; the tears took a walk down his face.

Sloan rose from her seated position and ran to his side. Kneeling, she took him into her arms.

"Oh my darling, no, no, that is not what I want. You never let me finish what I was about to say. I desire you; I want to feel your body against mine. I need for you to make love to me. I have suffered greatly in and out of the bed, as I know you have."

There is no greater hunger than bodily lust; food is secondary.

The staircase for the first time in his life proved to be no handicap as Clay's feet pounded the stairs, his wife safely cradled in his arms. Their lovemaking would continue into the early morning light, until Sloan's screams of rapture dwindled down to nothing more than pleasurable sighs.

Clay hated the thought of eating breakfast alone—or any meal, as far as that goes. Sloan's comment as she lingered in bed stayed with him. He could still hear her words:

"I haven't the strength to walk, let alone hold a fork; you will have to dine alone."

He thought she was finished with what she had to say, but she continued. "I finally realized why there are so many divorces; those women don't have you in their bed."

Clay grinned while he prepared a pot of coffee, Belgian waffles topped with blackberries, several links of pork sausages and never-to-be-forgotten fresh orange juice. He would not be dining alone; he and Sloan would share the bounty he prepared in the comfort of their king bed.

This weekend, he will share his time with no one other than his wife. He never thought he would enjoy the solitude minus the servants, but Sloan's decision years back to have the weekends to themselves proved idyllic. Now that he was back in her good graces he would disconnect anything and everything that would interfere with their time together.

Food now disposed of, Clay moved the trays out of their way. Sloan accepted the warmth of his arms as they cuddled in their king-size bed.

But Clay had something to discuss that was of great importance, something that should have been said shortly after Garth's death. But when Sloan disappeared into the bedroom shutting him out, it was put on hold.

"Babe, I know what I'm about to say will upset you, but it needs to be said. I purchased a gun shortly after Garth's suicide…"

Before he could continue Sloan was up and out of the bed displaying her objection, hands on her naked hips.

"There is no way I will have guns in my home. What are we, mafia?"

"Babe, I know your take on guns. But you need to hear me out. You know as well as I that Garth did not kill Krista. Don't you see, babe, the maniac that took your friend's life is still out there. How do we know you're not next? I did this for your protection and my peace of mind. Babe, I need for you to go along with me on this."

She began pacing, unsure of what to do. What if Clay was right? Could she suffer the same horrific death as Krista? Just the thought sent shivers down her spine.

"Okay, I'll go along with it, but it must be kept in your study, the place where even the servants are not allowed. The hidden compartment within your locked desk would be ideal. Don't look so surprised, Clay. Your father spoke of it in general conversation. I guess he thought you trusted me enough to tell me. I'm not putting you down over this; everyone has something kept hidden, whether it is something palpable or something stored in their head. That is a fact of life. And if it makes you feel any better, I never gave it another thought, until now. And rest assured I have no interest in its contents. If at any time I do feel threatened, trust me, I would find the strength to tear that drawer apart."

Clay wondered if there was anything that she did not know.

Oh yeah, she does not know he is her uncle.

CHAPTER TWENTY-SEVEN

Chase had been home for more than a week and had yet to report in to work, or even call his brother to let him know he was back in town. His thoughts would not give him a break. He had yet to unpack his travel bag from visiting with his mother and siblings. He was beginning to feel as if his life was at its end, that nothing really mattered, or at least nothing that has a sure cure. Dragging his ass was not his thing, and yet that was what he had been doing for the past week.

Why is telling the truth so damn difficult? It would certainly make me feel a hell of a lot better. Ah, but it's not only about me, is it?

The phone rang for the first time since his return. Chase thought of ignoring it, but the outside world had news to deliver. It could be a good delivery or a bad delivery, but at this point in his life how much worse could it get?

The sound of his brother's voice gave him a slight lift; he really did miss Clay.

"Well hello, big guy. I see you made it home safely, thank God. I pray you managed to get all your affairs taken care of. My father and I miss you terribly and it has nothing to do with our workload that is desperately calling for your expertise."

Chase heard his brother's chuckle. Clay was trying to make light of the workload, so as not to put a rush on his return. Chase had gotten to know his brother quite well, and with that knowledge came a love that could not be defined with just words.

"Hey, big guy, are you still there? Did I catch you at a bad time? Or has my chatter put a strain on your lips and you're unable to talk?"

Chase still had a chuckle or two left in him and he shared it.

"No, no, I'm still here. I was just about to call you. You can put your workload to rest, I'm on my way. And Clay, when it comes to missing someone, you and Phillip are high on the list. See you in a bit."

Maybe that was what Chase needed to hear, someone from the other side to get his dead ass moving. He had much to do. His apartment was crying for help. He had the talent to design his own pad, so he did not need Sunni's suggested help. It was one thing to be tied to her during social functions; he did not need her scooping through his things. And now that he figured out her true intentions towards Sloan, it was time to find another woman to escort to social functions; this lesbian would no longer be his disgusting partner. Clay had a string of women friends from which to choose; Chase could have his pick.

But now was not the time to think about Sunni or to tackle his apartment. He told Clay he would see him in a bit. But before he could take action, he became ill; Clay's name began ricocheting around inside his head.

How was he to come clean with all that had been laid on him? He loved Sloan intensely; it hurt just to think of her. Should he or could he tell her she was married to her uncle? And what about Clay, the big brother who threw a lasso around his heart? And what could he say about Phillip? Although no relation, he was as close as anyone could be to having the perfect friend and soon-to-be partner.

Chase's life could not have been messier had he not wiped himself after taking a dump. The only way to clean it up was with as few words as possible. He was sitting at present on a bar stool; he then stood as if facing his brother.

"Clay, I am not going to pussyfoot around with what I have to say. I know Phillip is your brother and not your father, and I think you should tell Sloan, who I grew up with in Mason's Mill, that you are her uncle. As to me, you are looking at your brother Marc."

So simple to destroy all those whom he loved. He made it to the bathroom before a spew of vomit exited. When finished he sat down on the rim of the bathtub and started to cry. His mother was so right. Why did he not listen to her wise old words, "Lies are no way to live a life"?

Chase brushed his teeth before he took a shower. He had finished with all he intended, except for the obvious, and that was now proving to be the worst dilemma he ever thought possible. Acting out his emotions was senseless; it was similar to crying over spilled milk. He decided to play it by ear. Surely the day will come when the truth can no longer be held back.

In a short space of time, he will come to regret that decision.

CHAPTER TWENTY-EIGHT

Sloan rested her hand on the doorknob, hesitating, not because she dreaded going in, but knowing if she did the tears would start again, the never-ending tears. The doorknob seemed to have a life of its own as the door slowly began opening to reveal its contents. Sun poked its ray of light through the partially opened blinds, giving the room the warm glow of a summer's day.

The door to the nanny's room was closed as Sloan moved to the center of her universe. Eighteen-inch border paper was centered on three of the walls displaying a circus arena. Clowns performing their antics, elephants parading, horses taking bows, dogs adorned with hats and coats jumping over balls and through loops, tightrope walkers secure with their safety nets, acrobats, and the ringmaster himself arms, extended and held high to welcome each and everyone with a guarantee of a day filled with thrills and laughter. Above the border were randomly placed balloons in all colors and shapes. This room was a happy, cheerful place, wrapped in the comfort of love.

Sloan knew this room well. Tears began to cloud her vision. Clear vision or no vision, the plush scarlet carpet and the dresser, chest, bassinet, changing table, playpen, rocking horse, toy box, and the table and chairs done in primary colors were pasted into her memory. Numerous stuffed animals were placed on shelves and in corners, and one slightly lazy monkey lay over the arm of a glider rocker. So many toys waiting to be played with. And finally against the fourth wall, void of wall coverings, sat the crib. The clown mobile swayed gently from the flow of air as the air-conditioner turned on. Slowly Sloan made her way to the crib. Eyes still unable to focus, she reached with one hand for the rail while the other hand rested on her swollen abdomen. Everything was so perfect, yet Clay detested the thought of being a father and refused to have anything to do with the baby, and that now included her.

She quietly mouthed the words, "I can't give up, I won't give up. There has to be hope."

Prayer and more prayers; no one was listening. She backed away ready to run and scream, but instead she stumbled onto her rocker. She placed her hand against her mouth forbidding it to open. The chair was beckoning, offering her sad, miserable body some bit of comfort. The lonely monkey was not forgotten; it clung to her breast. Sloan buried her face deep into its soft fur, stifling out the cries. Out of the speaker system a familiar voice sounded, a voice she loved deeply at one time.

"Sloan...where are you?"

She could not answer; the tears had a stranglehold on her voice.

"Sloan, damn it, I know you can hear me. Don't make me come after you."

Sloan had learned quickly to be alert to all sounds, no matter the distance. Now she was aware of Clay's heavy footsteps pounding the stairs. She could feel the force of her body trying to move, to be quick, but she remained immobile. Her mind screamed, *Run, you fool, run!* and finally her body cooperated. She stopped for only a second to close the door behind her.

The baby's room was located on the third floor, as far removed from theirs as it could be. Even though she knew Clay wanted no part of this reality, that did not make it cease to exist. Keeping close to the wall, Sloan moved as fast as she could along the seemingly unending corridor, and then down the staircase. She was now far enough away from the forbidden room to answer safely. Clay's footsteps were now rapidly ascending the winding staircase as he continued to shout her name. She appeared just as he reached the second floor. In an attempt to calm the trembling of her body, her hands gripped the balcony's mahogany rail.

They now stood face-to-face.

"Where in the hell were you? You know how many times I called your name?"

"Called? The correct terminology is screamed. It's really amazing how powerful your voice can carry throughout all fifty-seven rooms. Why should I answer? You can't possibly think my voice could be heard above yours. It's too bad your friends aren't around when you give one of your performances. I'm sure eyebrows would be raised and your social background would be questioned."

Clay's comment matched his mood. "Screw you, Sloan."

"You know, you have a problem. Not only do you have a filthy mouth, but your attitude needs an adjustment. If you needed me, you knew where I would be. I was rechecking my list to make sure I have everything I'll need."

"That damn list. You've had weeks to prepare. Anyone who can't have a couple of bags packed in seven weeks has a serious problem. Agreeing to this trip was a weak moment in my life. Never again will that happen."

An alarm sounded in Sloan's head, a warning signal to apologize or, to be more accurate, to "kiss ass."

"Clay, I'm so sorry. I'm just on edge worrying that something drastic will happen and that I won't be able to go, but it's really going to happen, isn't it?"

She felt stupid standing there like a small child and grinning like a fool. If she had not kept her hands attached to the rail, she would have clapped with excitement.

Clay's stance was firm. His eyes were void of warmth.

"Sloan, I changed my mind. I cannot allow you to go through with this trip. When you left Mason's Mill you said you'd never ever go back. It's best we keep it that way."

She gasped for air, choking on her words.

"Oh dear God, why do I ever expect things to go my way? I should have known you'd find an excuse, any excuse. Everything has to suit your needs, your wants. What about me? Clay, please don't do this. I'm sorry for the way I spoke. I'll do anything. Just give me this one thing, and I swear I'll never ask anything of you again. Please, Clay, please."

Weeping, she sank to her knees and grabbed onto his pant leg. Her pleading eyes locked into his. Seconds passed, and the spell of their eye contact broke. Further words were not spoken as he turned and headed back down the staircase.

First Sloan felt hate, then rage, but the tears were always the strongest. If she returned to the third floor, she could throw her legs over the rail and jump. The sixty-foot fall would make all her pain end; it would be a final solution to her problems. She ran up the stairs to the third floor. She'd managed to get one leg over the rail when she heard Clay's announcement to their butler.

"Truman, Mrs. Chadsworth is ready. Please see to her luggage. She will show you what she'll be taking. I'll see to it that Gus brings the limousine around to the front."

He then added an afterthought, "The sooner she gets out of here, the better I will feel."

She was so close. She wondered if she really could have ended her life. What if Clay had not spoken as loudly as he had, or if she had withdrawn into herself to the point she was oblivious to her surroundings? Would she have followed through? Had destiny intervened again?

Clay rode with her to the airport, but the limousine contained silence. Sloan bid farewell to Gus. She knew it was useless to kiss Clay good-bye; he had turned his back on her.

She was greeted by Clay's pilot, Andrew. He was a witness to their ongoing disagreements, which disturbed him greatly. Andrew considered Clay and Sloan to be more than his employers; he thought of them as friends. He had tried to help by suggesting Clay seek God's help to get their lives in order. He said this with the best of intentions, but Clay gave him a look that put an end to all future conversations in reference to Our Father in Heaven.

Clay gave final instructions and then without so much as a glance, he was gone. All that remained from his swift exit was the dust the limo left in its wake. The few times they'd traveled together in the last seven months, since they'd learned of Sloan's pregnancy, Clay had chosen to sit with Andrew. This time the pilot was minus its master. This trip could be the means to finding the answer to their problems. Maybe, just maybe, there was still hope for them and their baby.

As Clay's private jet prepared for takeoff from Kennedy Airport destined for Chicago's O'Hare Airport, Sloan's thoughts were of the Lincoln that would be waiting to take her to her final destination, a two-hour drive to her hometown, population 3,340 when Clay had taken her away ten years earlier.

Sloan reached inside her handbag. Her fingers caressed the small framed picture of Clay. He was so God-awful handsome, so perfect in form and feature, a study in masculinity and flawlessness. She turned towards the window, thoughts tugging at her heart. Did she expect more from him than he was capable of giving? She knew more than anything children had to be a part of her life, but Clay wanted no children in his life. Was this the source of their problems or was it something entirely different? Sloan knew if she wanted something desperately enough, she would find a way. Clay insisted she take birth control and as an extra precaution, he himself used protection. She remembered the day she ultimately would make a decision that would not only alter their lives, but result in a horror no one should ever have to endure.

They were preparing to go out for dinner.

"Clay, we need to have a talk."

He ignored her statement. "What do you think of my new suit?"

"It's okay, I guess. Clay, it's important that we talk."

"Okay? You guess it's okay? What kind of an answer is that?"

"I don't care about your suit. I care about what's happening to us, to our marriage. We need to talk."

"Why is it you always have something to say when someone is waiting?"

"Someone is always waiting. If it's not our personal friends Nico and Sofie and Chase with God only knows which woman of the night, it's a shitload of others. Don't you see, Clay, we never get a chance to be alone, much less have time to talk."

If Sloan had not been secretly meeting with Chase on what she considered her "Saturday special," she would have had a hard time dealing with his presence at the dinner table when their friends met on a twice-weekly dinner engagement. But the behavior of Chase's selected partner the last time was becoming a bit tiresome. (He finally told Sunni their platonic relationship had to end; he was looking to settle down and they both knew she wasn't going to be the one. Chase told Sloan another version: that Sunni expected more than he was capable of giving. Sloan had yet to be told that Sunni was a lesbian and that Sunni's hunger for fulfillment lay with her.)

But it made no difference which woman was given the privilege of Chase's arm; they had the same intent to smother Chase as if they were his blanket. Their friends would turn their eyes in the other direction.

It was at the last dinner party that Sloan had had enough. The dark-haired beauty for this particular evening could not keep her lips off of Chase's; the kiss was deep and long and Chase was showing no objections. Several minutes later they exited the dining area only to return after more than thirty minutes away. Sloan was furious; she tried on a weekly basis to put an end to what she considered years of his suffering (and hers) only to be turned down repeatedly. His endless bounty of women had to be getting what she was being denied.

She silenced her thoughts on Chase while she waited on Clay's response to having no time to themselves.

Instead of replying to her comment, he answered with a question. "Are you ready?"

Ignoring his question, she plunged ahead. "Clay, I want a baby. We can't party all of our lives. We need stability and a baby would provide that."

"My God, Sloan, we've been over and over this. Yet you persist in trying to bring another person into our lives."

"Another person? Good God, Clay, I'm talking about a baby. You're acting as if my intention is to bring someone in off the streets. This would be our baby, Clay, yours and mine. Most men and women look at it as a reinforcement of what they share, someone to love and strengthen their lives, build their future around. But then you're not like other men, are you, Clay?"

She gave him several minutes to think about what she had just said. It did not penetrate. Did she really think it would?

"I can see this conversation is again one-sided. Clay, please just tell me why you have no desire for a baby. You can't just say 'no children'—there has to be a reason. Tell me…talk to me…please, Clay."

His response was to tell her he was leaving, she could go or stay. Clay gave her a choice, but not in the way it counted. He slammed the door as he made his exit. His method of ending a dispute was to turn his back, slam the door and walk away. In the years they had been married, Sloan had never gone against him if he was firm in his decision. She had had enough; no more. She grabbed her gloves and fur, determined as of that night she would take matters in her own hands.

The day always started off the same. Clay would hand Sloan the contraceptive with a glass of water and watch as she took it. While he was away at work, she practiced day in and day out trying to retain an 81 mg aspirin, basically the same size as the birth control tablet. It was harder than it seemed. She did have one consolation, if she did not succeed soon, she would never have to worry about a heart attack, but there was the possibility of floating away from water consumption.

Sometimes Sloan would just stare at that stupid preventive heart pill thinking of super glue, anything to keep that damn tablet from sailing down her esophagus. It got to the point that she hated leaving the comfort of her bed to stare at that dumb orange thing that refused to cooperate.

But, here it was another day and the ritual continued. Sloan shook out yet another tablet, quickly working her tongue before gulping down a glass of water. She sat down absentmindedly, unaware that the pill had not taken its customary journey down her throat. As she stared off into space, really thinking of nothing, she felt something buried in her gum line. With her pointer finger she reached inside to remove the substance. Her finger came out tinged in orange. The pill had worked its way into the corner of her mouth. She'd succeeded this time, but would she get the same results with further attempts? Tablet after tablet refused to move from its designated spot. Whatever she was now doing, finally worked.

That problem now conquered, Sloan had to attack the condoms stored in Clay's nightstand. He'd purchased a hefty supply of condoms the day Sloan asked him for a baby. The memory of that conversation never went away and the mention of Hawaii always left a bad taste in her mouth.

A piercing from a sharp needle into each individually wrapped condom hopefully would do the trick. She shook the contents of the box onto the bed. Clay was down to four, but there was no need for concern: he was not about to do without sex, nor did she want him to. There may have been disdain in their relationship, but the body operated on its own; the mind was absent.

Clay seldom made eye contact when he placed the pill into the palm of Sloan's hand. If he had, he would have noticed the sly smile that played upon her lips. That pill and the pills to follow would not accomplish their purpose; Sloan would have her baby. She would not have to wait long for the results; she was due in two weeks.

Clay was the first to notice there was a no-show. The calendar had a check mark on the twenty-sixth day. Sloan's period was precise from month to month; never did her body waver.

He said nothing until he noticed the check mark had not been blackened by his wife's hand, indicating she had not come around. She could not lie or hide the fact; she blared out the findings.

"Yes, I know, I'm late. Something must have gone wrong."

She had never seen such anger. If looks could kill, she would be lying with the flowers. Clay accused her of having an affair. He called the Chadsworths' family physician, Dr. Frederick Marshall, the same doctor who had delivered him. Dr. Marshall was seventy-two years of age. He was of average height and beyond thin; he was a bag of bones. He was a man with a few strands of white hair still clinging onto its life's substance. His sagging eyelids, along with the dentures that moved with his every word, added to his already decaying appearance.

Clay screamed obscenities that Sloan had never heard of into the phone's mouthpiece. He accused their doctor of writing his wife the wrong prescription and threatened to sue him for liability. Included in that lawsuit would be the makers of the condoms, for they had to have been defective… On and on he raved. Finally there was a lull. Dr. Marshall somehow got a word in, for Clay continued to hold the telephone to his ear. Sloan could not imagine what the doctor was saying to him, but it was apparent he finally convinced Clay that no one was at fault; everything in life does not come with a guarantee.

Clay half-heartedly repeated what his doctor had said with an added comment: "He congratulated us."

Clay mentioned abortion only once. Sloan told him she would leave him before she would abort their baby. No matter how badly Clay did not want children, he did want Sloan.

When Andrew announced landing would be in about twenty minutes, it jolted Sloan back to the present. She caressed her extended stomach in an effort to soothe the movement of the persistent activity.

She was well into her eight month, when she knew she had to let her doctor know about her proposed trip.

She remembered that visit well.

She had positioned herself on the examination table after removing all of her clothing as the nurse instructed. Sloan could never understand why the doctor insisted on examining her breasts on each visit. She just went ahead and did whatever she was told, while thinking that probably all Dr. Marshall was capable of doing was looking and touching. Maybe that's how he got his kicks. Even if he could still perform, what woman in her right mind would bed down with him? He was beyond ugly, and even if he had his name on a bank, Sloan would never drop her panties for the likes of him...well maybe, if it was an absolute necessity, like now.

No sooner had Sloan told the doctor about the trip than his arms were thrown up in protest.

"You must be out of your mind to put your baby at such risk. A woman that wants a baby as badly as you would never consider traveling. No, Sloan, definitely not. You will have to postpone your plans until after the birth of your baby. I'll be damned if I'm going to be held liable for your irrational actions."

Sloan could stand no more. Tears escaped her eyes and fell onto the sheet.

"I have to get away. I must get away. Without this trip it could mean the end of my life. Damn it, don't you see, if I don't leave before the baby's birth, it'll be the death of a family. You can't force me to stay. I'm going. I don't know why I felt I needed your permission. You damn doctors are all alike. I do care about my baby's health. You just can't see beyond that point. What about me? My sanity is also involved."

Dr. Marshall seemed to ignore her, just like Clay. Men were proving to be all alike. Her performance would have forced any doctor to give in, just not him.

But Sloan was not going to take it lying down. She began slapping the probing doctor.

"Get out of my way...I'm leaving."

Shoving the doctor aside while remaining ever mindful to keep a firm grip on the sheet, she attempted to grab up her clothes to make a run for her life. Instead she tripped, her foot tangled in the covering. The doctor's quick action caught her. She was amazed at the strength of this frail-looking man. Wonders never fail.

"Sloan, honey, calm down! No one is going to force you to do anything you don't want to do. Okay...Okay...? If this trip means that much to you, then you'll just have to go."

Sloan released the sheet. She threw herself into the doctor's arms, naked. He stepped back red-faced to retrieve the fallen sheet from the floor. He could think of nowhere to place it without getting in his naked patient's way. He tucked it under his arm and headed towards the door. He had little else to say other than, "You better get some clothes on before the baby catches a cold." Sloan figured if he was trying to be a comedian to hide his embarrassment, he did okay. She laughed at his effort.

Sloan will soon be faced with memories of a past she vowed to forget. For a force stronger than anyone could ever imagine was pushing her forward, back into the past. She came to the realization her encounter with Clay was not by accident. Their meeting was planned long before she could think, talk or walk, for destiny held the cards to their lives. How it will turn out anyone can speculate, but with her help, just maybe Sloan can play out the hand they were dealt by returning to where it all began.

She did not call ahead; she wanted to surprise Harriet, her mother's best friend. Also on the agenda was to speak to Ben in reference to her frequent nightmares regarding her baby brother. And she would pay a visit to her family's grave site. Years back she had done what she intended; she had a special request for her family's burial site. She had to see the finished product as the work order was placed over the telephone. It had better live up to her expectations; if not, whoever had done the work will definitely do a modification.

Sloan confided in Chase about visiting her hometown and asked if he wanted to join her. She realized that this would have to be done without her husband's knowledge as he had yet to be told Chase was from her hometown.

Chase could charter his own plane after work on a Friday evening and be back at the workplace Monday morning with no one the wiser. It would certainly be an additional surprise as he just returned from seeing his mother this past weekend.

He would have given anything to be with Sloan for a full weekend, but to face his mother in Sloan's presence, he was afraid his worst fear would come true, that someone would slip up and his world would come crashing down. Besides, he had already spoken with his mother and advised her to keep a lid on his dishonesty as he had yet to address Clay, and he did not leave out the fact that Sloan was expecting. Harriet wept for the mounting deception, but what's a mother to do? She agreed.

Sloan will be visiting with Clay's mother when his body is discovered.

CHAPTER TWENTY-NINE

The day of discovery was deeply imbedded into Chase's brain. He was given the horrifying news after Clay and Phillip; Sloan couldn't keep it to herself. That memory sprang into action. It happened on one of their Saturday visits. They were sharing a cup of coffee in his apartment, his attention to detail told of a man more than committed to his work. His apartment was a showplace; Sunni had nothing on him.

But the chitchat between them was becoming a strain, notably on Sloan's part. She could not hold back; it was time for the unveiling. Sloan took Chase's hands into her own. She was bubbling with excitement.

"Chase, it's finally been confirmed, I'm going to have a baby. Can you believe it?"

His coffee found its way onto his shirt and slacks. No, he could not believe it, nor did he want to. He was pissed and he let it be known.

"Did you not tell me you were on birth control, and that Clay used prophylactics?"

Sloan hated the tone he was taking with her, but she stuck up for herself with a tone similar to his.

"Yes, of course I did, but nothing is guaranteed, you know that."

Chase displayed more than his disappointment, he blasted her with his anger.

"You pulled a fast one. You and I both know it. Clay is the one that's none the wiser. That makes you a liar. I can understand deceiving Clay because of your excessive need for a baby. But I would never have expected the same treatment. Trust is something I thought we shared. I cherished that part of our friendship. Damn you, Sloan, damn you."

He turned away and made his way to his bedroom, slamming the door behind him. It's one thing to shed a few tears, but he was banking on a downpour.

Sloan was now sitting alone. She'd lied to the man who was always there for her. Why did she lie to him? What difference would it have made if she had told him the truth?

He probably would have been just as happy as she. But a lie from Sloan was something Chase could not tolerate. Sloan now had her own Achilles' heel, that of a liar.

She pounded on Chase's bedroom door pleading with him to forgive her. She covered the floor with her body and wept into the small opening between the floor and the door. She was giving it her all, but after several hours with eyes swollen and a puffy face, she knew to give up. Chase, like Clay, turned his back on he; she was now truly alone. Sunni for some unknown reason would not be allowed to be a part of that equation, but her darling Krista would have been a definite.

Only when Chase heard the front door close did he really explode. Furniture was tossed, mirrors were smashed, and dimples made with his fist smeared the wall with blood; this distinct touch would not be in high demand. He had the balls to turn on the woman he loved, but lacked the balls to reveal the lies hidden within the Chadsworths' dynasty. How could he have done this? This was not Sloan's fault. She talked excessively about her desire to have a baby. He had no one to blame but himself, and now it was too late. Sloan got her wish; deception would not have had to play a part if Clay had come clean. And now all Chase was left with was prayer, prayer that the baby's body parts would be in working order. Sloan deserved nothing less.

Sloan decided she had nothing to lose. She would keep to her weekly Saturday get-togethers with Chase, although this time, she did sweat the outcome. She did not have the opportunity to knock before the door opened. Chase had her in his arms in an embrace that could not be mistaken for anything other than friendship. He pulled her inside, profusely apologizing. Yes, all was forgiven. He could do nothing else; he loved her. Everything returned to normal, if normal is what you would call some of their lives. Sloan was excluded, she did only what Chase asked of her. She was an innocent.

The web of lies has met its challenge; it could not get any more entangled. Or could it?

CHAPTER THIRTY

Chase kept glancing at his watch wondering about Clay's delay in coming to work; he of all people was usually the first to arrive. In short order Phillip poked his head into his office with the announcement that Clay had no intention of finishing out the work week. Friday was planned around his wife's departure.

Chase was losing ground with his life; he was unable to concentrate on the work before him. It did not take a drill sergeant to tell him he was a hypocritical asshole and an immoral bastard unworthy to be called anything decent. All the deception was eating away at his sense of worth. He knew that everything was about to come to a head, and he could not wait for this to happen. He convinced himself he was responsible for the majority of the dishonesty. It was time for a showdown or a breakdown, neither of which was very appealing.

Now that he was a full partner Chase did not have to account for this time away, but out of respect for Phillip, he did ask for the day off. Phillip, the friend he was, denied him nothing.

Phillip gave Chase a pat on his back and with a chuckle added something that was on his wish list. "Have a great weekend and enjoy all the things I wish I was capable of doing."

Chase grinned, adding his own comment. "You are capable; you just don't have the right woman to do it with." Chase was thinking of his mother as he knew Phillip was doing.

Chase dialed Clay at his residence. Knowing Clay, he had probably told the servants he would not need their services today due to Sloan's absence. The servants for years enjoyed their weekends off, thanks to Sloan. Today would be a bonus day. It was perfect timing, Clay would have the house all to himself.

Chase still had a measure of decency. It was not too late to correct all the wrong in his and all the lives involved in the charade.

Clay answered on the seventh ring. Sloan had mentioned that Clay was extremely upset with her return to Mason's Mill. He spoke with her only if necessary. Chase, of course, was the only one who would understand the reasoning behind his brother's distress. There was no way Clay would call his mother; that would surely open a huge can of worms, something he was not prepared to do. Chase tried to explore his brother's logic for holding back now that the disclosure was sure to come. There was none;

Clay was left with no alternatives. To Chase's way of thinking, his brother was going to wait and see the reprisal that was sure to come his way.

Chase was surprised with the pleasantry in his brother's voice.

"Clay, it's Chase. Your father just informed me that we will not be honored with your presence today. I also decided to take a long weekend. Are you up for some company?"

"Are you kidding? You're just the medicine I need without a prescription. Come ahead."

Laughter followed, but Chase's heart was not in it. This was going to be the most difficult day in his life. He could turn and run and never be seen again, but that would break his mother's heart, and never again will he allow her heart to be broken. He had to suck it up like the man his mother raised him to be.

The gate was open. Chase drove the great distance, his heart pounding within his chest. He would not stall; he would just throw it out and clear the air of the garbage.

The door to Clay's home was also ajar. Chase gave a yell, while staying rooted to the door's frame. Instantly Clay was within his sight. Chase was waiting to be invited indoors.

Clay shook his head grinning.

"What the hell are you doing standing at the door? When are you going to accept the fact that my home is your home? Now get your buns inside. I have something I want to show you."

Hands were shook as Clay led Chase into his study. Chase had yet to say a word.

"Wait until you see what I have. It is going to blow your mind."

Clay had already added an additional chair beside his desk; he wanted no distance between him and his partner. When they were seated, Clay extracted a key from his breast pocket and used it to open one drawer. Another compartment remained hidden from view. Chase held his breath. Clay held within his hand a .357 magnum. This gun could do some serious damage.

"What do you think? Is this not a neat weapon?"

Chase may have lost his voice, but his thoughts were still in force. Did Clay really expect an answer? Was he close to also losing his mind and getting ready to join him in the land of the lost?

When no reply came forth, Clay again jumped in. "Cat got your tongue? That's the reaction I had when I was shown the firearm. The sensation of holding that revolver gave me a sense of power never before experienced. Here, take it into your hands, see if you feel what I felt."

Chase threw up his hands as if he were being held up.

"I've never touched a weapon of that magnitude and I'm not about to start. The only guns I ever had in my possession were rifles, and they were used for hunting wildlife. Clay, this is some serious gun power. If it's your intent to kill, this will definitely do the job. Whatever possessed you to purchase such a thing? Surely you are not living in fear for your life. You have more people in your employ than a small company; there is no way someone could trespass onto your property without being seen let alone lay you out."

"Chase, get real. It's not for my protection; I bought it for Sloan. She will never have to keep looking over her shoulder wondering if the maniac that slaughtered Krista will cross her path. She now has all the protection she will ever need."

"Clay, you are clearly not thinking straight. Every time Sloan leaves the house does she pack the piece? The answer to that is a definite no. What is she doing at this exact minute? She is traveling. Where is her so-called protection? Or do you think the psycho's intention is to take her life while she struts in or around your property?"

It took Chase to point out Clay's stupidity. What was he thinking? His wife was out and about and her protection was sitting here in his hand.

Clay was now shaken with the thought of his wife's safety. The gun now felt heavy and ugly; he released it onto his desk. He wanted nothing more to do with it.

Chase was now able to recall his breath; the muscle of his heart also returned to its natural rhythm. He thanked God he was able to convince Clay that a gun was not the solution.

"I think you should return the weapon to the place of purchase. What do you think?"

"You are absolutely right; I will take care of this the first thing Monday."

Before another word bounced out of Clay's mouth, Chase charged ahead.

"Clay, I'm here for a specific reason. And what I'm about to say will likely tear at your heart. It could possibly destroy our friendship... I pray not, but I can't continue year after year denying my right as well as yours, to know my true identity. Once a month, I visit with my mother who lives out of state. She goes by the name of Harriet Anderson."

Clay's look was one of panic.

"Yes, Clay, I am your brother Marc Anderson. I know that Phillip is not your father but your brother and that Sloan is your niece."

Clay reclaimed the magnum. His hand was trembling.

Chase feared that his brother just might do him in, kill him off before he leaks this information to another soul.

"If you are thinking about taking my life, go for it. I lied to you from the start. I am full of remorse over that. But before you pull that trigger, there is one thing you should know. I envied those who had brothers to play and fight with, I pestered Mom frequently over this. Her explanation was simple but true: 'The father comes first and then the child. Are we not lacking the man?' She was shocked to find out she was to have a baby, but more embarrassed to tell me. I was just a toddler when we moved to Mason's Mill and she quickly became friends with the sheriff of our small town. Ben Davidson is the best thing that could have happened to her. I can't remember a day that he wasn't around, but I thought it was platonic. To this day, I wonder how I could have been so naive.

"Anyway, the 'story of you' came to life when our mother could no longer hide behind her horrifying past. Bringing new life into the world troubled her; she wanted a clean slate. She suffered greatly with the confession, pleading with me to forgive her and not to hate her. Forgive her, hate her? If anyone had reason to hate, she would have been the one, and yet she shines. I am proud to be her son. My only regret, as well as hers, is for the years that were taken from us.

"As to the name change, that was my idea, not our mom's. She was finished with all lies and she expected the same from me. But I had to prove my worth as an architect. When it came to a position in your company, I wanted no handout because I was your brother. I no longer count the years since you've taken me under your wing. You have been with me from day one. Never did you object to my opinions. And out of that came a friendship that neither of us can deny. Today, I would take a bullet for you — that is how much I love you. You are my brother and my best friend and nothing you say or do will ever change that."

Clay unconsciously dropped the gun onto his desk, his head now lying beside it. Chase had never heard his brother cry, but this wasn't just crying, this was far worse; Clay was about to convulse. Chase ran to the bar in Clay's study, not for booze but for a couple of bar towels rinsed in cold water. He pulled Clay upward, using one towel as a compress around his neck and the other to wipe his face. Time could not be counted in minutes, but hours.

And then Clay rejoined the living; if that is what you call living.

"I love her, Chase, I can't give her up. From the moment I saw her standing on that platform in your hometown, she grabbed onto my heart. I had to have her. Hopefully someday you will experience that feeling; only then will you truly understand what I am going through."

Only when Clay touched on the subject of finding that special someone did Chase fully accept that Sloan was now forever lost to him.

"Clay, if you don't mind, let's go back to when you met Sloan for the first time. Can you also recall the collision between you and another man?"

Clay's forehead creased for a brief second, as if forcing him to remember. It did not take long for the memory of that day to show itself.

"Every second of every minute of that day has a space within my heart. It will never be forgotten."

"Then I too must be a part of that space, for I am the man you successfully knocked down."

Thankfully this time Clay convulsed into laughter. Chase joined in, and as with all great happenings, they had a hard time controlling the tears that the laughter brought forth.

Shock now gave way to acceptance.

Chase finally got to say what his heart was feeling. "I think it's time we share what has been denied for so many years."

They now stood face-to-face. For the very first time they shared and showed their affection; their embrace was long and intense. They were now truly brothers; no one will ever separate them.

But the conversation was far from over.

Clay was truly at a loss as to what the next step should be.

"What am I ever going to do? I never wanted a baby and Sloan knew this. Now in less than six or seven weeks she is planning on bringing home a healthy baby. If it turns out that the baby has a problem, she will suffer greatly, and out of that grief, she just might come after me. She's liable to lash out, asking if there was something in my background that I had kept from her, and if that was the reason for not wanting a child. And if I do confess, it really will make no difference; Sloan and I will never again share a life."

Chase was never one to give up, and he will demand his brother do the same. As to Sloan, she was never truly his to begin with, and today with finality he will say good-bye. His brother will always come first.

But does Chase have a solution? You bet he does. He will follow the path of Phillip. Does father not know best?

"You will say nothing and do nothing. Clay, you've already stamped defective on your baby without giving your child a chance. You must wait it out; it's just possible your baby will be okay, and then you can banish the confession. And while we're on the subject of your wife, the only thing she knows is that I am Marc Anderson from her hometown. In all the years of socializing never once has she revisited that conversation. I don't think we have a thing to worry about.

"And you can also put your mind to rest about Sloan's visit with our mother. I pleaded with our mother to express shock and relief when Sloan comes knocking on their door. The most dreaded part was telling her that Sloan was pregnant. She wept uncontrollably; there was nothing I could do from this end…well, neither end, if truth be told. She prayed nightly that a baby will never be born of this union. She thinks that God is punishing her for her deception. There were no words to convince her otherwise, but she came through like the trooper she is and always will be. She agreed to act surprised. And if the day does come that Sloan demands an answer to my hidden identity, I will think of something, have no fear."

Will it ever end, this link to nowhere?

Clay regained the strength to claim leadership. He replayed everything that had been told to him from his father/brother, grandfather, grandmother, and then from the mother they now shared. Not a single detail was left out. Chase listened with a love never before felt with someone he had no contact for over twenty-eight years. Scorn did not enter into the picture.

The morning was preparing for another day. The grumble of stomachs began to sound. Clay's appeared to be the loudest as he made an announcement. "Well, it looks like we have an audience with something to say. How about lunch? I'm getting to be quite the gourmet cook. My specialty is to die for: hot dogs with chili and onions. Leave it to Sloan; she taught me about the finer things in life."

It was great to be able to laugh. Pandora's Box need never be opened again.

Their time together ended shortly after lunch The last words of the day came from Clay.

"I never thought anyone could compete with my feelings for Phillip, but you, my brother, have taken the reins. Thank you."

Chase turned away before his brother noticed the mist that floated across his vision. The distance from the Chadsworth Estate to the main road did not have his attention. He was thinking of the nights of lost sleep dreading the outcome of this day, and it was all for naught, for this day turned into one of his greatest. Sloan will continue to be held at arm's length, but that is a price Chase is willing to pay for his brother's continued welfare. He is and will always be his brother's keeper.

Never again will there be a day such as this, for just ahead the embodiment of Satan is about to take a stroll into the Chadsworth Mansion.

CHAPTER THIRTY-ONE

Sunni could not settle down; she was getting a high just thinking of her upcoming mission. Several words in the English dictionary sprang to mind to describe her feelings; *exhilaration* headed the list. Today, her troubles will be laid to rest. She had Sloan to thank for that, for without Sloan's constant chatter she would never have known about her proposed trip to their hometown, Mason's Mill.

She did not have much to pack, not on this operation: a Charter Arms .38 revolver purchased years back will finally come into play. She was dressed in killing attire, black leather pants with a matching short-sleeved zippered jacket. A black top in the form of a bra was barely visible. Her shoes resembled men's boots. Today, she will be riding in a sleek black Rolls-Royce. The car was rented, but Sunni could well afford to own one if she so chose. Nothing but the grandest machinery will enter onto the Chadsworths' property.

Sunni did feel a bit of concern that the gate was open. Could there possibly be someone visiting? Because of Sloan's persistence, the servants no longer worked the weekends. But Sunni wondered if that included Fridays. She would soon find out. Sunni lived her life taking chances, and this was one was no different. If Clay did have a guest or the servants were about, she could feign forgetfulness that this was the weekend Sloan would be away. Mottoes were for a purpose, and Sunni strongly believed in one: "Always have a back-up plan."

Sunni scanned the surrounding grounds as she drove through and beyond the gate. She prayed for no surprises and she received none. She would be alone with her victim.

She pulled the car around to the back of the mansion, an area hidden from anyone approaching along the front drive.

Tucked into her jacket pocket was her snub-nosed handgun.

She approached the front entrance as if she were the owner, although she did have to ring the doorbell. With her fist ready to start pounding, she was beginning to get annoyed at the length of time she had to wait for a response when the door finally opened.

Clay was overly surprised to see Sunni.

"Sunni, you are the last person I would have expected at my door today. Surely you knew this was the weekend Sloan would be away."

"There isn't anything I am not aware of when it comes to Sloan. That is the reason for my visit. Do you have a few minutes?"

Clay's thoughts began to take him in the direction of paranoia. *Is more shit about to be laid on me? Of course not; it's already piled so high, I'm wading in it.*

He opened the door wider and graciously invited his executioner inside.

"I just poured myself a drink. Would you care to join me?"

"I should say no, but what the hell, I surely won't be leaving my prints behind."

"Prints? What are you talking about?"

Clay was trying to figure out where she was coming from. It was then he noticed she was wearing kid gloves that hugged her hands like a second skin. But this was nothing out of the ordinary; you never knew what to expect when Sunni made an appearance. However, this time it was not the outfit, it was what she had gripped in her right hand.

"Let's unwind in your study. I have been dying to see the revolver that Sloan told me about. It's meant to keep the boogeyman away…right?"

Clay refused to show fear, although deep in the crevices of his mind, in a part seldom used, he was terrified. *What possessed Sloan to tell Sunni of the gun? Just its mention made her furious.* Sunni obviously had an issue, and he was sure it had nothing to do with the pistol. Something was greatly disturbing her. He could fix it; he could assume the role of his brother. Did Chase not take care of his problem?

"Okay, Sunni, since you're not here to socialize, it must be something else. What's so troubling that you have to hold a pistol? Trust me, you would have my full attention without it."

"Just shut the fuck up. You are one annoying bastard, do you know that? Just to see and hear your voice fuckin' pisses me off."

Sunni ordered him into the study. The gun displayed its authority; it was shoved deep into his back. His drink of scotch, still sitting untouched, will soon be consumed.

"Sit your fucking ass down and do not say a word."

Clay had yet to store his handgun. Could he possibly get it within his hands to get the drop on Sunni?

He was a quick study.

"Don't even think about it. I would have you down before you blink an eyelash. Now slide it over."

If he'd known that he had but a few minutes to use the breath God gave him, Clay would have fought to hold onto the magnum. And Sunni, who has never failed at anything, would have applauded his fierce attempt at his struggle for survival as she did her mother's.

Sunni was now a double-fisted pistol carrier.

Clay stayed rooted to his desk chair. He never so much as made a move, and he blinked only when necessary. Sweat began to pool around his shirt collar, and he was beginning to lose sensation in his hands, they were clinched so tightly together. Sunni may have control over his body, but his mind was his own, and he searched long into its maze of networks. Was there a purpose behind Sunni's madness, and if so, where was it going to take him?

He was about to find out.

"You know, I changed my mind about that drink. But don't let me stop you; I know how much you enjoy your scotch."

When a gun is doing the talking, you listen.

There was no debate as to which gun would be used: Sunni's was for the sole purpose of getting his attention; Clay's was to end his attention.

While Clay gulped what would be his last drink, Sunni cleared his desk of the non-essentials with her right forearm. She then planted her rear end next to the three remaining items: the now empty glass, the bottle the scotch had been poured from, and the telephone. The desk's surface had never been used for anything but practical materials. Sunni's skinny ass was definitely not a desirable item for any kind of use.

Sunni wanted Clay close when she told him of her intention. She reached out with her left shoe, tucking its tip under the ridge of his chair. The chair's casters offered freedom of movement, and Sunni pulled Clay and his chair directly in front of her.

She straddled his desk with her legs slightly separated, and then with the force of her right foot she shoved the heel of her boot directly into his manhood. His screech of agonizing pain blasted the dust off the entire wall of books and surrounding furniture. Cupping his genitals offered no relief and neither did the tears, and yet he could not take his tear-filled eyes off his abuser.

Sunni was bored and she knew the reason for the boredom: she could not torture him as she did the others.

She was beginning to show impatience. It was time to let Clay know the underlying reason for her visit.

"Life is a mother-fucking bitch when you can have everything your heart desires, and yet you are denied the one thing that will truly make you happy. And the blockbuster is, you have that one thing in your possession. I would rather have had Sloan all to myself, as my plans never included the likes of a baby, but in time that kid can easily be disposed of, maybe in the same fashion as her baby brother."

Clay was concerned with his throbbing balls, not the ramblings of Sunni, when he jumped from his chair, his fist making contact with Sunni's face. She may have been caught off guard, and was startled when its impact met her jawbone, but Clay would never have believed how quickly she regained the upper hand. The gun was ready to be discharged when he felt the nuzzle press into his cheek. Just a bit more pressure on the trigger and he could say farewell. He knew to sit without being told.

Sunni felt as if her chin had been repositioned. The pain was excruciating. It felt as if she'd had several teeth extracted without Novocain.

"You fucking bastard, look at what you did to my face. I should blow off your fucking fingers."

Clay was fed up with her nonsense. *Besides, if she does use a gun on me, that would mean she is a psychopath. This cannot be so; she is my wife's best friend.* He may have missed out on some of her babbling nonsense due to the intensity of his pain, but never could he ignore the comment about their baby.

"Sunni, I have no idea what's going on beneath that skull of yours, but for now I'm concerned with the remark you made in reference to our baby. Surely I misunderstood."

Sunni slowly repeated the words.

"I plan on doing away with the baby that was conceived in sin; you never wanted a fuckin' kid anyway. You should get on your knees and thank me."

"You're insane."

"You know, you just might be right. Did I mention that I smothered Sloan's baby brother to death? No, of course not. Although, I must admit it was a little difficult, and it wasn't because my conscience played a part. I was only ten years old at the time, and let me tell you, that kid put up a fight. It took all I had not to climb into his crib and sit on his face, but eventually he did give up his struggle. I was thankful; that little fucker wore me out."

Clay had never heard such a disturbing and appalling confession. Sloan had dreamt that her baby brother was murdered, and yet he shooed it away as a bad dream. He began to weep for her loss, but it was not over yet. He would have his say.

"Never in my life have I met anyone that reeked of such evil. You're a disease that sprayed its venom on an innocent toddler, and I'll be damned if I'm going to let you get away with that baby's murder. He will have his day in court, so help me God."

He was quick on his feet as he reached across his desk, grabbing at the telephone; he would call the police, he would rather be dead than allow Sunni to get away with murder. Sunni's reaction was to laugh.

"You won't think it's so damn funny when you're handcuffed and taken away, you crazy psycho bitch."

He began to dial.

"I think before you tell them about me, you should mention that you're a degenerate pervert, that you fuck your niece on a daily basis and numerous times on Sundays. I'm sure that will get you a lot of time in the slammer. Maybe we could be cellmates. We could share the same toilet, the same food, even the same women."

The telephone receiver dropped from Clay's hand. It dangled from its tangled cord onto the floor, and the sound that played back was that of a disconnection. His standing days were over; he slumped back into his chair.

He spoke just above a whisper. "How...?"

"How did I find out? Is that what you want to know? Let's see...oh yeah, it was that pompous asshole Garth, that fucker you would have given your life for, but instead that fucker gave me the means to take yours. Isn't that ironic? I had to find some deep dark secret that I could take to Sloan, uncover some kind of lie that would turn her against you. And who best to give me what I needed? Your trusted buddy Garth. But I had to find a way to get him under my control, and the only sure way was through sex, but not just ordinary sex—he could get that from anyone. That is when I introduced him to masochism. It was like guiding a baby to a nipple; once he had a taste, he wanted more and more. He became so addicted he could not do without. When one night I refused, he cried like a baby. I knew then I had him. I promised him a night like no other if he were to talk, and he babbled like an idiot, telling me way more than I could ever have expected. What's that saying from that movie *The Godfather*? 'Keep your friends close, but your enemies closer.'

"You look worried, Clay. Do you honestly believe I would betray you? I'm not Garth. I would never do that; loyalty is my greatest virtue. But that trust does come with a request."

Did Clay just hear what he thought he heard, that Sunni will keep this information to herself? He would do anything if this were so.

"You will need paper and a pen. You will write what I tell you. Are you ready?"

Clay scrambled for his writing tablet. But the ballpoint pen was soon released when he heard the words Sunni wanted him to write.

"You will have to kill me before I put those words to paper."

"I don't want you dead, you fuckhead. I just want you out of Sloan's life. You can live anywhere in the world, assume a new identity, start a new life, build another business or just sail around the fuckin' world. I really don't give a good fuck what you do; I just want your fuckin' ass to be gone."

"And I have to do this, because you want me out of Sloan's life. What have I ever done to you that would warrant such a request?"

"Because Sloan is my woman, has always been my woman, and you are standing in our way, just as Krista did."

"Oh, my God in Heaven…it was you! Krista was your friend, how could you? You need help."

"Oh, I see, I'm the one that needs help, but the pervert that preys on an eighteen-year-old and commits incest is normal?"

Clay somehow had to clarify how Sloan came into his life. The death of Krista would be taken care of at a later time.

"Sunni, you have it all wrong about me. If you will just let me explain…"

"Tell it to someone who really gives a fuck. Start writing or you will soon be missing the top portion of your head." Sunni had Clay's gun pressed firmly against the right side of his temple.

He reclaimed the pen.

My beautiful wife, I pray you can forgive me, but it's best to end the life that has brought you so many years of tears. Thank you for loving me; you will forever be my babe.

He did as Sunni commanded. But he was left with a nagging question: *What is her intention? Does she expect me to get into my car and just drive away and never again look back?* That kind of thinking was ludicrous, but then again he had no idea what was roaming around inside that sick head of hers. Whatever it was, he was sure to find out.

Clay looked at Sunni and nodded, a signal he had finished with what she had instructed. The sinister smile that crept across her face was not what he expected. He read its meaning; he had just signed away his life. Sloan will not hear his confession; he will not see or hear his baby's first cry. And yes, he would have accepted his baby no matter the disability. But his thinking cap had not yet been turned off: *If I can put her down before she gets off a shot, I just might have a chance for survival.*

But Sunni had her own confession and Clay was about to hear it.

"Before I turn over the weapon that will put an end to your life, there is one other thing you need to know. Should anything happen to me or I go missing, I've instructed my lawyer to deliver to everyone of importance, including the editor of the newspaper, information that will list the sins you and your family have committed."

She placed the gun in Clay's hand and stood before him and then, like the executioner she was, she granted him a say.

"Do you have any last words you wish to say before I pronounce sentence?"

But Clay no longer was a player in Sunni's madness. He left his body; he journeyed back into time. He was staring at the woman on the platform who would forever share in his life. His world was not over; it was just about to begin.

Sunni was baffled. Something was wrong. Where was the pleading for his life? Surely Clay did not want to die in such a manner. She was leaning over his desk and was within inches of his face. His eyes would tell her…but she was not prepared for the findings. Clay's eyes were blank; he was oblivious to his surroundings.

Now Sunni was truly pissed; she would not get the gratification that the other kills provided. Anger began to build. She would have to be the one to pull the trigger. She hated when fear played with her mind; getting caught found a place in her head, and it was getting hard to shake it loose. But she had no choice; Clay was no longer a willing participant. The residue from the gun that would collect on her gloves could possibly be transferred onto Clay's hand and fingers, maybe.

The explosion nearly blew his head clean off his shoulders. Sunni was slapped in the face with a surge of blood. She ran her tongue over her lips; she could taste his blood. Clay was the trigger guy and instead of displaying resentment, she experienced the same kind of thrill as when she tasted her mother's blood, and the feeling was incredibly delectable.

The mess when viewed by others would make many run to the bathroom, but to Sunni it resembled a one-of-a-kind painting, its primary color red, her favorite. Bone, tissue and brain matter splashed onto the walls, books and furniture. Sections of Clay's hairy scalp were like doilies plastered onto his furniture. Gathering the fragments of his face for a picture-taking would be more difficult than putting together a puzzle. The remaining bits and pieces of facial skin left behind clung to his shirt and lay on the desk top. The floor for the first and last time tasted its master's blood.

But it was the letter that was Sunni's main concern.

The discharge from the gun rearranged the position of his body and disrupted Clay's left hand that partially covered his handwritten note. The paper was splattered with blood but was still legible, and upon closer inspection she noticed what appeared to be a small section of Clay's ear; it had pasted itself onto the letter. She thought it appropriate, sort of like a signature as he'd failed to sign his name.

Sunni checked her boots. They were free of blood, so no footprints would be left behind, but from the waist up she was covered in blood. That was an easy cleanup, but not in Clay's home. She could not take a chance on leaving a hair or any fibers behind. The cleanup would take place deep into the forest, a place where no one would think to look.

She had just decided it was not a good thing to stay around to survey the damage left by the architect's hand when she heard the ring from another telephone line. The rings continued as Sunni closed the front door behind her, and their sound followed her down the steps and across the yard. She made her way to her car where, as always, she carried a change of clothes should they be needed. She put the car in gear. The woods were waiting for her arrival. She was free to kill again should it fancy her.

The last day of the work week had ended. Phillip's hand was still holding the receiver when he realized after twenty or so rings that his boy was not going to answer the call. He knew the reason: his boy needed the weekend alone to contemplate his fate. He did not need his father holding his hand during this time. Phillip, like his boy, will spend his entire weekend alone. But it was understood that Phillip will be by his boy's side when Sloan returns home Sunday evening. They will share in the heartbreak that is sure to come.

But Phillip's patience will wear thin; he will arrive early. When his greeting rings out and he receives no reply, he will venture into his boy's study.

CHAPTER THIRTY-TWO

Sloan crossed over the bridge into the shopping center. She parked her rental car at what appeared to be the only available space; not until she stepped out did she realize it was where she had parked her papa's truck so very long ago. *Did Papa have a hand in reserving this space? Did he consider this to be his permanent parking place?* For a brief second she was back in time, searching the crowds for a sign of her papa. He had to be somewhere, he would not leave without her, but he did leave.

Sloan began to cry. She reached into her gold and silver shoulder bag for a tissue. She was wearing a Christian Dior sky-blue maternity jumpsuit. She wore sandals with multiple gold and silver crisscross straps. Never did she wear her hair down during the months of July and August; instead, she twisted it into a double knot secured with several combs. She stopped for one purpose, to buy flowers for her family's graves; never again will she walk the streets that her family had walked.

She crossed over several lanes heading towards the grocery store. Upon entering she was guided to the floral shop by its sweet scent. The owner, along with three hired hands, carried the fifteen bouquets of flowers that came with the hefty price tag of $384.32 to her car. It was time to visit with her family.

Sloan drove past the sheriff's office taking no notice; she also refused to look at cabin number one. The roads were what caught her attention. They were no longer rocky; they had been blacktopped, making the driving pleasurable. *Did the town council finally decide to use some of Silva's money or did the state step in?*

She approached the cemetery at a beginner driver's pace. *What is going on?* Several cars occupied spaces highlighted with white lines. Sloan walked only when necessary, and this was one of those times. She pulled the car onto the area defined as the walkway.

"Heaven's Gate," the name of the cemetery, greeted her.

She clung to the steering wheel and began to weep; there before her were the headstones of her family, and a statue so extraordinary that God himself had to have had a hand in its making. Several years back, Sloan called a monument company that was close to Mason's Mill who specialized in custom tombstones. She asked to speak to the manager and told him she would mail a detailed drawing of what she expected. She clearly stated that she would accept nothing less than perfection. The manager told her that, upon delivery of the description, he would take the necessary measurements and send a contract listing the cost. Work would begin as soon as he received her signature of its acceptance and her check cleared the bank. Before hanging up, she had one other request: no one must know who the benefactor was; she must always remain anonymous. He agreed to her terms.

Centered and placed behind her family's rather small gravestones was a platform holding a colossal statue of an angel with wings extended to embrace the headstones of her family. The tears escaping the angel's eyes were perfected to the point of realism as they washed over her face, continuing downward onto her gown. Delicate teardrops clung to the facing of the platform with Sloan's simple inscription:

"Heaven is far more beautiful with your presence."

Ten years of tears engulfed her very being. The question of "why" continued to hover. Now she understood the reason behind the paving. The cemetery was now a tourist attraction. The tourists were in awe of the statue, as was she. Instead of being upset, Sloan felt blessed; her family will now have visitors to pay their respects while viewing the likes of something never before seen.

She was finding it difficult to maneuver in and out of all makes of automobiles, including the rental car. In a matter of weeks, she will have a baby to carry, but today it is bundles of bouquets.

Sloan pressed the mechanism that allowed the trunk to open. She gathered only enough flowers so as not to crush their beauty, but she would not have to make several trips. New arrivals noticed her condition and came forward offering their help. She smiled with gratitude.

A three-foot-tall black steel fence surrounded the perimeter of her family's burial site. Attached to the fence were a locked steel box and a sign reading:

"Please do not enter the enclosure. The family that were born and raised here died tragically in a house fire. We ask that you respect their permanent resting place and because the statue is one of a kind, we would appreciate that you not touch it. Thank you for your generous contribution."

Sloan wondered who thought of the gate and the lockbox. She prayed its sole purpose was for her family's perpetual care and that greed did not play a role.

Visitors apparently did respect the sign, laying flowers as near as possible to the Parkers' graves. Sloan ignored the posting; she flipped the lever, allowing her access. Those who'd offered their assistance with the flowers stepped forward. They laid the bouquets at the foot of the opening, but they did not cross beyond the gate. The sign said to respect those buried there, and to go against that request would be like trespassing onto sacred ground. For this young woman to go against the posting, there had to be a reason, and because of this, she was not questioned.

The tourists watched as Sloan placed a bouquet inside each brass cone. They felt her pain when she walked slowly to the center. She now faced her family and began to weep. The visitors turned away; some were wiping their eyes as they made their way back to their cars. Sloan will be alone to grieve in private.

She carried on a single conversation with each member of her family as if they were standing in front of her. She talked and wept for well over an hour. She promised them she would return.

It was now time to find the gravestones of the Doc and his wife; the extra bouquets were for them. Their placement was easy to find, as their graves were outlined with rosebushes, each a different color. Sloan noticed no other graves held in such high regard except for the obvious; her family finally received the respect they deserved.

Sloan stopped the car for the third time, tears refusing to stop their flow. She never expected to see her home again, but there it stood as it would have been from the beginning of time. The barn, untouched by the flames, still stood with a few years of added wear. *How could this be possible? Is there a picture floating around, or was it taken from someone's memory? And if so, why would anyone want to live in a house that took so many lives?* She would ask Harriet.

Sloan pulled into the driveway and parked behind a tan truck with a Dodge emblem. Sitting beside the truck was a Chevrolet Suburban. Harriet's Malibu apparently had seen its day. She took her time; she had not figured out what she would say for her long absence. She climbed the few steps, then stepped back as the sound of the doorbell rang out. The anticipation of seeing Harriet was almost more than Sloan's heart could take. The pounding within her chest was beginning to cause her alarm when the door swung open.

Hardly a Saturday went by that Chase did not talk about his sisters and brother. However, never did he say just how strikingly beautiful they were. Black curls fell beyond their shoulders; their blue eyes duplicated those of their brother Chase. They were taller than she expected, but then she had never spent time with or even personally met a ten-year-old, other than Timmy from her long-ago youth. That was a memory she did not care to conjure up.

Hannah, the taller of the two, was the first to speak, as always. She spoke before Sloan had a chance. She was very courteous.

"Hello. My name is Hannah and this is my sister Taylor. Are you here for a reading?"

Sloan smiled. Harriet was still doing what she did best.

"No. I'm a friend of your mother. Is she available?"

Hannah was still in charge.

"We know all Mother's friends, but we don't remember you. Are you sure you're at the right house?"

"I am, if you have a brother named Nicholas and your mother is Harriet and your father is Ben." Sloan could not stop smiling, she so wanted to give them a hug and a kiss.

Hannah was about to say something but Taylor jumped ahead.

"Mom, you have company. She said you are a friend — should we allow her entrance?"

Harriet was wiping her hands on a dishtowel when she made an appearance. The time has come for Harriet to show her acting abilities. She took her place alongside her daughters. She hesitated just long enough as if she were trying to figure out who was standing before her; ten years allowed her that excuse.

Harriet could not speak; she was at a loss for words. She would have a difficult time gathering Sloan into her arms. Her being short and Sloan's being tall had nothing to do with it; Sloan's pregnancy kept them apart. Instead, a substitute did what their bodies could not.

Their arms did the hugging, holding on tightly, crying and sobbing for all the years they had missed. The girls stood back, allowing them space. They had seen their mother cry a time or two but never to this extreme. They wondered where this beautiful woman had come from and what she was doing here.

The girls could take no more; Hannah again spoke before her sister.

"Mother, do you think it would be a good idea for your friend to come inside?"

Harriet and Sloan looked in Hannah's direction and started to laugh. With hands held Harriet guided Sloan to a firm but comfortable chair. After the introductions were made the girls hugged their mother, telling her they would join in when she finished reminiscing. The girls left the room hand in hand. Hannah had changed considerably since her talk with Chase; the sisters would remain close throughout their lifetime.

Sloan, with Kleenex handy, spoke her first words. "Your girls are beautiful, but is there not one missing?" Sloan smiled; she could not wait to tell Harriet about her life. Instead of Harriet showing surprise, she began to cry.

"Oh my God, is something wrong? Did something happen to Nick?"

Harriet shook her head, her hands covering her face as the weeping continued.

Sloan rose but struggled to kneel at Harriet's side. She took Harriet's hands from her face and wiped at her tears.

"You must tell me. Maybe I can help."

Harriet took her hands and placed them onto Sloan's face. "There is so much I need to tell you, I just don't know where to begin."

It was at this point that Ben and Nick entered the room. Father and son appeared to be in a deep discussion until they both noticed they had a visitor. Ben was not the actor Harriet was trying to be; he noticed Harriet wiping at her face as Sloan turned in his direction.

"Well, well, it looks like a ghost has reappeared. All I can say is it's about time."

Sloan was making an effort to stand holding onto the arm of the chair, but Ben, already aware of her condition, rushed to assist.

"Boy, do you remind me of Harriet."

He helped her to stand. Although Harriet had told Ben of Sloan's discovery, he was overwhelmed and he showed it. Because of his height and size, he was able to hold Sloan somewhat close. They both wept, he for her safe return, she for the warmth of a father-like figure.

Through tears she spoke. "I missed you both so much. I know now I should never have stayed away. Can you ever forgive me?"

Ben's eyes traveled over to his wife. It did not take a psychic to read what Harriet was thinking; she should be the one asking for forgiveness.

Nick tugged on his father's shirt. "Dad, why are you and Mom crying? Is there something wrong?"

Ben swiped his face with his big hand and then pulled Nick to his side. With his arm still around Sloan, he introduced his son. Sloan was amazed at his height; he was going to match his dad's stature or more. She should have shaken his hand since he was a boy, but she could not help herself, she leaned over to give him a kiss upon his cheek. His huge smile told of his approval.

Nick, like his sisters, knew when a visitor arrived and it was not for him, he was not to stay around.

"It was nice meeting you. Maybe you can stay around long enough to have dinner with us?"

"If your mom and dad will have me, I would like to spend the weekend."

Nick glanced in his parents' direction and knew by their expressions that Sloan would be with them the entire weekend. Elated, he ran from the room with his fist in the air shouting "Yes! Yes!" His sisters pulled him into their room trying to hush him. Sloan could hear them talking among themselves, when a show of excitement blasted down the hall and then into the living room. Sloan smiled; she was grateful they liked her.

It was time to get down to the purpose of her visit.

"Harriet, I know you are anxious to know where I've been all this time, but before I get to that I need to tell Ben something that has been troubling me, if you don't mind."

Harriet smiled her approval, thankful she did not have to talk, at least not yet.

"Ben, with what I have to tell you, I pray you won't think I'm losing my mind."

Ben guided Sloan to her previous chair. He could tell by her expression that it was quite serious.

"I'm all yours. Speak away."

"I've been having horrible nightmares in regards to Zachary. In those dreams I'm told that he was murdered." Sloan began to cry, her faithful Kleenex on standby.

Ben was stunned by her statement. He pulled up a chair and took her hands into his.

"Sloan, there is so much I could tell you, but I'm afraid to. In your condition you need as little upset as possible."

"Ben, you are the only one I can turn to. The figure that appears to me in my dreams tells me it is someone I know. You are the only one that could possibly help me. I need to free myself of these horrible nightmares. Please, if you know anything, I will forever be grateful."

She had the right to know all he knew; he would not hold back. Sloan leaned forward as far as her stomach allowed, giving him her full attention. When Ben finished she fell back into her chair. Someone took the life of her baby brother and years later murdered her family? This was not what she expected. She could not hold back the tears; a river would run.

Ben took Sloan gently into his arms and carried her to his and Harriet's bed. She would find sleep when the tears had fulfilled their journey. The light of Saturday morning would appear before she awoke.

Ben drew Harriet close, for she too had been sobbing. When he finally managed to calm her, he retrieved Sloan's belongings from her car and carefully placed them within her reach in their bedroom. Ben would share his son's room while Harriet had to toss a coin as to who would get the privilege of sleeping with their mother. Taylor won, but Hannah was okay with that; she surely had changed.

Sloan slowly made her way towards the faint sounds coming from the kitchen. The triplets were keeping the volume of their voices to a whisper while setting the table for breakfast. She stepped into the kitchen, hair pulled back into a ponytail and outfitted in a lightweight robe the color of a deep red rose. Her white slippers were toeless and backless, toenails painted a shade of mauve. She was starving and free of tears. Until she said "Good morning" no one was aware of her presence.

The triplets stopped what they were doing and raced to Sloan's side, a mass of arms entwined trying to embrace the beautiful woman. Ben and Harriet had their own arms in use, but they were for each other.

All three of Ben and Harriet's children began arguing on which two would sit alongside Sloan. The coin would come into play once again; they had to choose which side of the coin was their preference. Sloan did the tossing, and they were happy with that decision, no matter the outcome. Taylor and Nick won; Hannah showed a bit of a disappointment, but like the changed person she had become, she congratulated her sister and brother.

Prayers were lengthy due to the arrival of Sloan; they thanked Jesus repeatedly for her safe return. It was time to dive into breakfast. A platter of waffles with a choice of blueberries or blackberries, bacon and sausage with a pitcher of orange juice, and a pot of coffee was finished off with a plate of banana muffins that would satisfy everyone's palate. Sloan owned up to consuming the most.

For once conversations were not on hold until after finishing their meal. Sloan learned more about the triplets than Chase could ever tell. Story after story had her laughing so hard her stomach began to ache. However, at some point, all good things must end. Harriet was the one to call for time out. The trio knew to clean up, and when finished with their chore they were to do their homework due on Monday. Although tomorrow was Sunday, it was a day set aside for God and His teachings.

Sloan was anxious to tell how she came to meet Clay and about the baby she thought they would never have. Harriet and Ben sat quietly; not once did either of them come clean. The lengthy conversation about Sloan's fabulous life continued into lunch, finishing up at dinner. It was time to give attention to the triplets now that their homework was completed.

Sunday morning the sun poked its ray of light into the bedrooms to awaken the entire family. The delectable food that was prepared on Saturday was once again repeated. Sloan refused to pig out like the day before which made her quite uncomfortable. She had a long drive, she did not want to repeat that discomfort. And as always the triplets were the clean-up crew. The adults made their way into the living room; Sloan was already showered and dressed. She would soon depart for home after she got some answers about Marc/Chase and the deceit about his identity, but most of all she wanted to find out who was now residing in the home she had shared with her family.

Harriet was quick with an answer when it came to Sloan's home.

"Your home will never again be occupied; it was rebuilt as a tribute to your family."

Sloan could not hold back the tears. An honor such as this deserved more tears than she was able to give. Harriet was given a reprieve when it came to answering the question about Marc as the ringing of the telephone caught everyone's attention.

Harriet and Sloan could never be prepared for the horror that call will bring. It will render them in utter shock that neither will be able to cope with.

CHAPTER THIRTY-THREE

Harriet excused herself as she made her way to the telephone. Harriet considered it rude to talk on the telephone in the presence of a guest. She walked out of hearing range of her husband and Sloan, heading towards her bedroom. She noticed Sloan's bags were packed; she was ready to head home.

Harriet's hello had always been a sweet sound to Phillip's ears. He loved her immensely. He held back the agonizing tears, lest he not get the tragic news said.

Harriet recognized her lover's voice; she loved him as much as he loved her. She looked around to make sure the children were not within earshot as she closed her bedroom door behind her. However, before she spoke Phillip's name a rush of fear shook her entire being, leaving her weak and empty inside.

"Phillip, please don't. I know something horrible has happened. Please, please, I beg of you, do not tell me." She fell to her knees before he said the words that would end her life as she knew it.

Phillip really tried to hold back his tears, but he could not. He could have chosen to talk to Sloan and then he would not have heard or felt his lover's pain, but he was a man of honor, he did not have the heart to turn away when his lover needed to hear the words from his lips. He would leave it up to Harriet to tell Clay's wife.

"My darling Jena, I am so, so sorry. Clay's gone; he has taken his own life." He could not hold back the river of tears that began hammering on his face. His body could no longer hold his weight; he slid onto the floor, pleading with God as the receiver fell from his hand.

"Oh God, I beg of you to please help us. If I can't stand the pain, You must know the anguish Clay's mother feels. I will never again ask anything more, if you will please just help her. Please, dear God, please."

Harriet collapsed onto the floor. The telephone receiver now lay at her side, and she was no longer talking or listening. She clasped her mouth shut, trying to muffle the sounds associated with screams of anguish.

The wrath of God struck her where it would hurt the most. In her mind, the sin of adultery had cost the life of her beloved son, Clay.

Ben rose from his chair. "Sloan, if you'll excuse me, I'll go and see what's keeping Harriet. It's probably a client. She's still playing with them silly cards, but if it keeps her happy, what the heck."

"Leave her be. By the time I get my bags loaded into the trunk of my car, she will probably be off the phone and ready to say her good-byes. I think I've outstayed my welcome."

"Never, ever. We love you like our own. Now you keep yourself seated, and I will go and get Harriet. And don't you dare take it upon yourself to carry that luggage; that's what I'm here for, understand?"

"You must think you're still a cop, and in charge?" Laughter played upon their lips as Ben exited the room in search of his wife.

Ben found the door to their bedroom closed; he knocked. When he received no response, he edged the door open. He found Harriet sitting on the floor, her mouth covered with both hands. Tears were running full force; it was if a faucet had been turned on. He knelt by her side and took her hands into his. He did not have to ask what was wrong; she was quick with an explanation.

"I just received the worst news possible. Oh God, whatever am I to do?" The faucet continued to run. Finally, after several minutes Harriet mustered up enough courage to speak the words that in due time could possibly send her over the edge.

"Ben, it's my baby, my firstborn…he took his life. Oh God, how am I going to tell my best friend's daughter her husband is gone? All these secrets and lies, I knew someday they would come back to haunt me. But Ben, I never thought God would take my Clay from me. I had but six months of his life as a newborn, and then twenty-eight years later he shows up at my door. Four hours is all I was given that day, and never again did I see him. Instead, he gave me ten years in a box of letters; these will have to be my lifelong memories." The weeping continued.

Ben was dumbfounded; he could not believe what he just heard. Although he had not met Clay personally, if he was Harriet's son, he was Ben's as well.

"Oh sweetheart, I am so, so sorry. Can I help in any way?"

"It's time for all the dirty laundry to be washed clean. I need for you to stand by me; this is going to be the most difficult thing I've ever had to do."

Sloan was peeling back the pages of a magazine waiting patiently for her mother's best friend to reappear. Harriet was the only one, other than Lydia, she would gladly call mother if given the chance—she loved her that much. Sloan had been sitting for entirely too long; her feet were beginning to turn numb. She was struggling to stand as Ben and Harriet entered the room. Ben had his arm around Harriet. Sloan could tell she had been crying; her face was covered in red blotches. Sloan stayed where she was, her rear end now straddling the end of the cushion. She could tell Harriet or Ben or both had something to say, but what she had no idea.

Harriet, with a wad of tissues clasped in her hand, tried to talk, but the words refused release. Ben felt Harriet slip from his arm, but before he could grab hold, she slid to the floor.

The faucet turned itself back on. Sloan was quick to stand. She waddled over to Harriet's side; she would show comfort once Ben settled his wife onto the sofa. With Ben's offered support Sloan knelt as close as possible, taking Harriet's hands away from her face and speaking as if she were the mother and Harriet the child.

"There, there...nothing is so bad that a solution cannot be found. Look around, you have so many that love you. I think it's time to put an end to those tears and let your hubby and me help by telling us what has you this upset, okay?"

Harriet's tears lessened as she listened to this person she had loved her entire life. Nowhere in the universe are there words that could harbor the horror, but tell her she must.

"My darling Sloan, I would give my life to spare you what I have to tell you, but I cannot. The phone call I received was from Phillip Chadsworth."

Sloan's brow furrowed. She did not understand where this conversation was going. Why would Phillip call Harriet? She'd left Harriet's number only with Clay. Besides, if Phillip had something to say, he would have asked to speak with her, not with someone he had never met. Something was not right. Sloan began to tremble; fear once again had shown itself, not unlike the terror she experienced on her walk to town more than ten years ago.

"Sloan, I know you are wondering how I could possibly know Phillip. There is so much you should have been told, and in due time you will know all there is to know. But for now, you need to know why I am extremely upset and heartbroken, as will you. Your husband Clay was my son and the brother to your mother. He was not only your husband, but also your uncle. Oh sweetie, it breaks my heart to tell you, but my precious Clay committed suicide. I believe he lived in fear that the baby you are carrying would have some kind of deformity."

Harriet again began to weep for the loss of her son.

It did not take a man's hand to get Sloan to her feet. Just as she stood ready to scream out for her husband, she grabbed onto her stomach. The pain was wrenching, tearing at her backside. She lunged forward to grab onto something. Ben was her savior; this time he was quick with his hands. She let out a bloodcurdling scream that left little doubt her labor had begun. She clung to Ben, her nails digging deep into his forearms, as water poured down her legs and onto the carpet. The scream brought the three kids into the room, their mouths agape. Harriet was quick to get them back into their rooms. This scene was maybe for the coming of age, but then again, she would never consider this appropriate for a child of any age.

Harriet had no time to grieve for her son; his baby was about to be born. Ben managed to get Sloan to their bedroom, removing the comforter and then placing her onto the sheet before letting go. He was at a loss as to what to do next. Sloan began to scream again, only this time it was nonstop. She was thrusting about, twisting and turning while holding onto her stomach. Then she stopped and a funny look came onto her face.

"Oh my God, I feel something coming. Oh God, Ben, what do I do?" Ben yelled for Harriet to come quick.

Harriet had already attached herself to the phone, relaying everything to the doctor. When she heard Ben give a holler she replaced the receiver and rushed to the bedroom.

"It's okay, honey; I'm an expert at having a baby, well, babies. Ben, Dr. Rolan said to get plenty of clean towels and boil some water."

Relieved, Ben made a quick exit; his own babies' delivery was enough to last him his lifetime. Harriet gladly took over. How could she not? Her son's baby was about to be born.

"Honey, we need to get your clothes off. Do you think you can help me?"

She received a nod.

Harriet managed to grab several sheets from the linen closet, preparing her best friend's daughter for delivery. "If only" began running through her thoughts. They worked together; everything now seemed ready for the little one.

Harriet quickly said a prayer before she gave instructions.

"I am going to hold your legs tightly together; this can help delay the birth, but whatever you do, do not push. The doctor is on his way. I would rather he deliver the baby than I, okay?"

Sloan again nodded her head, and then began to weep. "Oh Clay, my darling, why did you take your life? I loved you so very much. Our baby will be all right, I know it will."

The weeping was the most pitiful Harriet would ever hear other than her own. She will struggle through a lifetime of hidden tears.

When Dr. Rolan was called for a home emergency, no door stood in his way; he entered without knocking. Introductions were pushed to the side.

"Okay, let me check to see just how far you're dilated, young lady."

Harriet told him what she thought; the baby's head was beginning to crown. The doctor was hoping he would have enough time to transfer Sloan to the hospital, but Harriet was right, the baby was on its way.

"Ben, you are going to be my errand boy, and Harriet, you are to be my helper. Any objections?"

When none were heard, the doctor quickly got to work. Ben did as told, as did his wife. Sloan held the screams to a minimum; the doctor thought she was one of a kind, for a first-time mom. He was a bit concerned with the bleeding, but that quickly ended when a baby boy rushed forth. The doctor looked onto the face of the most beautiful woman he had ever seen and announced, "It's a magnificent-looking boy." He quickly checked the newborn out; everything was okay and the bleeding had stopped, and the mother, now relaxed, seemed pleased with herself.

Sloan could not help but notice the glowing pride of her mother's best friend. She stopped the doctor's hand just before he was to snip the cord.

"Please...if you don't mind, I would like my mother's closest and dearest friend to cut the cord."

Harriet burst into tears; she will forever remember this day.

The doctor need not have guessed the baby's weight; Harriet's baby scale had been scrubbed, ready for use. Ben figured it would be needed.

"Healthy" described the baby boy to a tee; he tipped the scale at five pounds, six ounces. His hair might have added a bit more to his weight, for he had enough to tie into a ponytail; it was coal black and wavy.

The doctor handed him to Harriet so he could finish up with the new mommy. Harriet, with towel ready, got a glimpse of her first grandbaby; he was his daddy's duplicate. A lone tear that had not fallen earlier somehow dropped from her cheek onto her grandbaby's lips. Harriet knew it had stayed for a purpose; it was a kiss from his daddy, his first and his last. She began to weep uncontrollably. *My son will never see his son.* Concerned, the doctor turned toward Harriet. Was there something he had missed on the baby? He prayed not. But he was not given the chance for Sloan let out a long piercing scream.

"Oh my God, something is happening! The pain is tearing my insides. Something is terribly wrong."

Before the doctor could assess the situation another scream finished the ordeal as a second baby showed its face. Harriet was given the honor of not only cutting her granddaughter's cord, but she would be the first to hold both babies. She wept with joy; her son would have been so proud.

"Well, young lady, it looks like you are going to be quite busy."

Sloan was in shock. Why didn't her doctor tell her she was carrying twins?

Dr. Rolan was holding the third most gorgeous baby girl since Harriet delivered ten years ago. At five pounds, two ounces, this baby girl was close in weight to her brother, but her brother would not take the honor of all the hair; she was his match.

Dr. Rolan and his partner, Henry White the coroner, had decided they were too old to adopt and raise a baby. They would enjoy the children of their close friends.

Ben in his spare time set up a crib with fresh linens. Ben, without being told, got his butt in gear to pick up a mountain of diapers at the drugstore. As to all the other necessary items, Harriet had never had the heart to get rid of anything that belonged to the triplets; the washing machine would be in action for several hours.

After much discussion, but against the doctor's better judgment, Sloan insisted she and her babies would stay with Harriet and Ben and their brood, but only if they approved. Sloan did agree to one stipulation, that a pediatrician come by to check out the babies. Harriet was now gifted with being in charge of her two new grandbabies. She had lost a son, but God in His greatness arranged for Sloan to be at her home so she could be a witness to the birth of her son Clay's babies.

With everything that had transpired the most crucial thing was making the arrangements for Clay's burial. Sloan was Clay's wife, so she was the one to make the preparations. Harriet had to approach the subject carefully.

Sloan was restless; her heart was wounded beyond repair, and her tear ducts would remain open for many days and weeks. Harriet gingerly approached her bedside.

"Honey, is there anything I can get for you?"

"I want my Clay… Can you do that? Can you bring him back to me?"

"Oh sweetie, if only I could." Harriet's tears matched Sloan's. This continued for several minutes, Harriet holding Sloan's hands with no objections. Harriet thanked God for that rather small, but very important show of approval. Harriet held back as long as she could; it was time for confession.

"Sloan, I can no longer keep from you the lies that have governed so many lives. I just want you to be patient with me while I tell you. There are times you may want to interrupt, but I plead with you to let me finish; if not, I am afraid I will lose my courage. The years of deceit have traveled many roads. The beginning of lies started with me and continued until there was no turning back. I started living a life I never thought I would have. It began on a very cold and snowy day…"

By the time Harriet had finished telling her tale of so much happiness and then despair, Sloan had already moved over to her side. They wept in each other's arms. Amends and forgiveness need not be said; they were now closer than they had ever been. But Sloan was not prepared to forgive Phillip and Chase and especially Lydia, a grandmother she never knew she had. Harriet was given no choice, but Phillip, Chase and Lydia could very well have stopped the masquerade. She thought of her husband as a man with high principles, but to do what he had done made him less so by laying everything on his mother's shoulders. Sloan was left with no one to really trust, except for Sunni. She has always stayed a true friend.

The babies were cleaned and wrapped. Formula would be Sloan's choice for feeding. Harriet did not question Sloan's method as she laid each baby in their mother's arms. Sloan and

Harriet's tears were put aside for a later date; they needed to prepare for a funeral.

CHAPTER THIRTY-FOUR

It had been eight days since Phillip called Jena. He had heard no word back. After the investigation into a possible homicide proved to be inconclusive, the investigators had no other alternative but to rule it a suicide. Phillip had been staying at his boy's house; his boy's fragrance lingered throughout. Phillip's weeping was nonstop, tissues were scattered about, and the servants followed him about like tiny mice picking up the particles. They too loved Mr. Clay, but at the same time wondered if they would lose their employment. Nothing was said about Mrs. Sloan and whether or not she would be coming back. If it was their mate and he had blown his brains about the study, they seriously doubted they could live in that house.

Phillip's pacing finally came to an end. If Clay's widow couldn't make the decision to bury his boy's remains, then by damn he would make it. He would not allow his boy's body to continue to lie in a morgue. For all he knew, Jena may have kept it to herself considering Sloan's condition. The ringing of the telephone caught him off guard; he was ready to dial the mortician.

"Hello." The muffled sound Sloan heard was that of a beaten man, a man drowning in sorrow.

"Phillip, this is Sloan. I've…"

"Sloan…oh my God, honey, I am so, so sorry. This is the worst possible thing to happen to this family. I've been waiting and waiting for you to call. Are you all right, honey? I've been worried something fierce that something would happen to you and the baby."

"Phillip, I have nothing to say to you other than I have made arrangements with Krista's funeral director to handle Clay's remains. He is to be cremated and his ashes placed in the Chadsworths' mausoleum. This is to be a private affair. Those invited will be family members only. The burial will be this Monday at three p.m."

The sound the receiver made after Sloan's hang-up numbed Phillip's ear.

Phillip, with the receiver still in his hands, looked down at the buzzing the telephone was making, and then he fell to his knees bawling like the lost soul he had become. He would have bet his worth on Sloan's coming to him for sympathy; how badly mistaken he was.

Andrew had been waiting on Sloan to return

to the airport when he was notified as to what had happened to Clay. He was devastated to the point of crying. Andrew had wept when his wife gave birth to each of their two sons; not since then had his eyelids felt a tear. After he'd been given the sad news, he was told to take some time off; Sloan would call him when she was ready to return home.

Today was that day.

Harriet was finishing up with the last details delivered to each family member. She and she alone would be attending the burial. The children would be told at a later date exactly what had happened; until then, they would have to wait and wonder. She felt as if maybe she was wrong not to let them attend—after all, they were Clay's sisters and brother—but at the last minute she changed her mind. She prayed she wouldn't be sorry for that decision.

The babies born at almost eight months were as strong as full term. They were dressed and ready for their first car and airplane ride. Sloan was loading all the necessary baby items along with the suitcases belonging to her and Harriet into the trunk of the car while Harriet secured the babies in car seats. The babies would be traveling in the back seat as the law demanded. It was time to head out. Sloan's watch read 10:00 a.m. Accounting for the time driving, air time, and the drive to her estate to drop off the babies with the prearranged nannies who also had nursing degrees under their cap, she and Harriet would arrive in plenty of time for Clay's burial.

Phillip and Chase were awaiting Sloan and Harriet at the mausoleum. Chase called his mother with his condolences the minute Phillip called him with the news. Something was wrong and he not only knew it, he felt it. Someone killed his brother, and Chase will search him out until he puts him down, maybe with the gun his brother was set to return. Chase held nothing back. Everything he was told by his mother and the conversation he had with Clay hit where it hurt the most. Phillip's heart bled. He also told Phillip he knew he was his mother's first love.

Phillip had but one question while trying not to weep, not only for his Jena, but his boy as well. "Why did it take my boy's death to release the skeletons that have been hidden since he was a baby?"

"I wish I knew." Chase too was hurting as badly or maybe worse. He'd had a big brother for such a very short time.

Phillip was left with nothing; everything he lived his life for had now been taken. His thinking was, *Maybe love isn't the answer when it destroys the ones left behind.* He also believed that his boy was a victim of foul play, although neither he nor Chase could convince the authorities.

After Chase had spoken with his mother he asked to speak with Sloan. Sloan refused, but Chase was not the kind to give up that easy. He would continue to call until she spoke to him. After a count of at least forty phone calls, she grabbed the phone out of Harriet's hand and screamed into the receiver.

"If you call here one more time I will put in a call to the police department and report you as harassing me. Don't test me, Chase." The receiver hit the cradle with a loud crash. He did not get the reception he desired.

Chase will bide his time; one way or another he will get his say.

The priest was there to say a few prayers. It would be as simple as simple can get; fifteen minutes was all he was allowed. But "simple" did not apply to Sloan, for when she appeared and obviously was not pregnant Phillip and Chase's mouths fell open. But they did not make a comment for they knew Sloan would be anxious to announce the news. But Sloan surprised them; they were told nothing. Chase would not give Sloan the satisfaction of asking; he could play her game as well as she. He will let her get away from him this time, but he has his ways and he damn well will use them.

Harriet and Chase hugged through tears.

"Marc, I am returning home immediately. I don't need to stay to be reminded of all the lies that were formulated the day I gave birth to Clay."

Marc/Chase understood. He gave his mother one last hug and kiss and told her he would see her at his monthly visit.

Sloan was preparing her getaway and was being followed by Harriet, but Phillip managed to get a hold of his lover's arm before she departed for her return home.

"Jena, please, I must speak with you."

Harriet turned toward the man she had loved since she was sixteen years of age. She allowed him his say.

"I love you so much, it hurts just to say your name. Oh baby, I am truly sorry for all that has happened. If I could, I would give my life for my boy, you know that. Please don't let his death destroy what we have…have always had."

Once Harriet's tears started, there was no stopping them.

"Phillip, you are such a fool. Haven't you yet figured out why Clay died? He died because of us, because we couldn't keep our hands to ourselves. We, or I should say I, committed adultery. And because of our sins God took my baby, your boy/brother that you loved your entire life. Was it really worth it? Was it? I don't think so. Please, Phillip, let me pass, I have no more to say. I have a plane to catch."

Phillip refused to release her arm. "Jena, your way of thinking is all wrong. God didn't take our boy, someone evil took his life. Let me tell you what Chase told me, and then you'll believe."

"His name is Marc. Now let me pass."

"Sarcasm is not becoming to you; besides, I know what his name is."

"Then use it. Now if you don't mind, I have a family that needs me."

Then for the last time, Harriet looked deep into his eyes.

"It's over, Phillip. It really doesn't matter who took his life—he's gone. It took his death to show me how I've been denying my husband the love he deserves, and by God with every breath I take, I will make it up to him. Good-bye, Phillip."

Phillip's arm dropped to his side. There was no denying what Jena said was the truth, the whole truth, so help her God. It was truly over. There will never again be the two of them.

Phillip's tears rolled over his face and downward onto his five-thousand-dollar suit. He wept for so many things: the loss of his dear sweet mother, his beautiful sister Ali, his brother Clay, and now and forever, his Jena. His life will be the company his grandfather started, and just possibly Sloan will share her baby with him— after all, he is the child's great-uncle.

CHAPTER THIRTY-FIVE

Somehow word got out that Sloan had returned home. Sunni was pressing the button on the box anchored into the stone pillar. The butler Truman answered the voice box.

"Truman, it's me, Sunni. Tell Sloan I'm here. I'm sure she'll see me."

"One moment, Miss Harrison. I'll make your presence known." Within seconds the gate swung open allowing Sunni to enter.

Sunni drove like someone who had not seen their sweetheart in weeks, she was that excited. *Soon, my darling, I will make love to you, and you will scream out for more. This is a promise.* No sooner had those thoughts come into play than she was at Sloan's door.

Truman escorted Sunni into the sitting room while making pleasantries.

"For God's sake, I can find my way to her room. What's with all the formalities?"

"Miss Sloan said she will visit with you here."

Sunni was getting a little annoyed. She wondered what was going on. She removed herself from her seated position and began strolling about the room running her hand over the furniture as she passed by. Not a speck of dust on any of the furniture. Just as she turned around, Sloan had her arms around her.

"Miss me?"

"Oh my God, you're not pregnant. Oh, you poor thing, you lost the baby." Sunni was ecstatic but put on quite the show; she began to cry for her soon-to-be lover's loss.

"Sunni, there is no need for tears. My babies are just fine."

"Babies? Did you say 'babies'?"

"Yes, isn't it wonderful? I had twins, a boy and a girl. Wait until you see them. They are going to adore you as much as I."

Sunni's mind was working. *We'll see about that. There is no room in my life for kids. I guess I will just have to get rid of a couple smaller details.*

But instead of those words, Sloan heard, "I can hardly stand it; I must see them immediately."

"Well then, come on." Sloan started towards the nursery, located on another floor, where the babies were being tended by round-the-clock nurses.

"Oh, and by the way, I am so sorry to hear about Clay."

"I don't want to talk about Clay, Sunni."

"I know you don't. Who would? But really, to take a gun and blow out his brains... Just what in the hell was he thinking?"

"Sunni, there you are, doing it again. When I say I don't want to talk about something I mean it." As soon as those words left her mouth, Sloan began to weep.

"Oh honey, I am such a fool, my mouth always gets me into trouble. Please forgive me. Come on, wipe the tears. Let's go see the babies, okay?"

Sloan began wiping at the tears, although they did continue to fall. The tears stopped when she looked onto the faces of her babies, Jack and Leena.

The visit ended quickly; Sunni hated kids in any shape or form. But she used the excuse she had to get back to work. A project was to be completed today. Sloan was disappointed but understood. They agreed to meet for lunch the next day.

Days turned into weeks, then months. Phillip had had enough with Sloan's nonsense. He found out by word of mouth that his niece had not one but two babies. How proud his boy would have been. The pain of not seeing his great-nephew and great-niece was to the extreme. He called and talked to Truman.

"Truman, this is Phillip. Is Sloan there?"

"Yes, Mr. Phillip, she is in the ballroom playing with the babies. Shall I call her to the telephone?"

"No, she in all honesty will not talk to me, but I'm coming over to settle this dispute once and for all. Please do not tell her."

"No, sir; mum's the word. To tell you the truth, I've been praying for this day."

Truman was as much a part of the family as anyone; he knew what was going on. He was thankful this day finally arrived. He knew it would take at least an hour or better before Phillip showed himself. He was ready the minute Phillip's car pulled in front of the entrance, and he held the door open as Phillip blasted through.

Phillip began yelling at the top of his voice. "Sloan, I'm here to see to see my great-nephew and great-niece. I will no longer be denied my rights."

Sloan ran towards him.

"Phillip, are you out of your mind. You just about had my babies crying. What is wrong with you, have you gone crazy?"

"Sloan, I can't take it any longer. I love those babies and I haven't even seen them." With that said Phillip dropped his shoulders and began to weep.

Sloan had a huge heart and his timing was perfect; she'd begun to miss the old man.

"Oh, for gosh sakes, you carry on like it's the end of the world."

"It is for me if I can't be a part of your family. I love you, honey, don't you know that?"

"Oh Phillip, of course I do. Well, don't just stand there, come and give me a big hug."

Truman was peeking around the corner watching and praying, and then began to cry when they came together. All he could think of at that moment was how happy the days will be from then on, but what about Chase?

Phillip and Chase worked side by side; they were now full partners upon Phillip's insistence.

Chase was excited with the news that Phillip made amends with Sloan. It was now his turn, but would he get past the door? There was only one way to find out. He grabbed his jacket and headed out of the office; he would make Sloan listen if he had to sit on her.

Chase knew the combination to open the gate. He was at the door in a matter of minutes. Truman allowed him entrance as he did with Phillip; he again prayed.

Chase was not like Phillip though. He did not shout out; instead he went from room to room searching. He was well acquainted with the house and knew the rooms that were used most frequently. He found Sloan lying on her bedroom floor, playing with the babies. She could not see him, but the babies sure did. For some unknown reason, they both began to say "dada." He was overjoyed with their response. Did they really think he was their daddy? If only that were true. He would take them even if he were not—that is how much he already loved them. How could he not,? They were a part of the two people he loved the most, aside from his mother. Sloan did not pay any attention to their jibber jabber; she continued to tickle and kiss their little fingers and toes. What a fantastic mother. If only Clay were around to see it.

Chase knew that within seconds he could be thrown out. He needed to get a few words out before she got up off the floor.

"Sloan, we need to talk. I am fed up with your behavior."

She jerked her head toward him. "How did you get into my house? Did you force your way in? Is that how a gentleman behaves? Get out, before I call the police."

"Lately, it seems every time I want to talk to you, you want to call the cops. Well, dear heart, please do me the honors, or are you just a big bluff?"

Sloan, red-faced and angry with his remark, scrambled to get up. The babies worked their way up to a sitting position and began playing with a mountain of plush animals. Chase marveled at their dexterity; he would give anything to be their father.

"Get out, Chase. I mean it."

"All I want is to talk to you. Please allow me that much. If after I'm finished you still want me to leave, I will."

Sloan stood with her arms crossed, while tapping her right foot. Never had anyone irritated her as much as Chase.

"Well, what the hell are you waiting for? Say what you want to say and then get out."

"First, I want to apologize. When we began meeting on a weekly basis, we promised each other to always be honest. I broke that promise and I am truly sorry,. I hurt you badly. All I want is for you to forgive me. Do you think you can do that?"

"I hate you, Chase. You are a hypocrite."

"I am that."

"You can't be trusted."

"You are absolutely right."

"You think you can talk me into anything."

"True again."

"What?" Sloan lunged at him, tears beginning to form in her eyes. What she knew to be true was that she loved him.

Chase grabbed onto her hands and pulled her close. "Sloan, if only you could read my heart, it would say I truly am sorry."

Sloan collapsed into his arms.

"The authorities recommended that I not view Clay's suicide letter because of the condition of the note. They were referring to the blood stains left behind. Of course, I refused their suggestion. Oh Chase, I miss Clay so much it's tearing me apart."

"I know you do."

"I cry in the mornings, and I cry when I go to bed. It just never stops. I can't go on like this. I need help."

"Will you let me help you? Because if I can help you, you will be helping me. I too can't get him out of my head. I loved him, Sloan; he was my brother."

"I know he was, and I am also sorry for your loss."

They held each other until one of the babies began to cry. They in turn ran to pick him up. The laughter was genuine and full of love.

But Chase did not know what to call them. Phillip knew, but failed to tell him.

"Well, are you going to tell me their names, or do I guess?"

"Their names are Jack and Leena. What do you think?"

"Perfect. That is exactly what I would have chosen."

Sloan knew he would agree to anything, he loved her that much.

But Chase was not through with what she needed to know. He told her about the conversation he had with Clay the day he died.

"Sloan, he was going to return the gun the following Monday. Clay was smiling when he said that, because he said it would make you very happy to know that stupid gun was gone. He loved you more than any man I ever knew."

"Oh Chase, thank you. I really needed to hear that. I keep going over the suicide note that was turned over to me after the investigation. I know deep in my heart he would not have taken his own life."

Chase confirmed her feelings. "Someone killed him, I have no doubt. I will find the one responsible, so help me God."

"You do what you have to do. I trust you completely."

"Sloan, there is something else you need to know. And what I'm about to say is not taken lightly. I thought it through carefully before I came to this conclusion. Sloan, Sunni is a lesbian; she is in love with you."

"Oh Chase, that is absurd. Don't you think I would know if she were? I've known her my entire life."

"All right then, let's play it out. Has she at any time ever made advances toward you that you would consider inappropriate? Maybe it could have been in a joking manner?"

"Never, ever...wait...come to think of it, when we took a trip to Italy I remember waking up feeling violated. I went to sleep in a nightgown and awoke naked. I ran to Sunni's room telling her I was raped, but she convinced me otherwise. Oh my God, I need to find out if this is possible. I have to confront her, and I refuse to wait. Chase, I'm sorry."

"I feel the same…go. I'll let myself out."

Sloan called out for the nannies; they were there in a flash. She told them she had to leave to take care of personal business and she didn't know how long she would be gone. Of course they understood; that's what they were there for, to take care of the babies, day or night.

Sloan was out of the driveway before Chase could put his car in gear.

The drive was long; Sloan never thought she would get there. How dare Sunni touch her…if she really did. But of course she did. Sloan now knew without doubt. The driving was hectic. It was a workday, but Sunni had told her the days she was usually at home if she ever wanted to visit. She was thankful; today was one of Sunni's home days, or she just might have yanked her up by her hair right out of her office chair. And by the time she got through, the office staff would have known she was a lesbian.

Sloan turned her key over to a valet service and walked a couple of blocks. She mounted the steps to Sunni's apartment complex; she knocked several times, but received no response. She fiddled with the junk in her purse, searching for the key to Sunni's apartment. Now that she thought about it, Sunni had been generous with her key. Sloan remembered her words when she gave it to her.

"Honey, you can come over night or day. Slip into something comfortable and give me a call to let me know you are there."

Sloan was fuming as she inserted the key. She called out Sunni's name several times as she made her way through the apartment. Sounds were coming from one of the bedrooms. Sloan was now really upset that Sunni had company. Was it another woman? Could she say what she came here for?

She moved slowly towards the door, which was open. Hearing laughter, Sloan took a deep breath, praying she was not about to be a witness to sex between two females.

Sunni was sitting Indian-style near the wall laughing and talking to herself; she seemed to be in a place where only she ventured. Two pictures, small in size, were leaning against the wall. Sloan threw her hand to her mouth to hold back the scream. The picture of her family, the one she thought was lost in the fire, was the larger of the two. The other was the picture of her and Clay in their wedding attire. That was the picture that sat on the desk in Clay's study, the one she never realized was missing because she'd refused to enter that room since his death. Scattered about were some items Sloan had seen before: Timmy's whistle, Silva's red folder, something that resembled a knife, a ring, a wallet, a pair of eyeglasses, a blood-stained bra, and a pair of tiny blue socks that in all probability belonged to her baby brother.

Sloan took a quick look, praying she could remember all the things that lay about. She gradually began to back away, her body skimming the wall. She was desperate to get away before her hand could no longer keep her mouth from screaming out loud.

She made it safely out of the elevator and down the steps before she let out a piercing scream, a scream that told of an agony that was beyond help. People offered help, but Sloan shoved them away. The tears were tearing at her insides. She felt as if she were about to explode into a million pieces. She was frantically trying to catch her breath while attempting to get the trembling of her body under control. She shoved herself in and out of the crowds of people in her path, falling several times. Never at any time did she take an offered hand.

She finally reached the valet service, but the young man was hesitant to give back her key. Sloan knew she was in no condition to drive, but she wrestled the key out of his hand and barely missed falling backward. She quickly righted herself.

Sloan sat for a few minutes trying to think of what to do. It did not take long to decide, but she needed to get home to carry out the task. She was running for her life and all the lives that Sunni could possibly touch. Only when she was safely inside her home did she pass out. When she came to it had been almost five minutes. Multiple cold compresses were used. Truman was about to call an ambulance when she finally came to.

"Truman, please help me up. I need to use the telephone, and would you please call Chase from another telephone? I urgently need him."

Chase had just removed his jacket when the call came in. Truman shouted into the mouthpiece. "Mr. Chase, you must come quickly. There is something dreadfully wrong with Mrs. Sloan."

"I'm on my way. Truman, I trust you…if you think she needs a doctor, call one immediately."

"I just don't know, Mr. Chase, one minute she's crying hysterically and the next minute she is screaming. Mr. Chase, I would rather you make the judgment on whether or not to call the doctor. Please hurry."

Sloan had the telephone receiver clasped in her trembling hands. She could not stop crying. She dialed Ben's number and made a strong effort to control the crying, but no sooner had he said hello than she let out a wail not unlike a mother in hard labor.

Ben had no idea who was on the other end of the line, but whoever it was, that person needed help badly. He turned the telephone over to Harriet. She too heard the howling; it sounded like an injured animal. She was about to hang up and call the operator to send help to the person in distress, but at that moment, her abilities as a psychic came through.

"Sloan, it's me, honey…Harriet. You need to stop crying and tell me what is wrong. If you don't, I can't help you." She repeated it over and over; sometimes she too was screaming until she finally got through.

"I need to speak to Ben. Please, Harriet, I need Ben."

Ben took hold of the receiver and gently spoke. "I'm here, honey. It's Ben."

Through all the crying and hysterics, he finally understood what Sloan was saying. He staggered towards the Chippendale chair and fell into it. He was shocked. *It couldn't be…but then why not? Everybody else in town had checked out. But that would mean Sunni, at the tender age of ten or eleven, killed Timmy.* Ben could still hear Sloan weeping nonstop. Did she not have someone to take care of her? He screamed into the receiver, giving it his all.

"Sloan, I don't mean to sound harsh, but you need to stop crying. You need to give me all the information you have so I can turn it over to the authorities. Please, honey, you must get control. I know it is hard, but you want justice, don't you? You want to see her behind bars, do you not?"

Ben could tell she was really trying. He gave her as much time as she needed. She finally came through like the trooper he knew her to be.

"Yes, Ben. I want to see Sunni put to death for taking my family from me and all the other families that lost their loved ones. What do you need me to do?"

"What I am going to ask is going to be the most difficult thing you will ever have to do. But to get justice it will rely totally on you."

"I will do whatever you ask of me."

"You must get Sunni back here in Mason's Mill. Right now she is out of our jurisdiction. If you want results immediately, that is the best way around the legal system."

"I will do it. I will find a way. But you too have to be prepared. It could be only a day's notice. Do you think you can arrange that with the local authorities?"

"Don't worry about me. You let me know an hour in advance and I will be ready. We're going to get her, honey, and when we do, you will see justice at work. I'm proud of you, Sloan. You did what no one else could do, including me."

"No, Ben, you are wrong. Are you not going to be present when she is arrested? Of course you are. And I will see that you get the credit you are long overdue. Thank you for all your help. Just be ready when I call, okay?"

"You got it. Until then, take care you don't get hurt."

Sloan was now on a mission. There would be no such thing as a delay.

CHAPTER THIRTY-SIX

Chase could not get through the door fast enough. Tears were rolling around inside his eyes ready to be expelled. If anything were to happen to Sloan, he too would wish to be dead.

Truman was carrying a tray with something to eat and drink.

"Truman, where is she? I pray you did not leave it up to me to call the doctor."

"There is no need for that. She is quite fine, Mr. Chase."

"But did you not say something was wrong?"

Truman was now smiling. "Well, it seems she is now okay." He was still smiling.

"Truman, you about gave me a heart attack."

"Follow me. I was just about to bring Mrs. Sloan something to eat."

"Thank you for saving the day; you are truly one of a kind."

Chase was astounded that Sloan was sitting in the very chair Clay's body had been found in. Of course everything had been restored to its original order, but still he was more than surprised.

The first person Sloan noticed was Truman with the tray; tagging behind him was Chase. She could not get out of Clay's chair fast enough. She ran straight into Chase's ready arms.

"Oh Chase, you won't believe what I have to tell you." Sloan's makeup was smeared all about her face; she could not have looked more beautiful.

Truman set the tray of food and drinks on a table that stood by Clay's desk. He quietly exited.

"Okay, what the hell is going on? You had me scared to death." Sloan had a look Chase had never seen before; he could only describe it as euphoric.

"I couldn't be happier than I am right at this moment. And you want to know why? I know who killed my Clay."

Chase could not believe what he'd just heard. "How, when and who?" was all he could say.

"I went to Sunni's apartment and she was sitting amongst the things she collected after she killed her victims. Chase, she had my and Clay's wedding picture from this office. She even had my bra, the one I thought you had taken from me; I'll explain later about that misconception."

Chase took a chair, hardly believing something so incredible.

"So what can you do about it? Can you prove it? She probably has a special place she keeps all those items and gets them out only when she feels the urge to touch them. That there would be a true psycho."

"I have a plan. Do you want to know about it?"

"Sloan, this is some serious shit you are fooling around with."

"Do you want to hear about it or not?"

"Okay, what is your plan?"

"I am going to get Sunni to go back to Mason's Mill so she can be arrested."

"Oh I see, she will be so willing to go back to the place where all the killings took place. Sloan, you need to get your head examined. It would be easier to handcuff her and lead her by her nose."

"Oh Chase, don't be so stupid. I plan on going back there on the pretense that I want to put flowers on my family's grave sites. I'm going to ask her to come along."

"Sloan, I don't think this is a good idea. You could get hurt if she were to suspect something."

"I'm too smart for that."

"Yeah, just like knowing she's a lesbian."

"Okay, I won't deny you are right on that issue. All kidding aside, Chase, I promise I will be careful."

"When do you plan on going?"

"Sunni is off this Thursday. I'm going to give her a call right now. Keep your fingers crossed that she agrees to go with me."

Chase just shook his head, but he did not plan on Sloan going with just Sunni. He would be close by just in case.

Sloan was dragging the phone cord around with her while she talked to Sunni. Chase did not like this one bit. Sloan threw the telephone and ran toward him; he caught her in his arms.

"Hooray, she is going!"

Chase could smell her scent, feel her body pressing against his. He was aroused to the point of being embarrassed. Could she feel his erection?

He could not help it; he had to tell her how he was feeling at that moment. "I love you with every breath I take."

"I know." Sloan looked deep into his eyes. She loved him so, but she just was not ready to commit. She turned away, searching out the telephone; she needed a distraction. If Chase thought she wasn't interested, he had a lot to learn. If he hadn't released her when he did she would have torn at his clothes to take care of his ache as well as hers. She was trembling when she pulled away and continued with her conversation.

"I can't wait to see the look on her face when she is handcuffed; it will finally end my nightmares."

Chase so wanted Sloan to tell him she loved him also, but she did not. Maybe she did not love him like she loved Clay. Maybe she never did. Maybe he was reading more into it than there really was.

Thursday rolled its way into Sloan's life. She searched her closet for the best handbag to secure the victims' items. A tan saddlebag was perfect. She was now as ready as she ever would be.

On Ben's end, he too was set up and ready. He paced the floor in his house like he did when he found out Harriet was expecting triplets. Harriet kept telling him to sit; he was driving her crazy.

"Do you realize how long I've waited to get the person responsible for those hideous murders?"

"Yes, I know, Ben; it's been over eighteen years. I wish I had kept a journal of how many times you talked of this day. Well, you finally got your wish, now will you please sit down? Soon you'll be wearing a hole in the carpet. Besides, Sloan isn't due here for another hour."

"I think I'm going to check to make sure everyone is in place."

"Yes, you do that, and while you are at it, if Sunni were to show up early, make sure she sees you."

"So what if she did? I can't act surprised and say hi?"

Ben took his time as he headed towards the cemetery. The stake-out was being conducted where the bodies of many of those Sunni had murdered were buried. Men and women dressed in civilian clothes were scattered about, some kneeling as if in prayer, others placing flowers on the graves of their dearly departed, while others carried on conversations with their loved ones. It was well orchestrated.

Sloan was early. Chase was even earlier. He found an ideal spot to settle down. He was well hidden behind the trunk of a one-hundred-year-old oak tree no more than sixty feet from the Parkers' grave site.

Sloan pulled her rental car directly in front of the opening to the cemetery. The thought of murdering Sunni never left her thoughts during the drive, although she did have a problem: she had no weapon.

Sunni was the first to climb out. She stretched her arms. It had been a long drive. Sloan made her way to the trunk of the car. Inside lay fifteen white roses. There would be but a single flower to beautify the graves of each of her family members and the Harrisons.

Sunni took in her surroundings. "My God, I can't believe I let you talk me into coming back to this Godforsaken town. What I won't do for my best friend. But that's what friends are for, right?"

She walked directly in front of Sloan. "You know, Sloan, you are my very best friend, the one I've loved since we were knee high. I would do anything for you; you know that, don't you?"

Sloan could not stand it a minute longer. She did not wait for the signal of a redheaded woman to say hello as she left the cemetery.

"Would you kill for me, Sunni?"

Sunni was bewildered with that statement. "What do you mean?"

"Would you kill for me?"

"I don't understand."

Sunni began backing up and looking around. Everything appeared normal. The redhead noticed Sloan was not looking in her direction for the signal, so she took upon herself to look as if she was not looking where she was going and bumped into Sloan while offering an apology. Sloan immediately acted out her hatred, jumping on Sunni and knocking her to the ground, where Sloan then proceeded to kick her while mouthing the words that tore at her heart.

"How could you end the lives of my beloved Clay and my friend Krista? They made me feel special, that my life had meaning. And murder my baby brother...he was just a tiny guy, he did nothing to you. But that wasn't enough, was it? You had to take my family, and in the worst way possible. I pray you are insane;

if not, I have to assume some blame, for I considered you special, that no one could ever take your place. You were someone that would always be there for me. And to think I wanted so very much to be just like you. You make me sick. I will see to it you will have no mercy when it comes time for sentencing."

Sloan began to beat Sunni's face. Tears and saliva would run their course. She could not get enough of Sunni.

Sunni tried to fight back, not with fists but with words.

"Honey, please stop. I can't take anymore, enough is enough. I harmed no one, least of all your family. I would have given my life for them, you know that."

"And as surely as there is a God, you will indeed give your life if I have any say in your sentencing."

Two cops in plain clothing were about to grab Sloan, but Ben stopped them.

"Please, that young lady needs to get the anger out of her system. The person you are about to arrest killed thirteen members of her family."

They did as requested, allowing Sloan the time she needed after Ben told the story of how the murders took place. They looked away as if they were not a witness to the beating Sunni was receiving.

Sloan's hands were now covered blood; spittle was hanging from her mouth. She was exhausted, her hands no longer of any use. Ben walked up and gently pulled her to her feet, his handkerchief available to wipe her face.

"You did it, sweetie. There isn't a person here that isn't thankful, most of all yours truly. And by the way, I'm sure CeCe Thorman will no longer be an unsolved homicide."

The authorities yanked Sunni to her feet. Trails of blood were seeping from a multitude of open wounds onto her clothing and would leave their imprint on those who came in direct contact with her. Sunni knew then she was a fool to have trusted anyone. As she was being handcuffed, she was read her rights. She screamed obscenities at the woman she'd hoped would be her lover.

"You bitch! Do you really think you got the goods on me? There is no way you can prove anything. You have no idea just how much I could have satisfied you, you fuckin' traitor."

Ben nodded at Sloan, a signal she understood. Sloan passed by Sunni. Her hatred could not be mistaken; it was written over the smears of her blood-and tear-streaked face. She walked slowly to the rental car, taking her time and praying that Sunni was frantic with the thought of being caged for life or given the death sentence. She retrieved the items taken from the brutal killings of so many lives that had been snuffed way before their time.

The day after Sloan had found Sunni running her fingers over the collection she had taken from each of her victims, she revisited Sunni's apartment. Sunni was expected at work, and Sloan knew she could take her time searching for the things that could put an end to Sunni's lunacy. To say it was a difficult task would be an understatement.

Sloan had to work quickly, but she had already been there three hours with no luck. Sunni could come home at any time. The rooms were quickly dimming; rain was expected. Overcast began to cover the rooms in darkness. Light was needed if Sloan were to find what she was looking for.

Standing with her hands on her hips, she wondered why the overhead light in that one room was not working. She continued to press the switch on and then off, but nothing helped. The large ornate glass shade refused to give that much-needed light. As she moved closer, it looked as if something was hidden within. Sloan raced out of the apartment to secure a twelve-foot ladder from the janitor. The janitor offered to assist her, but she refused him kindly. She could manage on her own. He just shook his head. She found what she was looking for. The items were secured in a plastic bag.

She called Chase immediately.

"Chase, I found something I hadn't seen the first time: Krista's wedding ring and a birth certificate of a baby girl born to a CeCe Thorman. Chase, it is the same birthday as Sunni's. Do you think that woman is her mother, and if so, do you think she also did away with her?"

"More than likely. I guess she was pissed that her mother gave her away. Who knows? But that is something we can find out."

"But why kill Clay? He didn't do anything to her."

"He had what she wanted: you."

"Then why did she do in Krista?"

"She probably thought you were sleeping with her."

"How horrible."

"Not to her, it isn't. Enough. Will you please get the hell out of there?"

"Okay, okay. I'm going."

The earlier conversation brought Sloan back to the present.

As Sloan approached her once-beloved friend she dangled the extra-large bag in front of her face and spoke to the man who earlier had pulled from his pocket a badge showing he was the chief of police.

"The items you find in this bag will reveal Sunni's fingerprints. They were hidden within her apartment. And sir, when all this is over I would appreciate having the items that belong to me returned."

The chief of police nodded his assurance.

Sunni's hands were shackled behind her. She looked at the man disguised in regular clothing as he began writing something on a pad. She too had something to say, but before she spoke, she spat onto his highly polished shoes.

"You have no idea who you are dealing with. I demand that she be arrested for breaking and entering. She had no right to enter my apartment without my permission."

Sloan stepped up and shook Sunni's house key in front of the face she had loved, it seemed, forever. Now for the first time she recognized the evil lurking within. She became ill just thinking of how high a pedestal she had placed Sunni on.

"This is the key to your home that you so graciously gave me."

Sunni's right foot flew up and knocked Sloan to the ground. Sloan had had enough. It was over, and yet the tears once again showed themselves.

Chase was biding his time; he too allowed Sloan the time she needed to take a small measure of revenge. It was now his turn to offer the stability and comfort she would need from this day forward. He reached down to gather her into his arms.

Sloan looked into the eyes of the man who'd stolen her heart when she was but a teenager.

"I knew you would be here."

"Always, babe, always."

She rested her head onto his chest, her arm wrapped around his waist. Gently, he wiped away the tears with his fingertips.

"It's finally over, babe. No more tears, no more heartache. Never again will anyone bring harm to you; I will see to it. You are now my woman and together we will start over."

"Oh Chase, Clay really did a number on my heart. I truly loved him."

"Of course you did. I know you better than you know yourself. That is why I never took you to my bed. When the woman I love, loves another, I could never make love to her if she surrenders her body and not her heart."

Sloan could no longer hold on to the anger. She released into the wind the hatred she had carried. The justice system will see that the wickedness that dwells in Sunni will never again bring harm to another family. Sloan was ready to commit to a man she had loved way before her husband entered the picture.

"Before Clay came along, my heart knew I loved you, but fate stepped in and for whatever reason, directed me to love another. But as destiny proves, he had yet another plan and that was to bring us back together, for a love like ours will never be denied."

Together they gathered the flowers and walked to her family's graves; they were there to tell them they could now rest in peace.

The End

Author Evelyn Sciarratta

Mrs. Sciarratta resides in St. Charles, Missouri. She is a widow with five children, 17 grandchildren and eight great-grandchildren.

Rest In Peace is her first full-length novel.

The *Rest In Peace* trilogy is as follows:

> *Rest In Peace Book One: The Beginning*
> *Rest In Peace Book Two: Changes*
> *Rest In Peace Book Three: Starting Over*

The novel initially appeared as a synopsized serial newspaper feature in 1988. She's excited with the prospect that the new novels will bring as much enjoyment to readers as they brought to her as she was penning them.